Diverted to Dhapa

AVRIL DUNCAN

Copyright

This paperback edition is self-published 2023 by Avril Duncan
Utilising an imprint of Jasami Publishing Ltd.
Glasgow, Scotland
https://jasamipublishingltd.com

ISBN 978-1-913798-72-7

Jasami Acknowledgements

The Jasami team is integral to the production of all of our
work.
They are talented, creative and hardworking.
Thank you!

Executive Editor
Raquel Alemán Cruz

Editors
Claire Jack
Bailey Caughey

Cover Designer
Joy Dakers

Acknowledgements

My sincerest thanks to the following people:
My publisher, Michèle Smith at Jasami Publishing,
an inspiring new friend.
To everyone who helped prepare my book for publication
including Joy, Raquel, Claire, and Bailey.

Bill, my husband and *raison d'être*.

Debbie, Barry, Lynn, Ed, Sandy, Andrew, David & Shirley,
alias my adored family.

My two granddaughters, Elinor and Jojo –
I couldn't love you any more than I do.

Morag, Margaret, Kate, Helen & Jean, the India Intrepids.

Maureen Howley and Jane Boyd
for all their loving encouragement.

Irene, Freda and Felicia – in my heart.

And to everyone who reads my book:

May the road rise up to meet you
May the wind be always at your back
May the sun shine warm upon your face
The rains fall soft upon your fields
And until we meet again
May God hold you in the palm of his hand

Dedication

This Book is dedicated to Suman.
My little Indian friend.
May we find each other again one day.

Table of Contents

Prologue

Saturday

*S*tanding on a wooden chair, draped in a large grubby apron, Nokara blew into the mountain of froth in her hands. The child had used too much washing-up liquid and had created quite a bubble bath in the black, cast-iron sink. She giggled as a cloud of bubbles flew up in the air, gently dispersing as it fell back to earth.

A noise behind her made her turn quickly and the water drops, generously splashed onto the chair, made it slippery. Her bare foot slid over the side and she fell to the floor with a clatter, banging her head on the hard stone tiles. She was out cold.

Monday

The TV was on in the lounge and Jan, elegantly draped in a muted rose, silk sari, was sitting on the edge of her armchair, the pink velveteen blending beautifully with the flowing material. Her long, luxuriant, black hair was immaculate in every detail, and a cluster of diamonds clung around one ear, enhancing her flawless skin. She was nervously flicking through a glossy magazine, turning the pages automatically, disinterested in the stories and pictures they contained.

The door behind her opened quietly and a man entered the room. She turned her head.

"All done?"

"All done," he replied.

Thursday

Jan paced restlessly at the window, ignoring the bustling dissonance of life outside in the streets of Kolkata, her thoughts many miles away. The sound she was waiting for came at last, the bell a strident clatter in her ears.

"Come in, please." Her voice, soft and mellow, was in stark contrast to the noise of the doorbell.

Two people entered, the man in front, the child following.

She pointed to some rupees lying on the huge, ornate sheesham sideboard and the man moved over to snatch them up quickly, shoving them roughly into his pocket. He disappeared quickly through the door, closing it with a bang.

Jan turned to the child and smiled. "Come with me."

The young girl, standing just inside the door, was twisting her dress around her finger. She walked slowly behind Jan, staring wide-eyed at the sumptuous decor of the room they were passing through.

In the kitchen they stopped. Jan spoke slowly and softly.

"This is where you will stay. I'd like you to remain here unless I ask you to do something for me." She pointed to a small, curtained area in the corner of the room. "That is where you will sleep. There's a nice soft mattress for you. You need to keep the area nice and clean. When Cook comes in, she will explain your duties to you and keep you right. Okay?"

Speaking in Bengali, Jan was pleased to see the young girl understood her words and continued.

"What is your name?"

"Sunita."

"Well, Sunita, you have come to work for me now, so we're going to give you a new name. From now on, you'll be called Nokara."

Chapter One

SISTER IRENE MERCY GOVERNMENT
HOSPITAL, KOLKATA

In the early 1900s a family of nuns living and working amongst the poor and needy in Calcutta set up the Sahni Medical School. After independence from British rule in 1947, the college grew considerably and was renamed as the Sister Irene Mercy Hospital and Medical College in honour of one of its famous physicians, Irene Watwe. Now owned and run by the Government, it was one of the busiest hospitals in East India, attracting the poor and needy to visit its portals by offering highly subsidised health care.

The din was deafening. The vast reception hall was overcrowded with men, women and children, in long queues; some standing, some sitting, others lying on palettes, in wheelchairs or being carried. Doctors and medical attendants with clipboards in their hands intermingled with the crowds, their white coats in sharp contrast to the rainbow of saris in the hall.

A door opened at the far end of the hall and a group of students emerged, scurrying behind a doctor, clutching their bags, books and paraphernalia essential for their day's study. They held onto their loads tightly; no time to stop and pick up what they dropped. No time to chatter either, as the tall man at the front walked rapidly, neither looking behind to see if they were keeping up, nor slowing his step as he acknowledged various colleagues they passed along the way.

The moving group reached the big double doors near reception and passed through quickly as the doctor held the door open for them. They waited until he resumed his position at the front and once more scuttled in his wake along the wide corridor, lined with patients and relatives, squatting or hovering in groups, silently watching, their faces sombre with worry.

The students reached the children's ward and once inside, huddled into a corner around their leader as he prepared to give his instructions.

Dr Sami Nath, head paediatrician at the Sister Irene Mercy Hospital in Central Kolkata, was known as Sam to his friends. A member of staff for a number of years, he was inured to the long hike between wards and clinics, lecture theatres and surgeries. He smiled as he took in the students' breathlessness, and gave them a moment to catch their breath before addressing them with instructions for the day.

By lunchtime, with his teaching duties over, Sam decided to take a walk beside the lake, in the warm air, as an opportunity to escape the innumerable demands on his person, as well as eat his lunch in the calm before the storm of a busy afternoon of ward rounds and clinics.

Loved and held in high esteem by all his students, colleagues and patients, he was a friend and mentor to many. He had never, in all of his forty years, been tempted to form any deeper relationships in his life, until two years ago, when an encounter with a new, dedicated and beautiful doctor changed his feelings. Dr Suman Sudra, not originally from Kolkata, arrived as a new paediatrician in his department, and through her devotion, intelligence, and caring manner, quickly became an essential member of his team and just as speedily, an indispensable part of his well-being.

Dr Sudra, also escaping to the fresh air from the chaos of a busy morning, passed him by on a path some distance from the lake. Spotting him on a bench, she waved, laughing as he returned the wave enthusiastically with both hands. Fond of her colleague, she regarded him both as an outstanding doctor and a close friend and knew how lucky she was to be able to work with him on a day to day basis.

She quickened her steps and checked her watch, noting that the time had flown by unstintingly this morning and, as usual, she was late for a date with her younger sister, Vada, a student nurse at the college. She had promised to have lunch with Vada and was making her way along the paths that weaved in and around the hospital buildings to the girls' hostel where Vada was waiting.

It wasn't her tardiness or the wrath of her sister waiting that was occupying her mind as she hurried along a garden area, but instead a particularly difficult afternoon's surgery. She was due to assist Dr Nath with a procedure on a baby's eyes, an operation she had come across previously, but never in one so young. The child was suffering from a number of burns on parts of her body, most of which would heal over time with proper care and treatment, but one of her eyes had been burned too, with considerable damage to the eyelid and to the cornea. Dr Sudra knew that the child's mother had waited for four days before bringing her daughter to the hospital, and that the delay could potentially lead to blindness for this child.

"Suman."

Dr Sudra's head lifted quickly and she saw her sister hurrying towards her.

"I'm so sorry I'm late again," Suman began, "but you know what I'm ..."

She was interrupted with a laugh, as Vada linked arms with her sister and began to walk with her across the grass.

"Don't worry about that. Yes, I know what you're like. And I know how busy you are, but it's fine. You're here now. Do you want to eat inside or will we buy something and bring it out here?"

"I'd rather go inside. This sun's too hot and I can't see any shady areas left."

The two young women made their way into the girls' hostel that was home to Vada at the moment and joined the queue in the dining-hall for the self-service meal on offer. Suman dished herself a small portion of aloo posto with its tiny potatoes and poppy seeds, her appetite never very large at this time of the day, although Vada made up for her lack of enthusiasm by heaping a large amount of rice and macher jhol onto her plate. She loved the local dishes of Kolkata and the fish curry on offer today was her particular favourite.

Suman laughed. "How many are you eating for, Vada?"

Her sister grinned. "I still can't get used to eating three times a day. I just love it."

They made their way to a table and sat down to enjoy their lunch break.

"So," began Suman, "what are you busy with today? Have the exams started?"

"They start tomorrow. I've got some free time today for studying, although I've also got an anatomy class at five and a nutrition class at six. No practical training today, though. They want us to study most of the day."

"Well, see that you do study, Vada. These exams are so important. You should have cancelled our meeting today."

"No. I wanted to see you. I want to ask a favour."

Suman grimaced. "You need some money," she said with a shake of her head.

"No, definitely not," Vada replied swiftly. "You give me plenty of money; I don't need any more."

"Sorry, I shouldn't have said that. What favour would you like from me?"

"Well, I've got a two-week community placement coming up as soon as my exams are over, and they've told me I'll be doing some home visits, not too far away from here, for my first week, and a few days at a children's centre to help at an immunisation clinic there. I just wondered if I could borrow your scooter for the two weeks?"

"Of course you can. You've got your licence and you know you can borrow it any time. In fact, if you do well in these exams, we should think of buying you one of your own."

"I'd rather borrow yours, if it's okay. Once I've finished the four years and if I pass the finals, then I'll think about getting one of my own."

Suman nodded. "That's perfectly ok with me. But it's not if you pass your finals, it's when you pass your finals."

Enjoying their food and happy to be in one another's company, the sisters chatted well into the lunch hour before going their separate ways. Suman's pride in Vada's achievements was huge, her little sister not having had the same opportunities for schooling and study that she herself had. Vada had grown up in a rural village in Maharashtra with her mother and six siblings, whereas Suman's life had taken a very different path from the age of eight, something she rarely, if ever, spoke of. Nowadays, with Suman taking care of the family's financial needs, she was delighted to open doors for them that previously wouldn't have been possible. She had suggested a career in nursing to Vada, and her younger sister had jumped at the chance, never regretting the hours of study and the hard work it entailed. Vada loved everything about her life at the hospital.

Back in the paediatric unit, Sam was making his way to the operating theatre, pleased that Suman was going to be his partner for this particular operation. The baby had been burned by boiling water which had splashed into one of her eyes and his initial assessment had shown cell death in the eye. He had been dismayed to hear that the child's mother had been so slow to bring her daughter into the hospital, and he was not confident he would be able to save the sight in the little girl's eye. Infection had started and he needed to see how inflamed the eye was and how much fluid had gathered before he could initiate treatment. The delicate operation required a sharp eye for detail. *There is no better surgeon to work with than Suman for this tricky procedure*, he thought to himself.

Suman's training had taken place at the University of Edinburgh Medical School and in Edinburgh Royal Infirmary, where she had gained her qualifications in paediatrics and dermatology. In the early days of knowing Suman, Sam had quizzed her about her life so far away from India and her reasons for growing up in Scotland, not understanding why there were such vast differences between the two sisters. However, Suman had been very reticent in talking of her childhood and teenage years, and he had been left more curious than ever about her background.

She was twenty-nine years old, her thirtieth birthday not very far away. Her command of the English language was impeccable and often he was aware of a little Scottish lilt in her voice as she spoke. Vada, on the other hand, spoke mostly in Marathi, the local language of Maharashtra, where he had learned the sisters were from. Sam knew she was learning both English and Bengali to help with her nursing career, but also knew she used her local dialect all the time when speaking to Suman. He admired Suman's sister, though, both for her avid desire to learn and her commitment to nursing. A number of Indian girls enrolled as nurses more for a good pay packet than a desire to nurse, and he was very aware of both sisters' dedication and devoted sense of duty to properly care for their patients.

The investigative surgery on the baby was as tricky as both doctors had expected, but they were very pleased to see that the damage on the front of the child's eyeball, on the cornea, was now starting to heal. After checking the eyelids, the pupils and the back of her eye, they were very hopeful that this healing would continue and the child's sight would not be lost. Speaking to the assisting nurse at the end of the operation, Suman prescribed both steroid drops and medication for pain control to be given to the little girl's mother and added a reminder not to charge for any of the procedures or the medications the child was receiving. She mouthed a quick thank you and goodbye to

Sam as she hurried away to begin her own clinic in another part of the hospital.

Sam watched her as she left. Her support today had been invaluable to him, but it wasn't just her skills he was so drawn to. Everything about her had caused his initial attraction to grow, and he was aware of a strong need to really get to know her better on a personal level.

As Suman walked home that evening her thoughts were not a million miles away from Sam's; she mulled over the afternoon's surgery and, as she normally did, felt grateful that she had had the opportunity to work at his side. She always learned so much from him, and she felt appreciated as well as respected for the support she gave him. There was a spring in her step as she made her way around the back of the Academic Building and across to the apartment block she called home. Living on the twelfth floor of the Florentine Apartments, she liked being within walking distance of the hospital, and of course, near to her younger sister. She could be home in a very short time, a boon when she found herself tired and exhausted some evenings, or when she was on twenty-four hour A&E duty. A short walk, then collapsing into her bed, was much preferable to waiting for buses or negotiating the heavy traffic on the streets of Kolkata on a scooter.

Tonight, as always, she locked her apartment door behind her and put on the kettle for a welcoming cup of Scottish tea.

Chapter Two

SCHAANAPUR DISTRICT, KOLKATA, INDIA

Not more than seven kilometres from the hospital, as the crow flies, a large wooden cart was tethered to one of the outside walls of a makeshift bamboo hut in the village of Shabapur. Bimla, mother of two boys, Daivey and Raja, lay fast asleep inside the small dwelling. As well as the cart, rubbish lay in ordered abandonment around the hut, some of the piles as high as the roof. The rubbish had been carefully separated into different groups, a massive mound of rags and old clothes being the biggest group of them all. There was also a paper stack, made up of newspapers, cartons, cardboard sheets and paper bags, all folded flat and stacked up almost as high as the rag collection. Plastic containers took up one side of the hut, tied together into bundles and squashed flat to save space.

There were glass bottles, bottle tops, tin cans and metal articles, making identifying the job of one of the inmates of the bamboo hut an easy task for any casual passerby. Daivey, at the age of twelve, was the breadwinner of the family, his job that of a rag-picker, his place of work the enormous Dhapa Landfill site on which his home was built.

His cart was homemade, a long narrow plank of wood fastened onto four large, rusty metal wheels. Two handles with rags wound around them and sticking out at the front of the cart served as the means of moving the vehicle. The rags saved Daivey's hands from blisters; a full cart was a heavy load for a slender twelve year old to pull, and he welcomed the days when his brother Raja came to work with him to help with his recycling business.

Bimla was proud of her two boys. Daivey's hard work every day from morning to night brought in a regular income. Not a great income, but adequate to feed the three of them and buy necessities as required. Most of the money earned was handed over to Bimla daily, except for twenty rupees once a week, which Daivey added to a large jar on a shelf in the house. This cash was his savings, money Bimla allowed him to keep, and Daivey's ticket out of the slum village in which they lived. Faithfully saving his twenty rupees each week, over the last five years it had grown to the wonderful sum of five thousand, two hundred rupees. His ambition was to save enough to put a deposit down on a brick built house, somewhere outside the slum village of Shabapur.

For the time being, the young entrepreneur worked hard at Dhapa, collecting everything he could carry on his cart; items that he could sell on to the recycling traders living by the Hooghly River, near to the Circular Canal. Daivey's hands were calloused and his feet had long become hardened to the dangerous objects lying around and the small fires that burned in the landfill site, which stretched out for many miles. Thousands of people had made the site their home, the place where around four thousand tons of rubbish were dumped every day. Many folk like Daivey made their living there as scrap dealers or rag pickers or even farmers. Arable farming abounded on the site, with farmers growing vegetables like spinach and cauliflower on the swampy ground.

Bimla liked to think of herself as a farmer. She had been planting radishes for many years, liking the speed at which her radishes grew. From planting to maturity took only around four weeks, and by using rotation planting of the seeds, she could have a new crop ready for market every week. Eight-year-old Raja's job was to help his mother with the weekly planting and care of the crops, in between trips to the landfill site with Daivey when his older brother needed his help.

Today was one such day. Daivey and Raja took a handle each and began to pull the long wooden cart on its wheels over the bumps in the track, through the swampy edges and eventually onto the vast site itself, finding a spot where some new rubbish had been deposited during the night. Daivey looked out over the mountains of rubbish, spotting a vacant area where the rags and clothes looked newer and dryer; their colours standing out against the dark dreariness of the filth and squalor of the garbage hills.

The boys began filling their cart quickly, Daivey sorting out what he wanted and throwing it to Raja to pile carefully; the neater he piled the rags, the higher he was able to stow them on the cart. They worked fast, no words exchanged between the brothers, and after an hour, Daivey reckoned he had enough for the first session of the morning. He needed to take his haul home and store it for sorting later in the day. It took them twice as long to trudge home as it did to go; the cart being heavily laden and the garbage underfoot difficult to negotiate. Their arms were weary, but at no time did they stop or slow down for a rest.

There would be time to rest once the day's picking had been done.

It was on their third trip to the site that something unusual happened. Trips one and two had been highly successful; no-one had moved them on and the rags were good quality and dry. Daivey thought that one more trip would suffice for today. Plastic was his second favourite product to collect and, from his vantage point at the top of a large mound, he spotted an area with a lot of plastic lying about. He threw an armful of rags to Raja, feeling satin and wool in his hands; a good haul again today.

"Pile them quickly, Raja, and then we'll go and get some plastic to take back too."

Raja nodded, as Daivey scanned around his feet in case he had missed something good. He bent to pick up what looked like a large overcoat from the rags when suddenly he froze, his eyes widening in amazement.

"Raja," he called sharply. "Come here. Quick."

"What have you found?" Raja questioned. "Hope it's not another dead baby. I hate it when we find those."

As Raja clambered over the rag pile towards him, Daivey reached out an arm to grab his brother's hand and pull him the last bit of the way.

"Look," he whispered, pointing down into the mound of materials beneath him.

Raja had to bend forward to look and then, like his brother, froze where he stood.

Beneath them, peeping out from the folds of some filthy rags, were two little brown eyes. They could see a face surrounding the eyes, although the child's skin blended beautifully into the drab canvas of dingy brown colours around it.

For a moment in time, nothing moved. Then, realising he had to do something, Daivey began to gently pull the rags off the child, exposing more of the face, hair and neck. By this time he could see the child was a young girl. He scrambled quicker to remove all the rags, then lifted her gently out of the hole she was in and tried to stand her on her feet.

The girl was a little taller than she had looked amongst the debris, but she appeared scared, filthy and painfully thin. She began to shake and her knees gave way, making her fall back into the groove her body had made. Daivey clutched at her arms, pulling gently until he had her back on her feet.

"Let's get her to the cart," said Daivey, wanting to get off the top of the hill and away from anyone who happened to be watching. He looked at the girl.

"Can you walk?"

The child didn't answer; she just started shaking again.

Quickly, Daivey scooped her up and carried her over to the flat area where they had left the cart, Raja hot on his heels. With one hand he cleared a space for the child to sit on the cart. She fell back against the mound of material behind her. He tried again to ask the child a question.

"Can you talk?"

The child blinked, but said nothing.

Raja had a go. "What's your name? Do you have one?"

The girl's eyes moved from Daivey to his brother and, obviously feeling less afraid of such a small boy, she nodded.

Daivey jumped in quickly. "So you understand us, then? Tell us what your name is."

The girl recoiled against the command, curling herself into a ball and turning her face away.

There was silence from the boys for a long moment, until Raja broke it by asking, "So what are we going to do, Daivey? Should we put her back where we got her?"

The child's reaction was instant.

"No, please no," she pleaded, her voice gruff as if she had a sore throat.

Daivey could see tears starting and quickly reassured her that they wouldn't put her back into the garbage heap, but added that she must tell them her name and how she had got into the big landfill site.

"I think my name's Nokara," the gruff voice stated. "But I don't know how I got here. I just woke up here, all wrapped up."

"Did someone bring you?" asked Raja.

"Maybe. I can't remember much. Just a man's voice."

"What did he say?"

The girl's eyes turned back to Daivey.

"I can't remember."

"Do you know where you came from?" he asked.

"It was a big house. I was washing the dishes and then I fell off the chair. That's all I remember."

"Where's your mum or your dad?" Raja's questions were blurted out, short and sharp.

"I don't know. I haven't seen them for a long time. I don't know where they are."

This time tears fell from the girl's eyes and the boys turned away to hold a quieter conversation.

"What'll we do, Daivey?"

"I think we'll have to take her home with us. Ma will know what to do with her."

Nokara's tears had begun to subside and Daivey risked another conversation with her. He had noticed some marks on the girl's body beneath the grime and wanted to know about them.

"Are you hurt or can you walk?"

"I think my leg's broke. It's sore, and I got burned on the fires up there."

She pointed to a huge mound close by which Daivey knew was a very dangerous part of the landfill site. Containing an assortment of combustible materials, aerosols, gas cylinders, old plastic containers with dregs of cleaning liquids, human and animal waste and rotting food, that part of the site was awash with little fires, often flaring into larger conflagrations. Daivey whistled through his teeth.

"Were you in there?" he asked. "Were you put in there?"

The child nodded. "I managed to climb out and climb up here away from the fires and I hid amongst the clothes. But a lot of heavy things fell on top of me and my leg is sore. It's broken," she stated, as if it were an everyday occurrence.

"Right, get comfy on here and hold on tight. We're going to take you home to our Ma. She will know what we should do."

Trying to make the journey comfortable, with the least amount of bumps and knocks as possible, Daivey and Raja pulled and pushed the wooden cart all the way back to Shabapur.

As they neared the roughly-made hut they called home, Daivey was relieved to see his mother tending the garden and sent Raja on to warn her they were bringing a visitor. She was looking confused and worried as he approached.

"What's this I'm hearing, Daivey? Why are you bringing a girl from the rubbish tip home with you? What for? Who is she?"

Daivey tried to answer her questions and told her the tale of finding Nokara amongst the rags. Describing her injuries, he hoped his mother would take the child off his hands, allowing him to return to his job of rag-picking. He was now way behind with his work this morning - something he hated.

Unfortunately, Bimla had no such intention. An unknown child, in this injured state and covered in filth, was not something she was going to welcome into her home. The authorities that ran the village and its people could quite easily come bearing down on her, accusing her of goodness knows what. This girl might belong to someone, she surmised. She may have run away. Daivey was a good lad, honest and trustworthy, but someone may get the wrong end of the stick about all this and he was too young and naive to see anything wrong with helping a small girl in trouble like this.

"Take her back, Daivey. Someone may come looking for her."

Daivey looked stunned. "I can't take her back. She needs help and she's hurt. She's been dumped there and been there for a long time, by the looks of it. We need to help her."

"We need to do no such thing." Bimla began to get angry. "Take her back. You'll get us all into trouble. Take her back."

Daivey hesitated, realising his mother was scared and possibly correct in her assumption, but he couldn't feel it was right to take the girl back to the rubbish tip and leave her there.

He compromised.

"Well, I can take her back if you feel I have to, but can you maybe give her some water and food and clean her up a bit first? We won't get into trouble for that. Her name's Nokara and she thinks she's got a broken leg."

"Her name's not Nokara." Bimla's voice was puzzled. "That's not a name, Daivey. Nokara means 'servant'; so she's someone's servant. How did she get there, into the rubbish?"

"She says she was put there by a man," Raja intervened. "Ma, you can't send her back there. She's got a broken leg."

Bimla looked at her youngest son, then her eyes travelled back to Daivey, still staring imploringly back at her. She was in a quandary. Fear of trouble was uppermost, but underlying that was the trust her boys seemed to put in her ability and desire to help this unfortunate little girl. The boys' trust in her won. She sighed.

A few years ago, they had been a family of five, the boys' father and a little sister being part of the group. Losing her husband and her daughter to malaria had been hard, not just for Bimla, but for her sons as well. She knew in her heart why they wanted to help the child.

"Ok. Lift her off the barrow, Daivey, and bring her in. We'll see what we can do."

The brothers exchanged relieved glances and grins. They knew Ma would help, she just needed some coaxing.

Chapter Three

SCHAANAPUR, KOLKATA, INDIA

Bimla's hands were rough and hardened from her years of toil in the garden, but her touch was surprisingly gentle as she wiped the grime from the little girl's body. She had seen burns before, but not as bad as the ones she was uncovering on Nokara's skin. The girl was wincing as she chattered to Bimla, who was washing her in an old tub out at the back of the hut, away from prying eyes.

"I cleaned lots and lots of plates and cups for the lady, in nice hot water that came straight out of a tap in the sink. I did it with soap and made lots of bubbles. She was so beautiful, the lady. I had to call her 'Madam' and she wore necklaces and earrings every day. Her saris were sometimes gold, real gold."

Bimla's eyes widened as she shook her head. "I don't think they would be real gold. Probably just gold-coloured, made with gold threads. She must have been very rich, was she?"

"I don't know."

"Did she have a big house?"

"It was very big. My job was to clean the floors in all the rooms and dust the furniture. Even the kitchen was big. I had to wash the clothes and the covers on the beds, and my bed was in a corner of the kitchen. It wasn't a bed like the lady had. Mine was on the floor and I had to get up really early in the morning and push a switch to get hot water for Madam. There was another lady there, a cook who came to work there in the morning, and she made the food."

"Can you remember where this house was? When you were first taken there?"

"I don't know where the house was, but I remember I was in a car. I'd never been in a car before, and this was a big black one. The men who took me away from my mother were in the car as well." Nokara's voice broke as she mentioned her mother.

Bimla kept on questioning the child for some time but gleaned very little about where she had come from. Nokara couldn't remember her own home or the name of the lady she had worked for. Surmising the girl had been trafficked and sold into a wealthy woman's home to work in the kitchen, Bimla realised the child must have been very young when she left her own home and had no idea where it was.

"Do you know how old you are?" she asked.

Nokara nodded. "The lady said I was about eight years old. My birthday is in June, but I don't know when that is."

"Did she give you rupees for the work you were doing?"

"Rupees?" Nokara looked puzzled. "No, I didn't get rupees, just food. But sometimes I was hungry and I used to take food from the cupboard in the kitchen. I just took a little, so they wouldn't notice. They would have beaten me if they knew."

"Mmm," said Bimla. "Did they burn you, too? Is that where you got these burns?"

"No, they never burned me. The cook sometimes hit me with the broom when she said I was bad. It was the fires in the rubbish that burned me. I must have been sleeping in it and never felt it till I woke up."

Bimla stared at Nokara and swore quietly to herself, shocked that someone had abandoned the little girl to the fires of the landfill site, probably unconscious and unable to get herself out. Everyone knows of the fires that burn continuously amongst the combustible materials on the site.

"Why do you think your name is Nokara? Did your mother give you this name?"

"The lady gave me my new name. She said I was to be called Nokara while I was with her."

"So you have another name, your real name. What name did your mother give you?"

"Habiba. But Ma called me Habi, and my brothers and sisters did, too."

Bimla smiled. "Now, that's a better name. That means 'loved one'. So your mother must have loved you very much. And you can remember that you had brothers and sisters. We'll need to try to get you back home with them, Habi."

As she spoke, Bimla carefully lifted the child from the tub and dried her with a soft cloth. This she had to do very gently, the broken leg and the burns causing the child quite a lot of pain. She had instructed Daivey to find something for the child to wear from all the rags and clothing he had piled up in front of the hut. He brought her a dress, grubby and slightly torn, but wearable. A spare pair of Raja's undershorts were put on under the dress and, after a comb had been pulled through her long, tangled hair, she looked much more presentable than when she had arrived.

However, the injuries were worrying Bimla who knew that some of the burns were becoming infected, and the broken leg needed fixing. Medication was not something they had in their house. She worried that, without treatment, the child could become ill and suffer a lot more pain from the wounds. She sent Raja out to the fields to gather some plantain leaves and, when he returned, she told him to put the leaves in a bowl and squash them down to become mushy. This home-made lotion she spread softly onto Habi's burns and, although the child squirmed at the touch, she soon began to feel the soothing effect of the leaves.

Bimla knew that the effect would wear off soon, and was doing nothing for Habi's broken leg. She wasn't certain it was an actual break, but she could clearly see that there was something wrong with it. *Goodness knows how long she has had that,* Bimla thought, and wondered how it had happened. The temporary splint she had tied to Habi's leg was only going to hold it still for a short time. Her brow was furrowed deeply as she considered what to do next.

Watching while all three children ate a little food, Bimla smiled, sure that she had come up with the perfect answer, taking care of both the child's injuries and relieving herself of the responsibility of Habi. With this solution, Habi would be treated and then handed over to the authorities without Daivey suffering any comeback from the rescue.

Out of Habi's hearing, she spoke to her son.

"Daivey, you must take her on your cart to Sister Irene's, the big hospital. Once there, carry her inside and put her in the queue to be seen by a doctor. Then come away quickly and don't let her see you leaving. And don't speak to anyone. She'll get looked after by the doctors and afterwards they'll take her to a proper place where they can help get her home."

Daivey was not happy with this. "What about my work, Ma? I have to get back to Dhapa. Someone else will get all the good stuff that I should be collecting."

"You'll just have to take some time off, Daivey. She really needs treatment for the broken leg and her burns. I would have gone to Dhapa to collect your plastic, but you'll need the cart to take Habi to hospital. Don't worry, we'll all go to the site tomorrow and work twice as hard."

"What if someone sees me leaving her there? What if someone tries to stop me?"

"Well, you'll just have to get out of there as quickly as you can and run. I don't want you arrested for having an unknown girl with you that's not your sister. Get out and come straight home; speak to no-one. She'll be fine. The doctors will look after her."

Daivey grunted, unhappy at the task he had been given but unable to disobey his mother. Outside, he quickly finished unloading his cart and began to make a comfortable seat for Habi. *At least the cart won't be heavy to pull,* he thought, knowing how far away the hospital was. Once done, he pocketed the padlock he used every night to tether the cart to the hut. He would need it to keep the cart safe while he took Habi inside the hospital.

The Sister Irene Hospital was not unknown to him. On a previous occasion when his mother had taken ill, he had gone with her to the big Government hospital, overwhelmed by the immensity of the institution and the cool authority of the doctors, most speaking English to each other and wearing their crisp white coats. He did not relish another visit, but, with a resolute shrug of his shoulders, he lifted the little girl up on the cart and grabbed hold of the handles. They waved goodbye to Bimla and Raja and set off along the dusty tracks, crossing boggy fields and farmlands before reaching the main road to the hospital, where the cart became much easier to pull.

It took another hour of pulling before the big hospital came into sight, and Daivey's apprehension began to grow as he pulled the cart closer and closer to the huge cluster of buildings. Habi had closed her eyes and dozed for a while during the journey, but for the rest of the time chatted incessantly to Daivey. However, as the journey was nearing its end, she became quieter, not through apprehension like Daivey, but through the pain, which was beginning to engulf her as her burns began to ache like mad. Even underneath a light covering, the heat of the afternoon sun beating down on her for the last few hours was taking its toll on the sores on her body.

By the time Daivey tethered his cart to a pipe near the front door, she was crying softly with the pain.

"It's okay, Habi," he soothed, as he lifted her off the cart. "We'll soon have you inside and the doctors will take the pain away."

There were crowds of people everywhere, inside and out, and it took Daivey, carrying Habi in his arms, quite some time to push and bump his way past the people standing in the doorway. Once into the vast hall, he paused and looked around, unsure of where to go. Habi had stopped sobbing, but the tear marks were visible on her cheeks and her teary eyes stared around in fear at the vast, busy hall they were standing in.

"Hello, can I be of any help here?" a friendly voice asked behind them.

Daivey turned round to see a lady doctor in her white coat just a few feet away. He hesitated only for a moment, realising that his mother's instruction not to talk to anyone was going to be impossible.

"My friend is hurt and I need to get someone to see her," Daivey explained. "She's been burned and also thinks she has a broken leg."

"Oh, my goodness. Well, we need to get you seen as quickly as we can." She turned to Daivey, oblivious, so it seemed, of the long winding queues at each of the reception desks. "We'll never get a wheelchair; there's never any spare. Can you manage to carry her?"

Daivey hovered, not wanting to go with the doctor, but as she was moving away and beckoning to him, he had no option but to follow.

"I'm Dr Sudra, by the way, and I'm a children's doctor," she explained as they walked. "And I specialise in burns. So you've been lucky to bump into the right person. How did she get the injuries?"

"I found her on the Dhapa site, burned by the fires. Someone had dumped her on the site and abandoned her. I don't know how she got the broken leg. My mother said I should bring her here to the hospital."

"Your mother was right. She definitely needs help, don't you, darling?" Suman posed the question to Habi, giving her a lovely smile.

The child tried to smile back, but with difficulty, and Suman's footsteps quickened, trying to get her to the burns unit as fast as she could. Reaching her own consultation room within the huge ward, she unlocked the door and pushed it wide enough to let Daivey with his bundle into the room.

"Put her on the bed, over there," she said, beginning to wash her hands at a little sink in the room. "I'll get a nurse to come and take some details from you while I have a look at your little friend. But first, tell me your names."

"I'm Daivey, and this is Habi," he replied as he laid her gently down on the bed. "But I'm sorry, I don't know any details and I really have to go. Habi will be able to answer your questions."

Suman looked at Daivey, a speculative look in her eye. "Don't you want to wait and see how she gets on?"

"Well ..." he began. "My mother said ..."

Suman interrupted. "Was your mother worried that you might be held responsible for Habi?"

He nodded.

"Don't worry about that. I'm very impressed that you rescued Habi and brought her to me. We're not going to force any responsibilities on you. But please wait; I'm sure Habi would be happier if you were here for at least a little while." She looked at the child.

Habi reached out a hand and nervously grabbed his arm. "Yes, Daivey. Please don't go."

"Take a seat, Daivey. And help yourself to water." Suman pointed to a water dispenser in the corner of the room. "Maybe Habi would like some too."

Summoning a nurse to come and help, she pulled on some sterile gloves before beginning a very gentle examination of Habi.

"So, Habi. You've been having a bad time, haven't you? How did you come to be burned like this?" Suman asked the question softly as she worked.

The child, looking scared, answered Suman's questions as best she could, relaxing more and more as she realised that the nice lady doctor was not going to hurt her. The information she managed to give Suman was scant, but enough for Suman to form the same suspicion that Bimla had, that the child had been trafficked.

At last her examination was finished and she turned to Daivey to explain what was going to happen next.

"She has some bad burns, Daivey, but I've cleaned them up and put on some cream to relieve the pain. You'll see I've also put some gauze on the wounds and I'm about to start her on some medicine to help with the pain too. Hopefully she will begin to heal soon and we'll try to avoid infections.

She needs a lot of care at the moment, and I'm going to keep her here in the hospital for a while; maybe four or five days, possibly a week. Once I've had her x-rayed and her broken leg set, I'll check there are no more injuries and then get her into the children's ward. I've also given her an injection for tetanus and, after the leg has been seen to, I'll give her a sedative. That will make her sleep, hopefully for quite some time. I'll let you get back home now, as your mother will be worrying about you. Will you be coming back to see her again?"

Daivey hesitated, unsure of what to say. He scratched his head as a despairing look appeared on his face. "I don't know. I have to work and things are busy just now. I'll go now, but if my mother agrees, I'll come back."

"I hope you do, Daivey. It's quite likely Habi owes her life to you. You could have turned your back on her, but you didn't. You're a very kind person and a brave boy. Thank you, Daivey."

She put out her hand to shake his and saw he was embarrassed but smiling. She reached into a pocket and pulled out one of her personal identification cards.

"If you do come back, ask at one of the desks for me. Show them this card. If I'm around, they'll call me and I'll come and give you an update on Habi. I'll look after her, don't worry."

The trek home only took Daivey about an hour and a half, the roads being much quieter now and his cart a little bit lighter. During this time, his thoughts were fixed on the events of the day: finding Habi, taking her to the vast hospital building and his encounter with the doctor, who had had a huge effect on him. Never before in his life had he encountered someone so skilled, so clever, yet so kind, not just to her patient, but to Daivey as well.

He couldn't wait to get home to tell Bimla and Raja all about his afternoon, with a strong determination to return to the hospital one more time no matter what his mother said.

Chapter Four

JAN'S HOUSE, KOLKATA, INDIA

S unita sat up quickly. Someone was calling for her.
"Nokara! Where are you?"
The new housemaid scrambled up onto her feet and adjusted her uniform, a long black skirt and a white tee shirt. Kicking her blanket back behind the curtain of the sleeping area, she hurried through the kitchen door, along a corridor and into the opulent lounge at the end.

"I'm here, Madam." She curtsied as she spoke.

Jan stared at her new maidservant before speaking again. "Tidy your hair. I can see you've been sleeping. I'd like peppermint tea once you are ready and ginger biscuits."

"Yes, Madam."

Jan slumped heavily in her recliner with a long sigh as the child left the room. She was tired, unhappy and angry. This morning had not gone as planned. In the doctor's surgery, she received some very unsettling news.

'With child', was how he phrased it. Not believing the home pregnancy test that she had taken earlier in the morning, she had phoned for an immediate appointment with a doctor to validate what her brain had been rejecting for days. A wave of sickness threatened her at that moment, adding to her black mood. She groaned, both hands involuntarily moving over the bottom of her stomach, still as flat as it had always been.

A child in the family was not in her life plan. The highs and lows of motherhood were not for her. Life so far had led her in a very different direction, to a highly privileged lifestyle, with an expensive house, and some of life's luxuries. A life Jan had a desperate need to cling on to. She had no alternative. It was a need to embrace it or perish.

She pulled her phone from her pocket and made a call.

"Kali, I need your help. Can you come for coffee this afternoon?"

Sunita was carrying the tray with her peppermint tea and biscuits into the room as she ended her call, pleased with the outcome. The child laid the tray on a little table and curtsied before turning away.

Jan gazed after the child walking out of the room, as if seeing her for the very first time. Again her hand strayed to her stomach.

In the kitchen, Sunita began cleaning the dusty floor with a mop and bucket of water, paying particular attention to the corners and the dark areas under the furniture. A hard clout on the ear had taught her early on to pay attention to how she carried out her tasks and she knew now exactly what was expected of her as she worked. She was hungry, and the smell of Jan's lunch reheating filled the air, increasing the child's hunger pangs. The cook, departing some time previously, had left a very appetising meal for her mistress and given Sunita instructions on how to warm the meal. The child's own lunch, some cold rice left over from last night, was lying on a plate behind the curtain where she slept and she would eat only when the morning's chores were complete.

At one o'clock, she plated Jan's meal, a roti bread with rice, red lentil dhal with some cooked chicken and a spoonful of pickle on the side. She laid the plate on a tray. A jug of water was added, and a rolled up cloth napkin completed the tray's contents. Sunita lifted it carefully and carried it through to the dining room, where she knew Jan would be waiting.

Jan, however, was not yet in the dining room, and Sunita laid the tray on the table and began to unload it.

"No." She heard the curt exclamation from Jan as the tall, elegant woman came through the door. She froze.

"No, Nokara. I don't want any lunch today." Jan's face expressed the disgust she felt. "I couldn't eat it. Take it away, please, but leave me the water jug."

Sunita put the plate back on the tray, eyeing her mistress cautiously.

"And get rid of the smell of the food. There must be some fresh air spray somewhere."

"Yes, Madam."

Sunita bobbed a curtsey as she passed Jan, pausing as the woman continued, "Wait. I'm having a friend this afternoon for coffee. We'll need some cake and biscuits and put the coffee percolator on. That might help the smell."

Sunita bobbed again in acquiescence, a happy smile on her face as she exited the dining room. She had no intention of throwing Jan's lovely meal into the bin; she was going to have a good lunch today. She ate it quickly, sliding only a small drop left on the plate into the bin, in case Jan checked where her food had gone. Hunger appeased, she quickly washed the dishes before seeing to the ladies' afternoon coffee refreshments.

The doorbell rang in the middle of the afternoon and Sunita hurried to let the visitor in. As well-dressed and beautiful as Jan, Kali Dutta swept past the child and joined her friend in the main lounge of the house. The two women enjoyed their coffee and cake before Kali asked the question she was burning to ask.

"So, what was so urgent that you couldn't chat to me on the phone? Has Robert discovered how much you paid for the new carpets?" She laughed.

Jan smiled, "You know he never questions my spending. No, it's something a bit more serious than that. Something I don't think he'll like at all."

"Sounds intriguing. Tell me more. Is it something I can help with?"

"I'm hoping you will. At least, I'm hoping you'll point me in the direction of help." She hesitated a moment before blurting out, "I'm pregnant. I'm going to have a baby. Well, that's not quite true. I am pregnant, but I'm not going to have the baby. And I want you to tell me where to go to get rid of it."

There was silence for a few moments while Kali collected her thoughts.

"You don't want your baby?" she queried, incredulous.

"I won't be keeping it." Jan's face was grim.

"I don't understand. Surely this is good news for you both. Why don't you want your baby?"

"Kali, you know me better than anyone else. You know, with my history, I'm not cut out to be a mother. It's not that I don't want it, but a baby would not fit in here, not in this house. It would be too difficult. I want to be rid of this problem before Robert finds out."

Kali paused again, trying to think of what to say.

"I'm sure Robert wouldn't mind you having his child. And it wouldn't change your life that much. You can afford to hire help, so if you didn't want to do the mother bit, you could take on a nanny. Why do you want to put your health at risk with an abortion?"

Jan rose and took a few steps towards the window. She stood looking out for quite some time before answering her friend's question.

"You more than anyone must know how I feel. You know where I was born, how I grew up, and you know Robert, too, how he makes his living. Do you really think a man with his lack of feelings, his temper, is going to accept a child? Is this a place to bring a child of our own?" She turned round to face Kali.

"Children, to us, especially to Robert, are ..." she hesitated. "Expendable." Jan couldn't say any more and turned back to the window, unable to look at Kali, whose face was beginning to show frustration and puzzlement.

"Jan," her friend began, softly. "I've known you for a long time now, but you've never explained your background to me. So I don't know where you were born, or how you grew up. I assumed you were like me and your parents were Dalit. We lived on building sites, moving from site to site with no home to call our own and not much food around either. We had nothing. Was it something the same for you?"

"Sort of," Jan answered, her voice seeming to come from far off. "Except I grew up on the streets. I hated it. Scavenging in bins or stealing to find something to eat, and when we couldn't find anything, we went hungry and filthy for days. My father disappeared when I was really young and my mother took us to sleep under bridges to stay dry in the monsoons, or into the stations, making us beg for food or rupees."

Jan turned around to face Kali. "It was cruel, wasn't it? Having nothing to eat and nothing to wear except old rags that never fitted." She smiled wryly.

Kali sighed, dropping her chin into her hands. "Yes, it was cruel. I sometimes went to the stations, too. People on the trains would give you food if you were lucky."

There was silence for a long time, both women deep in the midst of their emotions and memories.

At last Jan walked over and sat down in her chair. She looked at Kali. "Were you picked up on the streets, too, like me?"

Kali groaned. "There were a few of us, friends, sitting at the side of the road, just talking. Some boys passing on motorbikes grabbed us and forced us up onto their bikes and drove off. I thought at first it was for a laugh. I thought they'd bring us back, or dump us somewhere to find our own way home. But they sold us to the traffickers and I had to go to work for Robert. I never got away till I met Asheesh. He bought me from Robert."

"How old were you?"

"Sixteen." Again there was silence and a stillness in the room as if the dust particles in the air were listening too; listening to the sadness and the helplessness of two young women caught up in the sordidness of real life.

"What age were you?"

Jan pursed her lips, remembering the day well. "I was fifteen. I ran away. I wanted something more than I had. I wanted a home, not just a tarpaulin to lie under. I wanted a better life and I thought I could find it. But I didn't. I ended up one night sleeping alongside the rail tracks and nearly being hit by a train that came hurtling by."

Kali's face was shocked.

"My God, Jan. How did that happen?"

"I'd had nothing to eat for days and was pretty weak. I couldn't get out of the train's way fast enough, but some other girls were there and they grabbed me and pulled me off the track just in time. Sometimes I wish they hadn't rescued me."

"Why would you say that? You don't mean it."

"I do. The girls took me under their wing, but they were street girls, prostitutes, selling themselves on the streets, and I went with them to do the same. I had no option. There was nothing else for me. And one night the traffickers chased us and caught all of us, then sold us to one of the brothels, right in the centre of Kolkata. I fetched the grand sum of six hundred rupees for my trafficker."

She laughed mockingly at herself. "I earned a lot more than that for my keepers, though, in my jail cell in the brothel."

"Your jail cell?"

"That's what it was like in there, locked in tiny rooms, where the men came in continuously. Twenty-four hours a day, no rest. And no escape, at least not till one of Robert's men came to the brothel and paid the brothel-keeper for an hour with me. I was seventeen by then and he liked what he saw. He liked the makeup they made me wear, and the sleazy clothes. He then wanted to buy me from my brothel-keeper, saying he thought his boss would like me and would give me a better job."

"And that was Robert?"

"That was Robert."

"And he liked you."

"He did at first. He wanted me for himself, not as someone to put in his brothels or his factories."

"And now he loves you?" Kali asked the question hesitantly, almost scared to use the word, knowing that feelings of love, respect and appreciation were for story books, not real life for women like her and Jan.

"I'm his property, Kali. As you well know. I'm here to do and say and be whatever he wants, just like all the other people he has trafficked. All the others under his control are the same, even the children he buys and sells. That's what this baby would be to him too. Someone to sell."

"No," Kali cried out. "This is not one of those children, Jan. This is your own, your very own child. It's not the same in any way whatsoever. You'll both feel differently towards your own child. You'll feel protective, and you'll love him or her so much. What if it's a boy? You couldn't do that to a baby boy."

It was a moment or so before she continued, this time in a more coaxing tone.

"Tell Robert. See what he says. Every man wants a son and, even if it's a girl, he'll love her too. He'd never forgive you if you got rid of his baby."

"I don't want him to know. That's why I'm asking for your help. In a different world, with a different husband, I'd be happy. I'd be thrilled that I was having a baby. But I can't risk it."

"This is guilt, Jan. Your hormones are already changing and making you think things you shouldn't be thinking. Put all these thoughts out of your head and forget about your past. It's perfectly normal that you and Robert would have a child of your own at some time. He'd be very angry with you if he knew you were getting rid of it."

Jan stared at Kali, a fierce look on her face.

"You have no idea how he'd be. And I have no intention of ever finding out how he would feel about it. I'm not going to tell him and you mustn't either. I'm not going to have this baby. Will you help me get rid of it or will I have to go to someone else?"

"Calm down, Jan. Calm down. If you're so hell-bent on doing this, then yes, I'll help you. But I wouldn't be a very good friend if I didn't even try to talk you out of it. I'll make some enquiries and find a good doctor who will do it, and do it safely. I'm presuming your own doctor wouldn't do it?"

"I can't go there. Robert would find out."

"Okay. It'll cost if you go private, but that's not a problem for you, so just be patient and I'll get back to you as soon as I can."

She rose from her chair and walked to the sofa to collect her bag. Reaching the door, she turned back to Jan.

"Call me if you have a change of heart."

There was no reply from the stony-faced woman, now looking down at her clasped hands. Silence filled the room after the bang of the door, lasting a good five minutes or more, the only movement during that time being Jan's hand sliding over her stomach and resting on it gently. She was disappointed by the attitude of her friend, fully expecting Kali to understand why she wanted to take this action, especially given their conversation about their past lives.

Sighing deeply, she was suddenly startled by a knocking on the lounge door.

"Come in," she called.

The door opened and Sunita entered, dropping a small curtsy to her owner.

45

"Will I take the dishes away?"

"Yes, you can take them away, and bring me a glass with a bottle of sherry from the dining room."

The child hastily withdrew after piling the dirty cups and saucers onto her tray and entered a few minutes later clutching a bottle of Harvey's Bristol Cream sherry and a glass, which she laid on the coffee table in front of Jan, still seated on her chair propped up with soft silky cushions.

Sunita cleared the final dishes from the room and shut the door behind her. Jan reached forward to pour herself a generous measure of the cream sherry and raised it to her lips, feeling in need of the effect of the alcoholic drink after her upsetting conversation with Kali. The sherry was warm as it touched her lips, but as she tilted her head back to gulp down the drink, she stopped suddenly, leaning forward and spitting it back into the glass. Then, frustrated with herself, she stood up from the chair and threw the crystal glass with its contents across the room, where it landed with a shattering crash against a small, black Chinese cabinet, the shards and the liquid flying out in spikes and splashes appearing on the wall and around the carpet.

She stomped over to the door, her face as black as thunder.

Why did I do that? she thought. *Why did I not drink the sherry? If I don't want this baby, why did I not just drink the sherry?*

There was no answer in her head and she pulled the door open quickly, shouting at the top of her voice.

"Nokara, Nokara! Get in here!"

The child came running, holding up her long skirt with both hands.

"Get that mess cleared up as quickly as you can. It's glass, so use the dustpan and brush, then wipe up the liquid. Don't cut yourself." In her anger at herself, her voice was getting louder as she spoke. Quickly, she grabbed the bottle of sherry with one hand and stormed out of the door.

Sunita's "Yes, madam," and curtsy went unnoticed as the lounge door slammed shut.

Chapter Five

SISTER IRENE MERCY GOVERNMENT
HOSPITAL, KOLKATA

Suman sat on the edge of Habi's bed, careful not to disturb the sleeping child. She took a quick look through the notes on Habi's clipboard, very pleased with the progress the little girl was making, her wounds all healing nicely.

The next problem she was going to have to think about, and very soon, was what to do with Habi. Within the next couple of days, it would be time to discharge her from the hospital, but, before then, she had to find a place to take the child. Her mind rebelled against putting her into one of the government shelters for rescued trafficked children. From past knowledge, she knew these were not the best places for vulnerable children like Habi.

In the hospital, there was an orphanage which was a wonderful sanctuary for babies abandoned at birth by desperate mothers who presumably were not in a position to care for another child in their families, or a young unmarried teenage girl not allowed to bring her baby home. This happened frequently; the stigma of unmarried mothers and abject poverty were still massive problems for thousands of families throughout India, and some believed their newborn would have a better chance of a good life if left for the orphanage to find a new home for them.

Suman knew the orphanage was a happy place, and the nurses were kind and loving, but it was bursting at the seams, with the cots holding more than one child at a time. Overriding that, Habi was not a baby or a toddler who could be cared for by the nursery nurses. She was too old for the orphanage.

If she was honest, Suman had hoped that Habi's friend Daivey would have returned to see how she was doing. She liked the boy. He looked like a hard-working, kind lad and she would have liked to explore the possibility of his family looking after Habi for a time. Daivey's mother had done a good job of applying medicinal herbs to Habi's burns and making a splint for her broken leg, so it might have been possible that she would accept a payment in return for looking after Habi.

Habi had made it clear that she liked Bimla, someone whose kindness had touched her after her rough treatment in the service of the lady she knew only as 'Madam'.

It's an avenue I'd like to try, thought Suman, *although at the moment I know very little about the family or where they live. I should have quizzed Daivey a bit more. Too late now.*

At home in her apartment that evening, Suman made a few phone calls. Two friends of hers were both volunteers at the orphanage in the hospital, and she was aware that they did other charity work in the city. She had in the past heard them speak of crèches working with street children and children's homes housing some of the most vulnerable children of Kolkata. She needed information about these and she found her two friends knew of a number of organisations she could explore, some situated not too far from the Sister Irene Hospital.

Armed with this information, she arrived at work early the following morning with the intention of taking a couple of hours off in the afternoon to go and visit the organisations she had highlighted as being a possible home for Habi. Unfortunately, her day did not proceed as planned. A number of children were brought into A&E needing Suman's attention and any other doctors and nurses that could lend a hand. An accident in an old, disused basalt stone quarry where some children were playing had resulted in a landslide of stones falling around them. Thankfully, no children had been killed but there were many injuries, broken bones and bad cuts, as well as the inhalation of the dust from the landslide causing breathing difficulties to a number of the unlucky children.

The day was full on, with no break in attending to the injured children until late into the evening. Suman decided to do a quick round of the wards where all her patients were.

"Are you headed home?" Sam asked as they took off their white jackets.

"Not quite," she replied with a smile. "I'm exhausted, but won't sleep tonight unless I do a last check around the wards. There's a few of the kids I like to say goodnight to. What about you?"

"Yeah, I'm pretty exhausted too, but my brain's still buzzing. I'll probably take a walk outside in the fresh air to unwind before going home. Can I come on your round with you?"

Suman looked surprised at this, but answered quickly. "You're very welcome. Anyone awake will be delighted to see you. The kids love you, Sam. You've got a great way with children."

"I love them too. That's why I chose to work in this particular field. It's great to be able to work with little ones just starting out their lives and be able to help them."

She smiled as they left the surgeries and began to walk towards the children's wards.

"And why did you choose to work with children, Suman?" he asked.

This time her smile was a wry one. "That's a long story, Sam. I might tell you all about it one day, but not tonight."

The walk around the beds was a quiet one, most of the children already fast asleep, but when they reached Habi's bed, they found her wide awake and sitting up with her back against the pillows, watching them closely.

Suman smiled.

"Hello, Habi. I thought you'd be fast asleep by now. Are you in any pain?"

"No, I was waiting for you. You always come and say goodnight to me, so I stayed awake. Have you come to say goodnight too, Dr Sam?"

"I certainly have, Habi. Dr Suman has been telling me all about you and I wanted to come and see how you were."

"I'm very worried," Habi replied.

Hiding his smile, he asked, "Oh, we can't have that, can we? Tell me what you're worrying about." He sat down beside her on the bed and lifted the small hand lying on the blanket.

"The nurses say that I'm better, and that means I have to leave the hospital. But I don't want to go because I don't have anywhere to go. So that's what I'm worrying about. Do you know where I will go, Dr Sam?"

"No, I don't, but I'm very sure that Dr Suman will not let you leave us until she finds a nice place for you. Am I right, Dr Suman?"

"You are. I'm working on it right now and have spoken to some of my friends, who are trying to find you a good place to go. So, until we find that good place, you'll stay here. Anyway, I won't let you go till I've taken your plaster cast off, as your leg is not quite healed. So you have to stop worrying and just get better."

"Will I be going to stay with your friends? Will they make me live in the kitchen and do the work?"

Suman sat down on the opposite side of the bed from Sam, and took the child's other hand.

"No, darling. You certainly won't be doing that. We'll find you a place where there are lots of other children to play with, and you can go to school, and learn to read and write. A place where the people will look after you, instead of you looking after them. Now, I think Dr Sam should tuck you up in your bed, and we'll both say goodnight and let you get to sleep. How lucky are you, getting a goodnight from Dr Sam?"

A very thoughtful Sam accompanied Suman on the rest of her round and out into the cool night air. He pre-empted her before she could say goodbye.

"Can I talk to you about Habi, Suman? I'll walk with you to your flat. I can go home that way, if it's okay with you?" He didn't wait for a reply before continuing.

"She's such a nice kid, isn't she? From what you'd told me earlier, I realised you'd become fond of her, and that you were going to try to find a home for her. But I can't help feeling you're taking on quite a responsibility there. What if you can't find a place for her? Would it not be better to get the authorities involved and get them to help find a children's home for her?"

Suman was silent, not knowing how to answer his questions.

He continued. "We've had children like her before in the hospital, Suman. You know that. Children who've been trafficked. And there are people out there trained to take them and look after them. Places they can go to be looked after. And I believe they even try to find the child's home to get them restored to their families."

A heavy lorry passing by appeared to be holding Suman's attention for a moment or two before she turned to Sam.

"Sam, to be honest, I don't know what I'll do if I can't find her a place, but I'll keep trying as long as I can. There's a reason why I feel so responsible for Habi. It's too late tonight to talk about this and I'm absolutely shattered. Could we have a coffee together at some point, or dinner, away from the hospital?"

It was Sam's turn to be silent. For months he'd been thinking on and off about asking Suman out, but had been reluctant even to try as he was certain he would be rejected. And now here she was asking him out, albeit not for a date. He was quietly delighted and accepted her offer with a smile.

"That would be good, Suman. And I'll be able to ask you about one of my little patients who is causing me worry at the moment. A very complicated case. You're just the person to advise me on what to do. What about dinner on Thursday? It's your evening off and I can do a swap with Dr Nadar."

"That would be perfect; thanks, Sam. Look forward to it. See you tomorrow."

She left him by the side of the road and crossed towards her apartment, giving a last wave as she turned out of sight. She was happy but anxious with this turn of events; happy because he was such an easy friend to talk to and a supportive colleague and she would enjoy having dinner with him. Yet she was also apprehensive because she had made the decision long ago not to talk about her past. This was something she didn't like to do and she couldn't understand why she had suddenly changed her mind.

Oh well, she thought, *maybe by the time we've spoken about his complicated patient, he'll have forgotten about my complicated life!*

Chapter Six

KOLKATA, INDIA

Activity on the street outside Jan's house was keeping her standing at the big bay window in the lounge. Her attention was riveted on a big, overturned lorry at the side of the road, and the small rickshaw, pushed against a wall, battered and mangled almost beyond recognition. The police were in attendance and a couple of cars drove away with what Jan surmised were the two drivers of the vehicles which had been in the noisy collision. She kept watching as the lorry was hooked up to the recovery vehicle, but turned quickly as she heard the front doorbell ring.

Nokara was making her way to the door in answer to the bell, but stopped as Jan's loud whisper reached her ears.

"No, Nokara. I don't want you to answer it. It might be the police, to ask about the accident outside. I don't want them in the house. Go back to the kitchen and keep very quiet, and don't answer any of the other doors if anyone knocks or rings," she added as Nokara disappeared into the kitchen.

The ringing continued, followed by knocking at the door. Jan stayed out of sight and remained as silent as she could.

"Jan," she heard her name called through the letterbox. "Jan, it's me, Kali. Are you in?"

"Are you alone?" Jan wasn't going to take any chances in case the police had managed to enter her garden, bypassing the security measures, and she shouted the question from behind her lounge door.

"Of course I'm alone," came the reply. "Can you let me in?"

Jan approached the large door with its beautiful stained glass window, gently lifting back a corner of the curtain which hung down the back to see for herself that Kali was alone.

"My goodness, you're very nervous!" Kali exclaimed as Jan opened the door and gestured to her to come in. "They can't come into the garden; you've got your security alarm on the gate. And I certainly wouldn't have let them in with me. They're dealing with the accident outside, not looking for criminals or their wives." Kali's attempt at humour was taken in the spirit that was intended and Jan smiled before leading her into the big, airy lounge. The two hugged for a moment before taking a seat.

"So," Kali began, "how have you been? You're looking peaky; have you been anywhere at all since I last saw you?"

"I'm probably looking peaky, as you say, because I can't stop being sick. Everything I eat, I throw up. Even when I don't eat, I'm sick. So no, I'm not going out at the moment. I'm keeping a very low profile and will do so until this is all over. Do you have any news for me on that subject?"

"Of course. I wouldn't let you down. I didn't want to phone in case Robert answered, but I do have some information, if you still want it. I thought maybe once you'd got used to the situation, you'd reconsider what you asked me to do for you."

"No, I haven't changed my mind in any way. I can't change my mind, which is why I asked for your help. So what have you found out for me?"

"Do you think we could have a glass of something or even a cup of coffee before we begin? My driver had to drop me a considerable distance away because of the accident, and I'm parched."

Again Jan smiled. "My bad manners. Of course we can." She walked over to a wall, elaborately decorated in a velveteen brocade wallpaper in deep shades of red, and pressed a button at the side of one of the huge pictures hanging on it.

"A call bell; that's new," Kali remarked. "Is this how you summon your young maid now?"

Jan laughed. "Yes, Robert had a bell system installed in the house so that I can call on her from any room I'm in. The kitchen now has a servants' bell indicator box, so Nokara knows which room I'm in. I think it's also so that he can call on me whenever he wants me, never mind Nokara!"

As if on cue, Nokara came through the door and curtsied.

"Two pots of Earl Grey tea, Nokara, and two glasses of white wine. As quickly as you can."

"Yes, Madam." The child gave a second curtsy and closed the door behind her.

"My God, Jan. It's getting like Downton Abbey in here! So English, and so upper class. And you…"

"And me?" Jan interrupted quickly. "Don't finish that sentence, Kali. I don't like myself very much at the moment."

The tall, beautiful woman was pacing the floor, but now sat back down, elegantly crossing her legs and facing her friend across the room.

"So, tell me, then. What have you managed to find out for me?"

Kali sighed, resigned to going forward with what she thought was a terrible idea. She opened her bag to bring out a couple of brochures and some loose pamphlets.

"Okay. I've got the brochures from the two gynaecology clinics I would recommend. They are discreet, they are safe, they work quickly and very confidentially. And, of course, they are very expensive. Read them through and then make a decision. I'm pretty certain one of these two would suit you. In fact, this one ..." She rose and offered one of the brochures to Jan.

"This one is run by a Doctor Dravin Khan, very highly thought of, according to his commendations."

"Khan? A Muslim doctor?"

"It says he was trained in India and he has good credentials. And, according to my source, the type of procedure you are looking for is one of his most successful operations. You need to phone and make an appointment. Check out both these brochures and, if any are suitable, there are some forms for you to complete. We can take it from there if you decide to go with one of these. You can have the operation done under a false name. They don't ask for identity cards and you pay up front. I think this is the kind of thing you are looking for."

Jan's face was blank, her eyes gazing far away into nothingness. Eventually she looked at her friend.

"Yes. It is. Thank you, Kali. I will read all of this carefully later and let you know what I decide. I appreciate that you did this."

She began to gather the brochures and pamphlets together and rose to insert them into a cabinet drawer. She locked the drawer and popped the key into her pocket.

"I want them out of the way before Nokara comes in with our drinks." She strode quickly across to the wall to push the button on her call system again.

"She's taking a long time to get them. Sorry about this. I do appreciate the help, but hate having these girls in the house."

Kali leaned back in her chair, relaxed now that the business had been done.

"She's very young, Jan. You should get an older girl and she will be able to do so much more for you. My maid is able to do my make-up and my hair and she looks after our clothes really well. If you had an older girl she could look after Robert, too?" she added with a knowing smile.

Jan bristled. "I don't encourage that. I keep all the servants away from him as much as I can. He has his own manservant, but pays no attention to the others."

"Very wise. Best if no one can identify him should anything go wrong."

"Well, nothing has gone wrong in the years I have been with him, so we shall just hope nothing ever does."

A light knock at the door heralded Nokara's entrance and the child began to serve the ladies their afternoon refreshments. Kali, with her usual curiosity, began to question the maid, asking her age, and where she came from.

However, Nokara had been well trained and replied to every question with a blank look and the words, "I'm sorry, Madam, I don't know."

Jan turned to Kali as Nokara shut the door. "I don't know why you're suddenly showing an interest in my new housemaid," she said with a laugh, "but she won't be able to tell you anything. She knows better. Don't you teach your staff to keep their mouths shut if asked questions?"

"Yes, of course we do. I was just curious about that one. What happened to the last one you had, the tiny one?"

"I've no idea. She had an accident and Robert had Ramdas take her away."

"Where did he take her? Was she okay?"

"I'm not allowed to ask questions like that, Kali. It's one of the reasons I hate having a maid. So, tell me about your new hobby. How is the jewellery making going?"

Successfully managing to divert the conversation with her friend into safer waters, the two ladies enjoyed their afternoon. Around four o'clock, Kali's driver returned to take her home and, once alone, Jan took the key from her pocket and got out the brochures she had locked away earlier.

She settled down to read about the two clinics. Still undecided at the end of half an hour, she locked the brochures back into the drawer and decided to defer making a decision today. Her head was telling her that a decision would have to be taken soon, as this was what she must do. Yet her whole body, with this new life growing in her womb, was screaming something else to her and she felt unable to deal with the conflict this was causing inside her.

Chapter Seven

SCHAANAPUR DISTRICT, KOLKATA

D aivey's pockets were jingling. *A good day's trading*, he thought. *Ma's going to be pleased with the money I've made today; it's been one of my best days ever.* He pulled the cart behind him, now much lighter than when he set off early this morning. Four times he had filled his cart and set off for the dealers' locations, the plastic buyers, the rag factory, the paper mill, and a few more. All were willing to trade and, better still, willing to haggle with him over the prices, resulting in him achieving good prices at most of them.

This took him a good bit of the day, but it was still only five o'clock as he neared his own village. *Ma would hopefully have his evening meal ready and she may*, thought Daivey, *be so happy with his takings that she would agree to a proposal he wanted to put to her*.

Raja saw him coming from a long way off and shouted to his mother that he was going to meet Daivey. She waved from the field at the side of the house, hoping against hope that Daivey had made good prices for his waste collections. Things were harder than normal for her, with the drought they were experiencing at the moment wreaking havoc with her crops. Money was tight with a few extra bills to be paid, all landing in her lap this week. She sighed, watching her boys head down the slope towards the house.

Daivey tied up his cart and made his way round to where she was, looking forward to telling her the news.

"Hi, Ma!" he shouted. "Can you come into the house? I want to speak to you."

What now? thought Bimla, a crease marring her brow under the big hat she wore when working in the fields. She laid down her hoe and took the hat from her head. Worn out and weary, her worries were making her more tired than she ought to be. Normally strong, hard-working and cheery, she knew she had been a bit more irritable with the boys as of late and hoped Daivey was not bringing yet another monetary problem her way.

"How did it go, Daivey?" she asked him as they entered the house together.

"Sit down, Ma," Daivey invited. "Sit down."

"Why have I to sit? Is it bad news? Or, is it maybe good news?" She smiled, unwittingly returning Daivey and Raja's own wide grins.

"It is, Ma. Have a look at this." Daivey thrust his hand in his pocket and pulled out what looked to her like an uncommonly large roll of banknotes. They were held together with an elastic band and he threw the bundle to his mother to catch. The hand went back into his pocket and a mound of coins was brought out this time, jingle jangling in his hands. He walked across to where she sat on the bed and laid them in his mother's lap.

"Count it, Ma. Tell me how much there is. It's the best prices I've had for a long time and I think there's more than we've had in these last few months."

"Have you not counted it yourself? That's not like you." She was teasing as she unrolled the notes and began counting the grubby rupee notes one by one.

With happy faces, both boys watched their mother as she carefully separated the notes across the bed, her own face lighting up more and more as she counted them. All counted, she started on the coins, stacking them up in denominations to make the count easier.

Looking up, she stared up at Daivey for a moment before saying, "One thousand, one hundred and two rupees." Her voice was a whisper. He nodded.

Bimla shook her head. "I don't know what to say. You've taken my words away. This is wonderful! One thousand, one hundred and two rupees," she repeated, quite overwhelmed.

"I know, Ma," he interrupted. "We were due a good week, but it's not just a good week, it's a great week. Go put your shoes on and we'll go into Shabapur and get some hot dahl pakoras from the street sellers. I know you love them. Come on, Ma. Quick, quick. I've got something I want to ask you, too."

Bimla's common sense was telling her not to waste this extra money on treats, but she knew her boys deserved one, especially Daivey. She knew how hard he worked, every day up at the crack of dawn doing his rag picking and waste collection. A sense of pride filled her heart as she scooped up the money from the bed. She pocketed some of the coins and then turned to unscrew an ornate knob from one of the poles at the end of her bed. The roll of notes was squeezed into the hollow tube and the knob screwed back on very tightly.

The bed was one of Daivey's acquisitions from the landfill site and he had joyfully collected all the pieces together and thrown them onto his cart, to clean up and present as a gift to his mother on her birthday. Bimla's bed was used as a couch during the day and her sleeping place at night. The boys slept on mats on the floor, happy to see their mother comfortable in her iron bed frame and worn mattress, another acquisition from the Dhapa site.

Slipping on her shoes, she linked arms with the boys and, with a spring in their steps, they headed into the village. At the evening market, the streets were alive with people and clamour, fairy lights adorning the stalls, incense and the smell of cooking filling the air. Many street food vendors had their big woks on, and Bimla, Daivey and Raja took their time to choose what they would like to eat. Each chose a dish and, as always happened, ended up sharing each other's food. Daivey's choice was an aloo tikki, generously adorned with red and green chutney, steam coming off the hot dish. For Raja, it was some Kachori, deep fried and sizzling, much to his delight. Bimla opted for some vada pav buns, one of her favourites.

Sitting on the edge of the pavement, they ate their delicious meals with relish, their fingers tingling with the heat from the freshly-cooked street food. As they were finishing, Daivey judged it to be the right time to speak to his mother about a problem he was trying to solve.

"Ma," he began. "I wanted to ask you something." He hesitated, unsure how to ask.

"Sure. Ask away," she prompted.

"You remember last week, when we brought the girl, Habi, home from the site?"

"I do." Bimla was wary about what was coming.

"And I told you all about the doctor who was so good to her, and to me?"

"You did. And I told you to forget all about Habi and the doctor. You did your bit, helping to get her to hospital."

"I know, but it's been on my mind. The doctor said if I wanted to go back and see Habi again, this would do her good, to see me, or even us, again."

As Bimla's mouth opened to answer this, he hurried on.

"So I wondered if you and Raja would come with me, back to the hospital to see Habi. I thought maybe, if the doctor was there, you could ask her for some medicine for your leg. We can afford it now, with all that money I got today. What do you say, Ma? Will you come with me?"

"Will I come with you? Does that mean you've already decided to go to the hospital? With or without me?"

"No, Ma. I won't go if you don't want me to, but I'd really like to go and see if Habi is getting better. And to take you with me. Your leg is not healing with the tamarind seed paste you're using. The doctor said if I ever needed help I was to go to her."

"My leg's okay, Daivey. You've not to worry about it. I told you it was a rat snake that bit me; it's not poisonous. I don't need a doctor."

"But she could have a look at it and maybe give you some medicine. Wouldn't you like to know what's happening to Habi, too?"

If she was being truthful, Bimla would have answered yes to Daivey's question. However, she was torn between a fear of getting involved in some way which she felt would bring trouble into the family, and easing her mind about the little girl who had been found with burns and a broken leg on the landfill site.

Daivey used her silence to his advantage. "We could go tomorrow morning. I've been speaking to Abdul, my friend who drives the rickshaw. He says he is going over that way tomorrow, so he could take us. The only thing is he's going really early in the morning. But please, Ma. I'd really like to go."

Raja added his plea to Daivey's. "I'd like to go too. Or I could stay here and go to the site for Daivey," he added after a withering look from his brother.

Bimla laughed, unable to stop herself.

"Yes, so you could, Raja. And I'd like to see you pulling that great big cart up the mountain all by yourself. No, I suppose if Daivey has his heart set on going, we'd better all go. It'll be a day out for us. What time is Abdul leaving, Daivey, and will he want money for taking us?"

"He's leaving about six in the morning, when the roads are a bit quieter. He didn't mention money, but maybe if we give him some, he'll bring us home again. It's a long walk for you, Ma, with your sore leg. I'll go and see him now."

It was well after six thirty the next morning when Abdul rattled up in his rickshaw to the family's house; they had almost given up on him. He was full of apologies, but gave no reasons for being so late. Bimla surmised he had been drinking the night before and had slept in this morning, and hoped his driving was going to get them safely to the hospital. When he stopped three or four times on the road to go and relieve himself in the bushes, she was sure about it. However, his driving was no worse than the other drivers' on the road and the boys were enjoying the experience of travelling along the roads of West Bengal, trying to point out to each other some of the architectural and cultural remnants from when Kolkata had been the former capital of the British Raj. They didn't know the names of the buildings, but were suitably impressed by their splendour.

With all of Abdul's stops and his late start, it was nearly eight o'clock in the morning when they arrived at their destination. The friendly driver dropped them off about a hundred yards from the hospital and promised to come back for them in a couple of hours' time. The gift of two hundred rupees from Bimla pleased him so much that he promised to come right to the main gate to find them around ten o'clock.

The little group set off walking towards the huge building that was the hospital, letting Daivey lead the way. They entered the big doors and headed over to the reception desks, where long queues were already beginning to form. Bimla was quiet, saying nothing, but she could tell that Raja was overawed by the crowds, and she could see the distress on his face as he took in the injured and sick people that were there with their relatives. The scene was similar to that when Daivey was last there, with some people lying on stretchers, sitting in wheelchairs, or squatting on the floor as if unable to stand. Bimla reached over and took her son's hand and he drew nearer to her as they joined one of the queues.

It took a while, but at last they reached the front of the queue and the male receptionist behind the long desk enquired as to how he could help them. Daivey stepped forward with a card in his hand, and gave it to the man.

"We've come to see Dr Sudra," he explained, hesitantly. "She gave me this card and said to ask you to phone her to come and see me, if she was around."

The man held the card up closer to his face and read it carefully.

"Well, I don't know if she'll be in yet. It's still quite early in the morning, but I'll give her a ring and see. You're certain she gave you this card herself and that you didn't find it somewhere?"

"Yes, sir. She gave it to me to use if I came back to the hospital. She is looking after someone for us."

With reluctance, the man picked up a pen and asked, "What's your name? I have to tell her who you are."

"Daivey Asura. I was here about a week ago. I brought in a girl called Habi and Dr Sudra is looking after Habi. I don't know Habi's other name."

Daivey was worried. Unable to read or write, he wasn't aware what the words on Suman's card were, and was afraid he'd be asked more questions, questions he couldn't answer. He took a deep breath and put his arm around his mother's shoulders.

"We'll wait over here while you phone. Thank you." He drew his mother and Raja out of the queue and over to a space on the floor not far away. He watched closely as the man made the phone call, his courage almost failing him and his heart thumping in his chest.

Moments later, the man called him over.

"Dr Sudra is here. She wants you to wait with me until she comes to get you. Just stand over at the window there, behind my desk."

"Thank you, sir. Thank you."

Suman was in her room, having arrived at the hospital only a short time ago. She was leafing through some of the mail when the call came through. Pleased that Daivey was back to see Habi, she was unaware that his mother and brother were with him, but was delighted to see them all when she arrived at reception.

"Daivey, this is so kind of you to come back to see Habi. She asks for you daily. And to bring your family; I'm really happy to meet you both. Come with me and we'll go along to the children's ward and have a coffee before we go to see Habi."

Settled in Suman's office with a mug of coffee beside her, Bimla was most uncomfortable and embarrassed. She was worrying about the casual way her son was speaking to this eminent doctor, as if he had known her for a long time and as if he was her equal. He wasn't being disrespectful, but Bimla was very concerned that such a professional person as Suman might take offence at his informality.

The caste system in India had long been illegal, but most definitely not abandoned. Bimla, conscious of where she belonged in society, didn't like Daivey showing such familiarity to people like Dr Sudra. Suman was unaware of Bimla's worries or thoughts, the caste system not being something that entered her own thoughts at any time unless it adversely affected any of her patients. She chatted to Bimla in Bengali, only lapsing into Marathi or Hindi when she struggled for a translation.

"How did you get here so early this morning?" she asked.

Daivey answered for his mother, on a high now that he was again speaking to this kind lady who was looking after Habi. "We came in a rickshaw. And we're going home in one. It belongs to a friend of mine and he was coming this way."

She smiled. "I'm pleased about that. I was worried in case you'd been walking for hours."

She turned to Raja. "I've heard all about you, Raja. You help Daivey at his work on the landfill site, don't you? And you helped to rescue Habi. I'm very grateful to you for doing that. Sounds like she wouldn't have survived for long where she was."

"She had a broken leg and lots of burns. Ma tried to help with them." Raja was as excited as his elder brother and Suman smiled as she turned to Bimla.

"I know. You did a good job in treating her wounds, Mrs Asura. What did you put on the burns?"

"Banana leaves. I've used this for my boys and it's good for burns. How is the child, Doctor? Is she any better?"

"Yes, she's much better and almost ready to leave hospital. I'll take you to see her once you've had your coffee. She'll be very happy."

"Where will she go when she leaves here?" Bimla hesitated, not sure how much to say to Suman. "I ... em, I asked her about her home, but she didn't know where her home was. Has she remembered?"

"Unfortunately no, she doesn't have any idea where it is. I don't know at the moment where she can go, but I'll keep her here until I find a good place to take her. I would try to find her own home, but she hasn't given me any hints on where it might be. I gather she came from someone else's house where she worked as a servant. Did she talk to you about this?"

"She just told me that she was kept in the kitchen, but couldn't tell me where the house was or who she was working for."

Daivey joined in the conversation. "Ma thinks she was trafficked, and made to work for some rich lady."

Bimla added quickly. "Well, we don't know that for sure, Daivey. It just sounded like that to me." She gave Daivey a quick warning look, concerned that he was voicing this fear of hers.

However, Suman nodded. "Yes, I think that too. So we must look after her well until she finds a permanent home, wherever that may be. Would you like to come to the ward and see her now? She will have had something to eat and will be watching for me coming on my rounds."

Daivey interrupted. "Could you maybe have a look at Ma's leg before…?"

Bimla jumped in quickly to try to stop Daivey from continuing. "I'm fine, Daivey." She turned to Suman. "Please don't worry about me, Doctor; you've got enough to do. I'm fine." She frowned at Daivey.

However, Suman refused to accept Bimla's assurances.

"I can easily have a look at your leg before we go. We've got plenty of time. Tell me what happened to it."

As Bimla explained the problem of her snake bite, Suman began to examine the wound just above the ankle.

A number of questions later, she stood up and crossed over to a small medicine cupboard in the room. She unlocked it and reached in for a tube of ointment and a couple of bandages from the shelf.

"It's a nasty bite and it's become infected." She knelt down again. "I need you to keep washing it every day with clean water, and apply some of this ointment afterwards. I'm going to put a dressing on it just now, and give you another bandage to use when you're washing the first one. I'm really glad you let me have a look at it. That ointment works miracles and should help to clear it up. The tamarind paste you put on it is good too, but this ointment will hopefully work a lot quicker."

Gratefully, Bimla accepted the paste and the bandages and offered to pay, but was quickly silenced.

"No cost. I'm happy to help."

Suman helped Bimla to her feet with a smile, and turned to the boys, hovering at the door.

"Have you had enough to eat, boys? Pop these biscuits in your bag for later." She picked up the plate of biscuits her assistant had brought in with the coffee tray and scooped them into Daivey's bag.

"All set?" She held the door open for the little group as they left the room.

Suman walked with Bimla, the boys behind, as they made their way along the wide corridors, filled with families waiting to see their relatives. As usual, many were sitting or lying asleep on the stone floor, presumably having been there for quite a long time. A few ill-looking patients were in the corridors as well, hoping to get a bed as soon as one became available. They stood out of the way for Suman as she approached with her small entourage, and looked with curiosity at the attractive doctor in her white coat.

They soon reached the ward, with Suman having spent the time questioning Bimla on a number of things she wanted to know about their home life. Once they were standing at Habi's bedside, Suman was sure of one thing; she was going to pursue her idea of Habi going to stay with this family, even if it was for just a short time. Their honesty, alongside their love and respect for each other, was clear, as were their penurious circumstances, which did not deter Suman from thinking they would look after Habi in the way she wanted the child cared for.

Habi saw them coming and the excitement on her face was apparent to all. She tried to welcome them all at the same time, saying their names at the top of her voice and then stopped, subsiding into tears. Suman sat down on her bed.

"What's all this, Habi?" she asked gently. "No need for tears. Daivey and Raja and Mrs Asura are just as happy to see you as you are to see them. They've come to ask how you are, not to see tears. Come on, let's have that lovely smile."

Softly wiping her tears with a hankie, Suman began to realise the depth of the child's loneliness, having no one but Suman and this little family in the whole world. She hugged Habi tightly, then stood back to let Bimla sit on a chair at the side of the bed. Raja jumped up on the bed to sit, and began chattering, asking lots of questions of Habi, whose eyes were shining.

"Your burns are nearly gone, Habi," he announced. "What about your leg, is it better too?"
Habi pulled back the light blanket covering from her legs.

"I've got a plaster cast on it. It's to be on for six weeks. You can draw something on it if you like. Dr Suman wrote her name, and wrote me a poem, a funny one, and drew a funny face on it. And the nurses all wrote their names and drew something for me, and some of the other girls in here drew me some Mandala circles. Is that the right name, Dr Suman?" Suman nodded.

Raja pulled himself forward quickly and whispered in her ear. She laughed and answered proudly, "Yes, I'm allowed to call her Dr Suman. I don't have to call her Dr Sudra because she's my very best friend. Apart from Daivey, who rescued me." She leaned forward to take his hand and pull him down to sit on the bed as well.

"I rescued you too." Raja was indignant and received a dig in the ribs from his older brother.

"Yes, you both did," Habi agreed. "And your Amma, too." She smiled shyly at Bimla, who leaned in for a hug, returned tenfold.

After about ten minutes, with both the boys intent on their artwork on Habi's plaster cast, Suman quietly asked if Bimla would like to come out of the ward with her for a chat.

"We'll leave her with the boys for a short time, and then I'll bring you back."

After a quiet word with one of the nurses, Suman led Bimla into a small side room at the end of the ward, and pointed to a chair for her to sit on. She herself just perched on a table sitting against a wall, and crossed her ankles.

"What did you think of her?" Suman asked. "A bit different from the last time you saw her, I expect?"

"Yes, a big difference. She's so much better. Will her scars go away, and will she be able to walk normally once her plaster cast comes off?"

"Yes to both questions. Mrs Asura ..." She stopped. "May I call you Bimla? I feel I know you so well even after this very short time."

Bimla coloured slightly, but smiled as she answered. "Of course. You do me a great honour."

"Not at all. I'm indebted to you and your boys for bringing me such a lovely little patient. I wanted to speak to you about Habi, though, as I'm concerned for her future and I thought that perhaps you could help me out."

"Me, help you? How can I do that?" A wary look had entered her eyes.

"You know Habi's circumstances, and you share my suspicions about what happened to her. I think it might be almost impossible to find where she came from and where her family are. In these cases, when we have lost or abandoned children in the hospital, we would normally hand them over to the authorities to go to one of their shelters for orphaned or trafficked children." Suman shook her head before continuing.

"I don't want to do that. In fact, I feel responsible for her, more so than for any of my other patients. I don't want her to feel alone and have no one to care what happens to her. So I wondered, do you think it would be possible for you and the boys to take Habi into your home, for a little while, to look after her for me? She has spoken a lot to me about what she would like and where she'd like to go, and your home is the only place on her list. She doesn't know anyone else. What do you think about this?"

"Dr Sudra ..." Bimla began.

Suman interrupted. "Call me Suman."

Bimla's eyes widened in surprise, and she was silent for a few moments.

Her next words were spoken slowly, with thought. "You're a very kind lady, Suman. Daivey told me when he came home from the hospital last time that he met a very special person and I didn't understand what he meant. But I do now, and I'd love to be able to do whatever you ask of me.

However ... I have to say no, and tell you my reasons for saying no. I'm a single parent. I have no husband, so life is quite hard. We don't always have enough money to get by and I can't get work, as no one will employ me. I've never learned to read and write, so I grow crops in my small garden and sell them and I put my boy Daivey out to work collecting the garbage. Raja helps us both. We try to bring in enough money to feed and clothe ourselves and Daivey sometimes has a good week, which brings in extra money. But I then have to pay something towards all the debts my husband left me with."

Bimla paused for a moment, wondering if she was telling Suman too much about family, but she needed to explain the exact reasons she couldn't do what this warm-hearted doctor was asking of her. She carried on.

"Sometimes it's a struggle. My boys don't go to school. I can't afford uniforms for them and I can't look after them if Daivey doesn't bring in money. I'd love to take Habi in. I lost my little girl many years ago, and Habi would brighten up our house as Sonya used to do. But I must say no. I'm so very sorry. Put her in the children's shelter and she will get to go to school. She's a bright little girl."

As she finished speaking, Bimla's hands were clasped in her lap and she remained in this position with her head bowed, unable to look at Suman.

There was a silence for a moment while Suman gathered her thoughts, realising that Bimla was a strong, proud woman for whom life had not been easy. She also realised that to offer her money, which she intended to do, was maybe not going to be as straightforward as she had thought. She was afraid Bimla would reject this as being 'charity' money, which Suman suspected she'd never accept.

At last she spoke.

"Bimla, you've given me a lot to think about and I want to say I have a deep respect for you for sharing all that with me. I know it wasn't easy for you. So can I maybe put another, different suggestion to you, before you make your final decision about Habi?" Suman crossed the small room, drew up a chair and sat down beside Bimla.

"I've been checking out a number of places for Habi, trying to find one I thought suitable. Some of them are quite expensive, but they don't offer what I had hoped to find, a homely place where she could stay and find someone who really cared for her and who would send her to school. I've also checked out foster homes for her, but, again, I couldn't find one I liked enough. And they're also very expensive.

I've thought about how to solve the problem and I believe you could help me do this. Habi could go to school and you could send your boys to school at the same time if that's what you'd like to do. I have a trust fund available which would pay a suitable salary to the person who takes Habi in. It would be a job, Bimla, as well as a favour to me. You would be employed to look after Habi, and receive a decent weekly wage for the work you would be doing. Do you have a school near you that the children could go to?"

Bimla's eyes were alight as she stared at Suman. "Yes, there is a small school near our house, but we would need to visit it first to see if it's a good school. I think it teaches boys in the morning and girls in the afternoon. Daivey could continue with his job at Dhapa in the afternoon. He would not like to give this up, as he has a good business which he loves."

She sighed deeply. "Could you really do this for us? Really?"

"I think so. I'll find out a lot more and get a contract for you, from the trust fund. I'll come and visit your home and maybe if you find someone to help you read the contract, you could invite them too?" Bimla nodded quickly in reply to this question.

Suman asked another one. "Do you have space in your house for Habi? A room to sleep that is not with the boys?"

"We could make one. Daivey suggested we add an extra room some time ago and has collected all the things we need to do this. He and his friends could do it quickly. But are you certain there will be enough money in this fund and in this weekly wage for us to do all this, schools for the three of them and all Habi's other needs? It would be a lot of money."

"I'm certain," Suman assured her, hastily plucking a figure out of thin air. "The wage might be somewhere around three to four thousand rupees a week or perhaps a little more. But I'll check to be certain. Do you think that would be all right?"

Suman's question went unanswered, but not because Bimla was unhappy with this figure. Her mouth was open, but no sound was coming out!

Chapter Eight

KOLKATA, INDIA

Thursday evening arrived far too quickly for Suman. She was rushed off her feet at work with no time to plan or prepare for an evening out with Sam. In the late afternoon, hurrying to her apartment, she realised that she would have to dig out something nice to wear from the back of her wardrobe, as Sam had informed her earlier in the day that he had booked a table for the two of them at La Cucina in the Hyatt Hotel. Delighted with the choice, as she knew its reputation, it also provided the rare opportunity to wear more formal attire.

Looking stunning, Suman's choice of clothing was an ankle-length dress in a vivid blue; the dress showing off to advantage her slim, neat figure. Not having had much time to worry about her hair, she wore it loose, hanging in long, sleek curls down her back, a style that suited her well.

Sam, too, was in a happy mood, as he was looking forward to spending the evening with her and finding out a bit more about her mysterious past. Laughing over her choice of food from the menu, he explained his amusement when she looked puzzled.

"Salmon Scottato was exactly what I thought you'd order. You seem to love everything Scottish. I hope you're going to tell me why."

She smiled, realising that the questions about her background had started very early in the evening. She tried to turn the conversation back to Sam.

"And your choice of linguine leads me to think you like Italian food and possibly Italy as well. Have you ever been to Italy, or across to Europe? Your English is excellent."

"I have indeed been to Europe, to a number of different countries, including the UK. I've got relatives living in London and have been a number of times to visit them. And yes, I've been to Italy as well, although no relatives there, just a wish to see a bit of Europe. I went to Munich in Germany and Paris, of course, plus a stop off in Greece on the way home. I love to travel. Are you the same, are you well travelled too?"

"Sort of," she replied hesitantly, hoping she could deflect the questions back to him again. "From the age of nine I lived in Scotland and was taken to London for a visit, and over to France when I was a bit older, but I haven't travelled as much as you. Tell me how you liked Europe."

"I loved it. I'd do a lot more travelling if I could, but you know what it's like at the hospital, work takes up so much time it's hard to get holidays. I've never visited Scotland, though. That's an unusual country to go to. What took you there?"

"Family," she answered slowly, the moment saved from any more explanations by the arrival of their drinks.

The moment did not last very long and she gave into the inevitability of the conversation forever returning to her earlier life, or at least until she told him what he wanted to know.

Over a bottle of an Italian Bertani Soave wine interspersed with the arrival of the different courses of their meal, Suman, more relaxed now, began to open up a little about her unusual life, beginning with details of her early childhood growing up in poverty in a very rural village in the state of Maharashtra in India. From there, she told him how she had been taken to Mumbai, and then on to Holland for a short time, eventually arriving in Scotland under the guardianship of a foster mum called Ellie. She spoke in loving terms of Ellie and her husband Geoff, and said that one day she would introduce Sam to the pair of them, as they were coming to Kolkata to visit her very soon.

Reading between the lines, Sam realised there must have been something really bad in her past as he watched her normally warm, bright eyes cloud over when she spoke of Mumbai and Holland. She had only fleetingly mentioned them in her story, but he saw the change in her and was desperate to ask a number of questions about that part of her life. He refrained, but it took a lot of willpower to stop the words coming from his mouth.

She could sense his dilemma and, taking a big breath, said with a smile, "Go on, you can ask me some questions."

He leaned forward, cupping his hands together and resting his chin on them with his elbows on the table, drawing as near to her as he dared. His voice was gentle, his doctor's manner coming to the fore.

"Are you sure?"

She nodded.

"Mumbai and Holland," he began. "You used the word 'taken'. Was this against your will?"

Her eyes stared into his for a very long moment and, to his utter dismay, a large tear appeared in one of her unblinking eyes and rolled silently down to land in her lap. Sam was terrified.

"No, no, no," he said urgently, passing her a large white handkerchief from his pocket. "Please don't answer my question. I shouldn't have asked that."

A few seconds passed as she wiped her face with his hankie and regained control of her emotions.

As she passed the hankie back she looked at him. "You're a good friend, Sam. Thank you."

"No worries," he replied, adding a little more wine to her glass. "And, as your friend, can I recommend the wonderful roasted almond cannoli for dessert? I have personal experience of this and know it's the best in India."

He was right, the cannoli was scrumptious and brought to an end a most enjoyable meal, discounting the small emotional hiccup during the main course. In the taxi home, not wanting to touch any more raw nerves, Sam thought it safer to discuss a problem he was having with one of his patients, a child of five who had been brought in with suspected polio. With the last confirmed case of polio occurring more than two years ago, and the vast majority of India's children vaccinated against the disease, he was sceptical about the diagnosis and asked Suman if she would be willing to have a look at the child tomorrow. He was pretty certain the problem was acute flaccid myelitis, another inflamed spinal condition, almost as severe as polio, and was keen to know her thoughts on it.

"To be honest, Sam, I've never come across AFM. I've seen polio and assume AFM has very similar symptoms. Does the child have paralysis anywhere?"

"No, but she does have a number of other symptoms, including a weakness in one arm. It was caught very quickly, so I'm monitoring it closely. I had an MRI scan done on the child today and tomorrow I'm doing a lumbar puncture test. Fancy assisting me with that?"

"I'd certainly be glad to help if I can. I'll have a look at my diary and see what my day is like tomorrow, and if I can come I will."

Their two heads were together for the rest of the journey, the discussion all about the horrendous viral disease that Sam thought he might be dealing with. The symptoms, diagnosis, treatment and prognosis were all debated between the two doctors until the taxi arrived at Florentine Apartments.

Sam climbed out of the taxi with Suman, his intention being to say goodnight and walk home from there. So it was a surprise when he heard her suggest a walk through the gardens and a seat on a bench beside the magnificent hibiscus flowers growing in abundance there. As they sat down, he looked at her now serious face and frowned.

"Suman, I'm so sorry I upset you earlier ..." He stopped quickly as she put a finger on his lips and smiled.

"I know, Sam. But I think I do want to tell you a bit more about myself. I've come to know you so well and I trust you implicitly. I'd like to be more open and honest when I'm with you. I want to be more ..." she paused for a moment, screwing up her face in thought, "... more myself."

He said nothing, not knowing the right words.

She continued. "I'm not sure where to start, so tell me what you think you know and I'll take it from there."

"Okay." He spoke softly. "I can't help feeling that something very bad happened to you when you were young. You've alluded to it once or twice and I've suspected from what you've said that you were trafficked. You spoke of being taken."

She sighed deeply. "Yes, I was. I was trafficked at the age of eight." Suman wasn't looking at him now; her eyes were miles away, staring into the flower beds in front of them.

"That day, I went down to the river with my friends to get water. It was Holi, and we were looking forward to the village celebrations at night. When I got back, my mother and father told me that some government officials from Mumbai had come to the village and they were offering my parents the chance to send one of their daughters to a school there, to learn to read and write and be taught a profession of some kind in a girls' boarding school. My father thought it would be a great opportunity for me."

She looked round for a moment with a wry smile. "The money they were offering him helped with this decision."

"And your mother?" Sam asked.

"My mother was not allowed an opinion. She had to go along with it. But I saw in her eyes how terrified she was."

A few minutes passed as she sat remembering and he sat without a sound at her side until she felt able to continue.

"I was put in a big truck, there and then. My mother had already packed a few things for me. I wasn't alone; there were two other girls from my village taken too, and we were driven for miles and miles, all through the night, and ended up in what I now know was Mumbai. I watched money being exchanged when the men handed me over to others and I never saw my two friends again. I changed hands a few times for money before I ended up in Holland."

"Why Holland?" he asked.

"Lots of brothels in Amsterdam," she answered, her wry smile showing again. "And good prices for girls my age."

He closed his eyes for a second, the pain reaching his heart. When he opened them, his hand reached out for hers and held it tight, struggling to keep his emotions in check as she continued.

"I had a guardian angel; a girl called Angena, who looked after me, and my luck changed one day when she met Ellie by accident in a night club we'd been taken to. The gang masters were going to kill me, but she convinced Ellie to rescue me and ..."

There was a long pause before the next words came out in a rush. "Ellie rescued me and took me to Scotland."

Suman freed her hand from his and stood up at this point, as if to say that this was enough for her and she needed to go. He stood too, reaching out quickly to pull her into his arms and hold her tightly. She laid her head on his shoulder and allowed him to hold her, but made no sound.

After a moment, she took a step back and looked up at him. She could see his face was wet and reached out to wipe the tears with her thumbs.

"Sam, I've had a lovely night, but I can't have you crying for me. Doctors are supposed to be able to control their emotions," she teased. "I'm going in now, but if you still want to be my friend, it's my treat next time." She smiled at him. "I might even cook for you."

At that, Sam lifted his head and somehow managed to return her smile. "Cook for me? You can cook?"

Her smile widened. "I'm not that bad, you know. I can cook a mean haggis, neeps, and tatties. I even make a fabulous cranachan."

"Well, since I have absolutely no idea what any of these things are, I'll take you up on your offer!"

Chapter Nine

JAN'S HOUSE, KOLKATA, INDIA

A few days after Kali's visit to drop off the brochures, Jan was uneasy. Still queasy in the mornings with her pregnancy and knowing she should do something quickly about ending the nausea, she had not yet made a decision about which clinic she should visit to remove the problem once and for all. Knowing that the sooner it was done the better, she was also aware of an even stronger instinct taking over her body. That instinct was exactly what nature had intended it to be, the need to protect the foetus growing inside her womb.

Each day that passed, she became less and less inclined to make the phone call to book an appointment at the clinic. This morning she even found herself wondering what size the foetus was, and worse, what gender the baby was. On her laptop, she typed in a question about the size of a twelve-week foetus, and got what should have been a very reassuring answer that, at this stage of her pregnancy, the baby was only about the size of a plum. Even more worrying was the fact that she carried on typing questions, wanting to know all about what was happening inside her.

She had to make the decision soon. It appeared that one more week would take her into what was termed the second trimester. A panic began to surface inside her, knowing that each moment she delayed, the worse this was going to be. She brought out the brochures again, choosing one at random and opening the page to where the telephone number was.

She got as far as dialling in some of the numbers, then hung up quickly. No, she was not yet ready to do this. Hastily pushing the brochures back in the cabinet drawer, she rang the bell on the wall, summoning Nokara to the room.

As the child entered, another wave of nausea overcame her and she hurried past Nokara with the words, "I'm going for a lie down on my bed. Please bring me a cup of chai and then, after that, I don't want to be disturbed."

Heading upstairs, she barely made it past the bed and into her en-suite bathroom to retch into the bathroom sink. Exhausted and sore, she lay down on the side of the bed, curling her knees up, unconsciously forming the foetal position with her body. The cramps in her stomach after the retching were painful and she moaned slightly, her hands instinctively holding her stomach.

Her eyes were closed and Nokara thought she was asleep as she brought in Jan's tray and laid it on the bedside cabinet beside her mistress. She jumped as Jan's voice said quietly, "Thank you. Can you please put a blanket over me? I'm very cold."

"Yes, Madam." The child opened the wardrobe door and brought out a soft, furry blanket, closing the door with a gentle click. Turning back to the bed, Nokara hesitated, her gaze being drawn to Jan's body lying curled up on the bed, facing away from her. Unsure what to do, she stood rigidly still until, after a moment, Jan asked, "What's the matter? Why are you not putting the blanket over me?"

"Madam, I …"

"What? What is the problem, child?"

"Madam, you're bleeding." The words were blurted out.

Jan's eyes widened, a chill running through her body as she lay totally still.

"Well," she said at last. "Put the blanket over me and go back to the kitchen. I will deal with it. Say nothing to anyone."

"Yes, Madam." She did as Jan had ordered and laid the blanket over her mistress, hurrying from the room and down the wooden staircase.

The moment the door was closed Jan turned and put her feet over the side of the bed, wrapping the blanket tightly around her as she stood up. She was very aware now of what was happening to her, and fear entered her soul, alongside the unexpected realisation that she didn't want to lose this baby. At last she admitted to herself that what she actually wanted above anything else was to carry and keep this tiny little being inside her. Her mind began searching for what to do. Should she lie down again? Should she phone a doctor or go to hospital? She took a deep breath, trying to stop the rising panic, and walked to the window. She needed to think, to plan her next steps.

"Nokara, I'm going to be away for a short time. If anyone asks for me, you must not tell them anything about what you saw today. Nothing. Do you understand?"

"Yes, Madam." The little curtsy followed, unseen by Jan as she lifted her bag from the floor and made her way to the front door.

"I'll wait outside for my taxi," she explained. "Just shut the door behind me and lock it. I'll see you when I return."

The black taxi did not take long and she climbed into the back seat.

"I want to go to the Sister Irene Mercy Government Hospital, please. Do you know where it is?"

"Yes. But it's a long way away, and will cost a lot of money."

"How much will it cost?"

He calculated quickly. "I'll need three hundred rupees to take you there."

"I will give you two hundred rupees if you take me there and three hundred if you drive very quickly but very carefully."

The driver was grateful to be earning three hundred rupees for the journey, and set off with extreme caution and care. However, he was extremely disappointed on arrival to be told not to wait on his client.

"I don't mind waiting, even for a long time, Ma'm. You will want to go home again after your visit," he assured her.

"I'm visiting a friend and might be a very long time, so there's no point in you waiting. I may even stay all night if she is really unwell. I have your number and will phone you once I'm ready to go home. Will that be okay?"

"Yes, Ma'm, thank you." Reassured he would be getting the return trip, he drove off through the crowds of people walking and milling about in the hospital grounds, leaving Jan behind trying to look as inconspicuous as she possibly could.

Knowing there was little possibility of any of her friends or her husband's friends being here at the hospital, she had nonetheless put the scarf of her sari up over her head and was holding it over in front of her mouth as well.

Just in case. She entered the main doors of the huge hospital and headed for the reception area, hoping against hope that she would be attended to quickly. Her cramps were bothering her again and she started to worry that the bleeding from earlier would also return.

The queue was not too desperately long, and thankfully she only had to wait around fifteen minutes. Grateful it was a female on the desk, she spoke softly to the girl, trying to keep her problem as confidential as she could in such a busy place.

Although she wished she was visiting her normal private health clinic, she had realised some time ago that this wasn't possible. The clinic staff would insist on informing Robert about what was happening to her, and billing him for her care. She couldn't risk that. For him to find out that she was pregnant and said nothing would result in dire consequences. She had no idea if the baby was still there or not, but if, by some miracle she was still pregnant, the less he knew the better.

There was no doubt at all in her mind what Robert's reaction to the pregnancy would be. Contrary to Kali's assumption that he would be delighted with a child of his own, Jan knew that nothing could be further from the truth. The subject had been discussed between them only once, with Jan being told that any babies of hers would be taken away and sold to the highest bidder.

The receptionist asked only a minimal number of questions and Jan had prepared her answers in advance; a false name, address and phone number and a fictitious next of kin. She gave her name as Mrs Hingorani, as she knew of a distant relative living in Delhi with this name and it was the first one that came to her mind. The next question she was asked was about her health problem and as soon as she explained about the bleeding, she was informed she would have to go to the gynaecology ward. A wheelchair was offered and gratefully accepted and, within minutes, Jan found herself being pushed along the wide corridors of the hospital by a porter and entering a busy waiting room, where she was then left sitting. From where she was positioned, she could see into some side rooms where it looked as if there were clinics being held. She also spotted a door marked 'Day Surgery', with the door firmly closed. A large, two-tiered trolley sat in the corridor nearby laden with medical instruments, upturned bowls and some threadbare towels, looking abandoned.

Jan shuddered, afraid of what was going to happen to her. Thankfully she didn't have long to wait. A nurse came out of one of the closed doors and approached her, asking her name. Again she gave the name Hingorani and was then wheeled into a side room. Her heart sank as she watched the nurse leave and close the door. Sitting in the room were two male doctors, their stethoscopes dangling around their necks.

The older of the two men rose and spoke. "Good afternoon, Mrs Hingorani. My name is Doctor Thakur and this is …"

She interrupted him quickly. "Doctor, I'm very grateful that you could see me, but I'm afraid it's my husband's instruction that I'm seen by a lady doctor. Can you please arrange this for me?"

The doctor hesitated, rubbing his chin for a moment.

"I'm asked that a lot in this clinic, Mrs Hingorani, so I understand why you are asking. However, I can assure you that I am a very well-qualified gynaecologist and surgeon. Please know, I am happy to help with your problem."

Jan shook her head, tears appearing in her eyes and her face a picture of dismay.

"Please don't worry." Dr Thakur held up his hand as she was about to speak again. "I really do understand and will go and see if one of our female doctors is available."

The two men rose and hurried out the door, leaving Jan unable to apologise or thank them. A few minutes later, the duty nurse wheeled her back into the waiting area.

It was another twenty minutes before she became aware of a young woman in a white coat heading her way. It was another doctor, female as requested, and after she had introduced herself as Dr Ghosh, she wheeled Jan into the small consultation room again, calling out to one of the nurses to accompany them. The session with Dr Ghosh was short but thorough, with Jan shedding some tears as the cramp pains became worse halfway through.

Dr Ghosh was most sympathetic and explained. "I'm going to give you a pregnancy test first and foremost, Mrs Hingorani. Although it's possible you've lost your baby during the bout of bleeding, there's also the possibility that you haven't. A number of women bleed in the early stages and towards the end of their first trimester. It's also very common to have these stomach cramps. That's because your uterus is starting to expand and everything is getting stretched around it. So before we do anything else, we'll see whether or not you are testing positive. If it's negative, we'll discuss what we do after that, and if it's positive, I'll send you along for an ultrasound scan to see what's happening in there. Are you all right for this to happen?"

Jan nodded, a ray of hope filling her mind because of the doctor's words. The test itself did not take long, although she was warned that she would be given a blood test as well, not just to confirm the result but also to check on Jan's general health. Dr Ghosh smiled at Jan as they looked at the pregnancy test stick together, with the two lines appearing, showing a positive result.

"I won't say congratulations yet," she said, "but it's looking very good. Now we have to find out what's causing the bleeding. I'll sort out the ultrasound scan for you right away, and then we'll pop you into a bed in the ward. I'll be keeping you here overnight just to keep an eye on you and all being well, you'll be able to go home tomorrow. Is there someone waiting outside for you? Can I get them in for you?"

"No ... eh, no. My husband is working and I came by myself. But it isn't a problem, I will phone him. May I use my phone in the corridor?"

"Yes, of course. But maybe you should wait until you've had the ultrasound and then speak to him, when we know a bit more. I expect he's anxiously waiting to hear how you are."

"Yes, he will be. Thank you so much, Doctor. You have no idea how much this means to me."

"You're very welcome, Mrs Hingorani. I'll go and organise the scan. Just wait here for the present time."

It wasn't long before a trolley was wheeled into the small room and Jan climbed up onto it, glad of the chance to lie flat for a short time. She was full of mixed emotions: relief that she was testing positive, and fear of the scan showing something wrong. However, the uppermost thought in her head was the impending night in the hospital. This was not going to be possible for her. She had already been away from home for a considerable time and would have to return there before nightfall. Robert did not permit her to be away anywhere overnight and she was going to have to invent some story of where she was this afternoon.

The visit to the ultrasound room took a lot longer than Jan hoped, but the happy news she received gave her such a lift that she tried not to think about it. She was told the foetus was still there, alive and well, and that she was around eleven weeks pregnant, not twelve as she had thought. The nurse doing the scan even allowed her to listen to the baby's heartbeat and her own heart pounded with joy.

Dr Ghosh reappeared as they wheeled her along the corridors towards the gynaecology ward where she was to spend the night under observation. Reassuring her that she was in the good hands of the nurses and the overnight doctor, Dr Ghosh left with a promise to return in the morning to see how she was doing.

By this time, Jan's panic was escalating. Still wearing her sari and with all her belongings around her, she knew that the time had come when she must try to get out of the ward and away with no one seeing her. As it turned out, this wasn't a difficult thing to do. With very few nursing staff to be seen on the ward, and those left busy trying to look after a number of patients at the one time, she knew they wouldn't notice if she slipped away. There were also a number of relatives of patients present in the ward, and she took her chance when a group visiting a patient nearby decided to leave.

Keeping a close eye on the nurses on the opposite side of the ward, she grabbed her belongings, put her shoes on and joined the group of four as they passed by her bed. She reached the door with no one noticing her departure and moved as fast as she could without drawing attention to herself, back along the corridors and down on a set of stairs, trying to find a back door she could exit from.

In this she had no luck, but suddenly found herself back in the large reception hall where she had entered the hospital. She paused for a moment, taking her mobile phone from her bag and dialling the number of the taxi driver who had brought her here. He answered her call right away, as if he had been sitting waiting for it.

Arrangements were made for him to pick her up outside the hospital gates and she was returning her phone to her bag when a child's voice nearby broke through her senses, causing her to freeze, the chill going up her spine like a lightning rod.

"Dr Suman, there's the lady I told you about. It's Madam."

Jan stared at the child sitting in a wheelchair, clutching the sleeve of the doctor by her side. Her heart began to pound in her chest, and for a second she thought she was going to faint. Instead, her hands began to scramble about, trying to lift the scarf from her sari up to hide her face, and the mobile phone she was holding fell to the ground, sliding a few feet away from her.

People around stopped to stare as she lifted her sari up a little off the floor and ran as fast as she possibly could to the entrance of the hospital and out the door, across the gardens to the gate. She never stopped to look behind and never heard Suman's voice shouting for her to stop.

Suman gave chase, but unfortunately lost Jan in the crowds outside the door. She ran across to the gate, but could see no sign of the lady she was chasing. Jan, by this time, had raced across the road outside and was now obscured by the onslaught of traffic passing by.

Suman turned to go back into the hospital, disappointed at not managing to catch up with Habi's 'Madam'.

She would very much have liked a few words with that lady.

Avril Duncan

Chapter Ten

SCHAANAPUR DISTRICT, KOLKATA

Suman was lost. Staring around the huge landfill site that was Dhapa, she was mesmerised. There were high mountains of rotting rubbish as far as the eye could see and little fires burning all around with putrid smoke rising in swirls. The smells were overwhelming and she wished she had brought a mask from the hospital in her pocket. Dotted around were the rag-pickers, scrabbling to find riches amongst the rubbish - anything they could sell to the traders.

Having heard people refer to Dhapa as 'Hell on Earth', she now understood why. Thousands and thousands of tons of waste were dumped here every day, fermenting into a putrid landscape. Suman thought about the pollution it was causing and about the type of lives the people inhabiting the area must be experiencing twenty-four-hours a day. She knew from reading about it that around thirty to forty thousand lived on or near the site. Some made a living as scrap dealers, rag-pickers and recyclers like Daivey and his family, others worked as farmers using the fertile pockets of land to grow their crops.

Reaching the crest of a hill of rotting garbage, she was already starting to find it more difficult to breathe; the result of the horrendous fumes coming from the untreated waste. *No wonder they get sick and come to hospital,* she thought. Diarrhoea, TB and typhoid were the usual causes of the casualties who went to be cured. The thought of the monsoons coming to this area, as they did annually, turned her stomach as she imagined all the garbage soaked and the stench that this would create.

Daivey had told her of the cremation site at Dhapa, set up not just for the people living in the many villages around the landfill site but for the many unidentified bodies found by the waste pickers foraging for sellable items.

She turned to go and made her way down the hill of garbage, walking precariously to avoid slipping and hoping that someone would be able to direct her to Bimla's house in one of the landfill's villages. A couple of men with large sacks on their backs looked up as she neared and she stopped to speak to them.

"Am I near Shabapur?" She spoke in Bengali, assuming this would be their language.

"Shabapur?" one man repeated. She nodded.

He pointed into the distance and waved his arm around in circles. "Shabapur is there. Near Hooghly River."

"How far is it? How many kilometres away?"

He shook his head and gave a shrug of his shoulders.

She tried a different question. "How many minutes for me to walk there?"

Again he shrugged. The other man, by this time interested in the conversation, came to the rescue.

"Go down off this hill and walk towards the Circular Canal down there," he pointed as he spoke. "Maybe fifteen, twenty minutes. Not far. It's a small village with many farms. Who are you looking for?"

"The Asura family," she replied.

He shook his head.

"Daivey?" she tried.

His face lit up. "Ah, Daivey. Yes, I know him. He lives on the second farm you will come to. They sell radishes."

"Thank you so much. I appreciate your help."

She set off in the direction he indicated and waved the two men goodbye. At the bottom of the hill which she had climbed to get her bearings, she was more than delighted to see her scooter still there and in one piece. She had tied it firmly to a wooden post in the ground and padlocked it, hoping it would be safe with nothing missing when she returned.

She put on her helmet and climbed onto the seat. With a loud roar of the engine she headed off over the rough tracks through the site, putting some distance between herself and the putrid smell of the waste. Even the air seemed to become slightly more breathable the further from the mountain she drove. Her long hair billowed out behind her as she weaved her way round the bends and in and out of the groups of people working at this lower level. It didn't take long to find the village, although she did have to stop to ask someone else if she was going in the right direction.

Bimla's house was just where she had been told, and the home-made sign that said 'Radishes for Sale' was clear to see. She wheeled the scooter into the garden area, a static sea of green leaves and red radishes making a beautiful picture. Bimla came out of the house and greeted her warmly.

"Please come in," she invited her guest.

Suman followed her inside, noticing the artistic rangoli pattern made of colourful powders outside the front door. In the room they entered first, Bimla lifted a metal dish from a shelf in order to perform Aarti, the welcome ceremony offered to special guests entering a house. A small candle was lit in the centre of the dish and Bimla filled the plate with pieces of coconut and some rough grains of sugar. She circled the dish three times before lifting some of the coconut and sugar to lay them in the palm of Suman's upturned right hand.

Suman put the food into her mouth, and began to crunch noisily. She then clasped her hands together.

"Namaste," she said to Bimla, "I am honoured to be welcomed into your house."

"I'm very happy you are here," Bimla replied, indicating a wooden chair in the corner of the room. "Please sit down."

Formalities over, Bimla offered her guest a drink of water, which Suman regretfully declined, afraid the water was not bottled and purified like the water she had brought in her bag. Aware she had possibly offended Bimla by refusing the water, Suman more than made up for this by complimenting her on her well-ordered, clean, and inviting house. She could see after a glance round that, although it was constructed of corrugated sheets on the roof and wooden planks and slats on the front and sides, it was a substantial size and looked like a very solid structure. She could see a number of rooms from where she sat; there was a kitchen area and what looked like the boys' bedroom, plus something she was astonished to see: a very clean, tidy bathroom with a small metal bath-tub and toilet. Whether or not it was a working toilet she didn't ask, but was very happy to see it there alongside what appeared to be a strangely-shaped wash hand basin with a bucket of water sitting by its side.

Before entering, Suman noticed the fruits of Daivey's labours outside, with the high mounds of recycling materials all around the house, some in grey plastic sacks which had once been white but were now dusty and torn with frequent use. Inside was just the same, with many items looking like reclaimed articles brought home by the boys to be cleaned and used. It was highly probable that the seat she was sitting on had come from the site too.

Matting was lying on the ground, making a comfortable floor to walk on and the most surprising item of all was a television set erected on top of a box against a wall.

Suman couldn't resist asking, "Does your television work, Bimla?"

Bimla laughed loudly.

"No, no. It's only for showing off to the boys' friends when they come in. They spend hours trying to fix the wires inside, hoping that one day it would work. We have electricity in the house occasionally, when the overhead cables bring it in through the roof, but it doesn't happen often. We've never been charged for it, so we don't worry."

The two of them enjoyed a lengthy chat, sorting out all the details of Habi's impending stay with the family, and both seemed very pleased with the outcome of this. Suman then suggested they take a ride on her scooter to visit the school that Bimla had told her about.

Pre-warned that they were coming, the headmaster welcomed them into the school. Finding him a quiet, intelligent man, Suman took to him quickly. He showed them around the six classrooms, which were crowded with children of all ages, and assured them that three more pupils would be more than welcome to register and attend when they could do so. The three would be starting school at elementary level, never having attended school previously, but he claimed this would not be a problem, as each class contained children with mixed levels of ability. Suman could certainly see that very small pupils intermingled with older ones.

"Do the children learn any English?" Suman inquired.

To her delight, the headmaster nodded and then answered her in English.

"They certainly do. We begin teaching them English at level two, and at that age they seem to pick up the language pretty quickly. I'm presuming there was a reason you asked me that. Did you live in England at any time?" he queried.

"Well, I don't know why you suspected that," she answered with a wide smile, "but you're nearly right. I was brought up in Scotland and did my schooling there, and attended university in Edinburgh. Have you been to the UK yourself?"

"I have indeed. I lived in Birmingham for a short spell. It was your accent I noticed, even when talking Bengali. You have a very distinctive accent. A nice lilting tone."

She laughed. "That's the Scottish in me. I picked up the brogue very quickly and it'll never leave me. Thank you so much for all your help this afternoon and well done for what you're doing here. We'll probably meet again when the children begin their classes." She shook the headmaster's hand as she spoke, with Bimla following suit. Poor Bimla had been looking very lost during the last few minutes when the two were speaking English.

"Sorry, Bimla," Suman apologised once they were outside. "That was rude of me to speak in English. Did you like the headmaster? Are you happy with the school?"

"Yes, I did, and I'm so happy that Daivey and Raja will have the chance to go to this school and learn so much. I can never thank you enough. Maybe one day they will speak to you in English too?" Bimla asked the question with a smile and Suman linked arms with her as they made their way back to the playground where they had left the scooter.

"They will, Bimla. They will."

Chapter Eleven

JAN'S HOUSE, KOLKATA, INDIA

Jan's bedroom door was shut and had been for some time. Nokara was worried, leaning forward to put her ear against the door, trying to hear if her mistress was up and about. A tea tray prepared about three hours ago had been firmly rejected and Nokara was unsure whether or not to knock and enter with this new one. Normally, Jan liked a very regular supply of refreshments, especially her ginger biscuits. The girl held her breath and risked a short tap on the door.

"Come in."

Nokara balanced the unsteady tray in one hand and turned the knob to enter.

"Your tea, Madam." She curtsied.

A sleepy Jan turned over in bed and opened her eyes.

"Just lay it on my bedside table, thank you."

Once the child had left, Jan risked sitting up against her pillow. She was hot and thirsty and badly in need of a drink, but was worried the nausea would return. Her movements were slow and careful. She poured the peppermint tea and took a sip, feeling grateful that the sickness seemed to have abated for the moment.

Refreshed by the tea and feeling stronger, she slid her legs over the side of the bed and attempted to stand. The wobbly legs had gone too and, taking some steps, she realised that she did feel much better than earlier. In the bathroom, she turned on her shower and got a towel from the shelf on the wall, waiting for the water to warm up a little. The tepid water cooled her body and she was enjoying the feeling of being cleansed and fragranced.

All of a sudden she became aware that someone had entered the bathroom and, with an abruptness that made her jump, the shower curtain was flung to one side and pulled from the rings, ending up torn and precariously dangling from above. With dismay she saw Robert standing there, his face like that of a mad man, his eyes dark with anger. She tried to reach for the towel to cover herself, but he grabbed her hand and flung her back against the tiled wall of the shower, her body hitting it with a massive thud.

"Where have you been?" he thundered.

She cowered where she stood, wrapping her arms around her body in an attempt to cover her nakedness.

"I've been shopping, but came home, as I didn't feel well." Her voice quivered. "I went to bed for a while."

His hand shot out quickly towards her face and she reeled from a stinging blow on the side of her head, which again caused her to fall back against the shower wall, this time ending in a drop to the floor. She clasped her face where the blow had fallen, but didn't look up at him or meet his eyes.

"You're a whore and a liar," he said softly through gritted teeth. His eyes narrowed. "I'm having you watched. Why did you go to that hospital today?"

"I haven't been well. I thought if I saw a doctor I could get something to make me feel better."

With a rush he bent over and grabbed both her arms, roughly hauling her up onto her feet. His face came within inches of hers and she closed her eyes, terrified of the alarming look on his face.

In a menacing voice, he said, "You have a private doctor. Why did you go to that particular hospital, a substandard place, only for scum and prostitutes and nobodies?"

She winced as he said the word 'prostitutes'. Seeing this, he took hold of her throat with one hand, his thumb putting pressure on her larynx.

"Prostitutes," he repeated. "Whores. Did you go to see a young, handsome doctor and ask him to examine you? Did he touch you? Did you sell yourself to him?"

Robert's other hand came up to her throat as well and tightened as he spat out his words at her, his face inches from her own. The more she struggled, the tighter his hands squeezed. She was unable to answer him and suddenly, unexpectedly, he let her go. His body, still fully clothed, lunged forward to pin her against the shower wall and his hands were everywhere as he assaulted her, brutally and maliciously, the water continuing to pour down on them both. He stopped only to unbuckle his trousers. She closed her eyes, knowing what was coming. It was more violent and more vicious than Robert had ever been before and her thoughts went wild, worrying about the baby inside her.

The rape over, she watched him, dazed, as he stepped backwards out of the shower, grabbed her towel to mop the water from his face and then moved quickly away. She waited until he was out of sight and then she sat up, wrapping her arms around her knees, her head coming forward to rest on her arms. She was not aware that she was shaking from head to toe and neither was she aware of the water still cascading down onto her body.

Long minutes passed before she rose, her legs like jelly, and reached over to turn off the water. Stepping out of the shower onto a bathmat, she took a second towel from the shelf, pulling it tightly around her whole body, only a small part of her face still showing. Holding it close, she stumbled into her bedroom and sat down on the bed.

Outside in the corridor, as Robert left the room still mopping his face and head, unknown to him, two small eyes watched from behind a tiny slit in one of the other bedroom doors. Nokara was as silent as a mouse, keeping herself hidden as he strode past her, the fury still blatant on his face. She pressed herself out of sight as he passed, not moving an inch until she heard him slam the door to his own bedroom with a very loud bang. After a few minutes, she opened the door a little bit more and peeped out.

He was nowhere to be seen, and the young girl pulled the door fully open and tiptoed over to Jan's bedroom. As she had done earlier, she pressed her ear against the door, at first hearing no sound. She leaned harder. A soft weeping was coming from inside and she pulled back, unsure what to do. Aware that Robert was close by and could re-appear at any time, she was tempted to scurry back down to the kitchen and hide for a while. Cook had gone home some time ago, so there was no one she could ask for help.

Her desperate need to please her mistress and look after her came to the fore and she very gently knocked on the bedroom door. The weeping stopped, but no voice told her to come in. She knocked once more. Again, no answer.

Cautiously turning the knob and opening the door a little, she peered round to see inside. Jan was sitting on the bed with her back to the door, her towel still clasped very tightly around her. Nokara entered and quietly approached her mistress. Jan turned and stared at the child with narrowed eyes as she came into sight.

Nokara curtsied. "Can I take your tray away, Madam?" she asked, her gaze taking in the vivid red mark on the side of Jan's face.

She received no reply to her question. Jan turned her face away as an inadvertent sob escaped from her.

The young girl moved slightly closer. "Are you hurt, Madam? Can I help you?"

Chapter Twelve

SISTER IRENE MERCY GOVERNMENT
HOSPITAL, KOLKATA

S uman and Vada walked across the hospital courtyard, making their way into the vast hall through a staff entrance. The sisters had enjoyed chatting over lunch in the cafeteria, with Vada reading out a letter she had received from Hira, their eldest brother. Now in his thirties, Hira considered himself head of the family since their father, Mukesh, had passed away some years earlier. The eldest of the ten siblings, Hira was holding down a very good job in a large carpet factory in the town of Achalpur, in the state of Maharashtra, very near to where their family home had been.

Now married with a family of his own, he had moved his mother, Kanya, into the new home he had bought in Achalpur, where he could look after her alongside his wife and two children. In Hira's letter, he spoke of a promotion at work which was prompting him to consider adding an extension to his house, the reason being another baby on the way. The two sisters were delighted for him and knew that Kanya would be very proud as well. They talked of visiting Achalpur; it had been some time since they had seen their mother and all their siblings and were considering suggesting a huge get together for them all at some time later in the year when the monsoons had passed.

Waving goodbye to Vada, Suman walked to the Children's Ward, where her clinic would be starting shortly. In her office, she noticed a stain on her white coat. Chastising herself for dropping some of her lunch on it without realising, she slipped out of the coat and reached for a cleaner one hanging on the back of the office door. As she put on the coat, she realised there was something in the pocket, something solid.

Goodness, she thought. It was the mobile phone she had picked up when Habi's 'Madam' had dropped it. She was annoyed at herself. It had been her intention to follow that incident up, but she had been caught up with her daily work and it had slipped her mind.

The mobile phone, of course, had completely run out of battery and Suman was unable to open it. Seeing it was a Vivo V20, one of the most popular mobiles in India, Suman was sure she could find someone to lend her a charger. She put the phone back into the pocket and checked her watch realising that she still had around twenty five minutes before her clinic began. She left the office and hurried across to the admin department where some of the secretaries were working on their computers. One of her favourites, a very friendly, helpful girl called Ann, looked up and saw her coming. She stopped typing and turned to face Suman with a huge smile on her face.

"Dr Sudra, hello. Now, what favour can I help with today?"

Suman laughed, shaking her head. "I'm so sorry. I'm forever asking favours, but you're so good at doing them for me that you're stuck as my number one port of call. And this is a biggie, a really big favour. Should I not ask you? Are you tremendously busy?"

"No, you shouldn't ask me," Ann smiled broadly, "but you're going to anyway, aren't you?"

Suman nodded with a laugh, and explained.

"There was a young woman, probably in her late twenties or early thirties, who visited the hospital on Friday. I saw her leave around half past four which means she may have checked in about an hour or so before that. Assuming she wasn't a visitor, I wondered if you could check the records between, say three and four o'clock for a lady checking in. I'm hoping you could give me a list of all the names."

"That's an impossible job, Suman! There must have been hundreds of women checking in to clinics and appointments at that time." She paused, seeing Suman's hopeful face. "Well, not impossible, but certainly a massive job. I'll try to do it, but I can't promise anything. How would that be?"

Suman nodded. "Thank you."

"Before you go, have you any idea what department the lady was visiting? Or at least can you tell me which part of the hospital you saw her in?"

Suman scratched her head. "That's what I can't do. I only saw her in the main hall, passing reception as she left. I've no idea what she was here for. The only clues I have are what I told you."

Ann sighed. "It might take me some time to get this to you."

"That's no problem. Whenever you have time. And don't let me get you into trouble, this is a personal thing and nothing to do with work."

Ann put her hands over her ears. "I never heard you say that, Dr Sudra. But you definitely owe me a coffee for this."

Suman made her way back to her own office with just ten minutes to spare and hurriedly prepared her files and notes for the clinic she was holding this afternoon. For the second time in just a few days, she was taking the evening off, this time to take Habi to her new home with Bimla, Daivey and Raja. She had a number of misgivings about taking the little girl so near to Dhapa, but had reconciled this with the knowledge that the house was a good bit away from the actual garbage and the fact that Suman knew she would be well looked after.

The clinic was a busy one as usual, and she had a number of complicated complaints to deal with, including a procedure to correct a tongue-tie problem in a little three-year-old girl. Carrying out a frenotomy procedure on the child, which involved a tiny snip in the tissue under the tongue, resulted in some tears, hastily stopped with a small packet of sweets which Suman always kept in the drawer of her desk. The little girl left the clinic with smiles, clutching the bag of sweets proudly in her hand.

Following up on Sam's invitation to come and see his young patient, the small child with suspected AFM, Suman visited in the morning, finding Sam in a very sombre mood, distressed that the little girl did not look as if she was going to survive. After a quick examination, Suman agreed with his diagnosis, but could only comfort him by saying that there was nothing he could have done differently to bring about a better outcome for the child. She left him with a heavy heart, knowing he felt as emotionally responsible for his patients as she did herself. Losing a child in their care was the worst part of their job.

The afternoon was busy. The problems were coming in thick and fast: a child with pneumonia who was admitted to the ward, a few youngsters with skin infections, a boy with cleft problems, various insect bites and a few other childhood complaints which had managed to escalate quickly due to poor healthcare provision in a number of the rural areas of Kolkata. If these illnesses could only be tackled at a local level when first occurring, she thought, she would not be treating them in such an advanced condition.

Suman's years growing up in Scotland and attending a great university in Edinburgh had created in her a burning desire to give back some of the love and care she had received from Ellie, Geoff, and their families. Visiting India at the age of fifteen to reconnect with her own family had furthered this resolve. It was Suman's wish to help the poor and very needy children in the country of her birth. No other ambition had ever entered her head.

At six o'clock, Habi was waiting for her. Wearing her new clothes with one shiny red sandal on her left foot, Habi was quick to point out this accessory to Suman as soon as she arrived to pick up the child. Sitting on the bed, the foot was thrust out in front of her to give Suman the best view of the new red shoe. Duly admiring it, Suman asked where it had come from and who had given her the red suitcase that matched the shoe.

"Doctor Sam gave me the case and two shoes, for when my plaster is off," Habi informed her proudly. "He wanted to put them in the case but I wanted to wear one today.

And the nurses gave me other clothes as well as this dress. They're packed in my suitcase."

"Well, you look beautiful, Habi. I've got some other things you might need, so we'll take these with us as well. Do you like wearing your new shoe?"

"I feel very funny in one shoe but it will be good when I've got the other one too. Will Daivey and Raja have shoes too?"

Suman smiled at the question. "Oh yes, they'll have shoes too. You need these to go to school. Are you looking forward to seeing Daivey and Raja?"

"I think so," the little girl replied. "I had brothers before, when I lived somewhere else. But I don't know where they are now."

Suman hugged Habi tight and lifted her from the bed into the waiting wheelchair. They chatted all the way to the main entrance and Habi was delighted when she saw a car sitting in front of the hospital with Dr Sam at the wheel, waiting to take her to her new house. He had offered that morning and Suman had been pleased to accept, knowing how fond Habi was of him and how nice it would be to be driven there and back in such comfort.

Knowing the way to Bimla's house, Suman gave directions to Sam, guiding him along the side roads and rough tracks until they found themselves drawing up close to the small farmland that was filled with Bimla's radishes. The boys were waiting for them and shouted to Bimla once they saw the car approaching. She came out to join them, welcoming Habi, Sam and Suman to their little house. Daivey and Raja were more interested in Sam's car than in Habi for a while, until called to order by Habi, who asked them for a tour of the house and garden. Daivey did the honours, lifting her from the wheelchair and carrying her in his arms. She was shown the extension they had started to build and was told that this would be her bedroom once it was finished. Until then she would share her sleeping place with Bimla.

Habi was delighted. A room of her own was something she had never had before and when told she would be sleeping in a bed with a very pretty cover on it, she was ecstatic. Sam, Suman and Bimla laughed as she issued an order that Daivey and Raja would not be allowed to sit on her bed.

"The extension is coming along nicely," Suman congratulated Bimla. "I see it's nearly finished."

"Yes, a number of the neighbours have been helping Daivey with it and I think it will be finished this weekend. We'll get Habi into her own room and bed as soon as we can."

"I think she'll soon be running your household, Bimla. The boys are already doing everything she tells them."

Bimla laughed. "I know. But they're so looking forward to having her here and having a little sister to look after. And so am I," she added. "You've no idea how much. I know it won't always be easy, and we might have some difficult moments as all families do, but she's a ray of sunshine to us all. Our lives are going to change a lot, for the better. I can't begin to thank you."

Suman put her arms around her and thanked her warmly for what she was doing for Habi.

Sam was in agreement on the way home that this seemed an ideal solution for the little girl and for the family as a whole.

"Bimla was telling me that she's got an official contract for her new job, and a very excellent salary." He looked round at Suman, sitting innocently beside him in the front of the car. "That was very clever of you to source such a thing, Suman. I didn't know it existed. A foster mother's allowance, is it?"

"I believe that's what it's called."

"Suman, I know you better than you think I do. There's no such thing and, if there is, I don't believe that's what Bimla's getting. You're a very generous, kind person, and I admire you so much."

"I'm not a generous or kind person at all. Well, maybe a little." She smiled over at him. "But what I do actually has another name. It's called payback, Sam. Payback."

Chapter Thirteen

SISTER IRENE MERCY GOVERNMENT HOSPITAL, KOLKATA

It was a number of days before Ann got back to Suman with an extremely long and very comprehensive list of women who had attended any clinic or department in the hospital on Friday. The information came on spreadsheets, clipped together in order of the time they checked into the area they were attending, including the two A&E departments. It also came with an apology from Ann for taking so long, but when Suman had a cursory look through the list, she could see exactly why it had. The amount of information must have involved many hours of Ann's time, with details of time of arrival, name, address, phone number, date of birth, and reason for attendance at the hospital.

So if Habi's 'Madam' had checked in anywhere in the hospital during the hour in question, her name would be on this list. Making a mental note to tell Ann how much she appreciated all this work, Suman popped the list into her desk drawer and locked it. She would have time to work her way through it later in the day when she was off duty.

Suman had also acquired a charger for the mobile phone that had been dropped and, trying out a number of ways to unlock it to gain access to the information, she had unexpectedly succeeded. Sadly, once in, Suman could see the phone was pretty new, with scant information on it. There were only two numbers in the contact list and she had tried ringing them both with no success.

Checking the phone log, she saw there were very few calls in or out and no answer when she tried to call these numbers. No other apps had been downloaded to the phone, and no emails either. Text messages threw up a bit more information, with two texts coming from someone called Kali, and one reply that had been signed off with the letter J. Suman presumed that J was the initial of the phone owner and she tried sending a text to Kali, explaining that she had found J's phone and asking Kali to contact her. However, there had been no response so far to any phone calls or texts.

Kali was presumably a friend of J, thought Suman, so it was disappointing that she had not replied. She found it all very frustrating, except for one very shaky clue on which she was pinning all her hopes.

In one of the texts between Kali and J, Suman had read a reference to an unspecified event which mentioned the words, 'sugar, dissolved - no'. Being a doctor, Suman was familiar with what this reference meant. In a home where money was very scarce, women would sometimes use a homemade recipe as a pregnancy test. According to rumour, sugar mixed with urine would give a result. If the sugar melted, the test was negative; however, if the sugar turned clumpy, the test was presumed to be positive.

She knew that there had never been any scientific proof that this homemade test had any credibility, but felt that she now perhaps had a rather dubious clue on where to start looking. Tonight, she was going to look through the list of ladies who had visited the maternity or the gynaecology clinics during the hour preceding her chance meeting with 'Madam' and, hopefully, would find some women with this initial. What she would actually do then, she wasn't entirely sure, but felt she had to try.

That evening, with her cup of tea beside her and different coloured pens in her hand, she read through the lists, beginning with maternity and gynaecology, where she found only eleven women with the initial J. Discounting two of the ladies because of their date of birth, she was left with nine. She made nine phone calls, making the excuse that a phone had been found at the hospital and she was trying to find the owner so that she could return it.

All the ladies who answered confirmed that they had their mobile phones safe and sound with them and had not dropped it at the hospital. Indeed, all of them were answering using their mobile phones. Of the nine phone calls, only two had not been answered. By ten o'clock that evening, Suman was almost ready to give up. Checking out some J's visiting other departments she had worked her way through a good number of them and admitted it was a bit of a wild goose chase that she had embarked on.

The baby clue could have been a red herring, but something was drawing her back again to the list from the maternity and gynaecology clinics. She closed her eyes and went over the events of that afternoon when Habi had recognised the woman. She pictured the woman in her mind, trying to guess her age as accurately as possible. It had been quite a short-lived sighting, but Suman had a very adept memory and could conjure up an image in her head. She narrowed the woman's age down to somewhere around her late twenties.

This meant that she was looking for a date of birth less than thirty years ago. She consulted the list again and found a number of birth dates within two years of thirty. She highlighted these names, forty four in all. Most had given the reason for attending the hospital as an antenatal or postnatal appointment, with a few saying they were in labour and ready to be admitted to the maternity ward. Another lady had mentioned vaginal bleeding and abdominal pain as her reason for attending and another two had pelvic problems. Suman thought she would phone these three who she felt could be ticked off the list quite quickly.

She began with the two ladies who had pelvic problems, a Mrs Jameela Banerjee and a Mrs Haleema Hasan. Unfortunately, when the ladies answered her call, they confirmed they had not dropped their mobile phones and were, like most of the others, using it to speak to Suman.

The next lady she phoned was the one with vaginal bleeding and abdominal pain. Registered as Mrs Myla Hingorani, she had been added to the patient list of Dr Thakur. Not so hopeful about this one, the first name being Myla and not beginning with a J, Suman tried phoning anyway. Strangely, a recorded message came back saying, "This number has not been recognised". *Interesting*, Suman thought, and made a note to try to speak to Dr Thakur should she meet him in the next day or two.

Suman went on to make more calls, some with no reply, most proving futile. At this point she called it a day. It was getting too late in the evening to phone any more numbers, and her hopes of being successful were diminishing fast. She was tired after her busy day and decided it was time for bed.

The next morning dawned warm and sunny as normal and, after a hearty breakfast of idlis, Suman set off for the hospital nice and early. The list was in her pocket, but knowing that today was going to be an extremely busy day with a number of minor surgeries planned, she surmised that this was not a good day to be playing the amateur sleuth. Most surprising, then, was the fact that one of the first people she met when heading towards her office was Dr Thakur. She fell in step beside him as he walked along the corridor and, after some pleasantries, she asked about his patient, Mrs Hingorani, from last Friday. He did not recollect the lady straight away, but after some thought he remembered she had been a patient who had requested a female doctor instead of a male. He bore no grudges about this; it was just a fact of life in his professional role that women often requested another female when doing an internal examination.

Suman asked if he could remember what she had looked like. Describing the lady as 'a stunner' in a very beautiful sari, he said that he had been surprised to see someone like her in his surgery. A Dalit lady, he informed her, dressed very expensively with lots of jewellery, he passed her on to his female colleague, Dr Ghosh, who, he believed, examined her and then admitted her to the ward for an overnight stay.

Realising that he was describing Mrs Hingorani very much as Suman would have, she was disappointed that this could not be Habi's 'Madam' if she had stayed overnight in one of the wards; Habi spotted her as she was leaving the hospital at around four in the afternoon. Back to the drawing board, she decided.

However, on seeing Dr Ghosh in the cafeteria a couple of days later, Suman thought it worth having a word and was extremely surprised to find that Mrs Hingorani had not in fact stayed in the hospital. She had disappeared prior to being checked into the ward. Dr Ghosh gave Suman a condensed version of Mrs Hingorani's visit and the nervous demeanour she had displayed the whole time. Suman thanked her colleague and realised that she had probably found the lady she was looking for.

Unfortunately, it looked very likely that the details 'Mrs Hingorani' had given when checking in were not her true identity.

Oh dear, she thought with a sigh, *one step forward and two steps back.*

Chapter Fourteen

FLORENTINE APARTMENTS, KOLKATA, INDIA

It was Sunday morning, India's day of rest, when banks closed and a good number of offices and industries locked the doors to their employees and forced them to have a day off. India, including the vast city of Kolkata, was said to move at a marginally slower pace on a Sunday than on weekdays. However, Suman, watching the traffic on the road outside her window, didn't believe this was true. The road was as jam-packed with vehicles as always, their horns tooting as they ducked and dived any which way to try to get through the massive traffic jams. The noise was almost deafening when she opened the window.

Her mind returned for a moment to Edinburgh, where she had lived for many years, and she thought how quiet the Scottish city had been in comparison to Kolkata. Not that she had thought Edinburgh was quiet at the time. Sundays brought out the tourists in their hundreds in Edinburgh, most wandering along the city streets or taking in the castle and the gardens on Princes Street.

Nonetheless, she thought, Scotland had never been like Kolkata. She had so much affection for Auld Reekie and her life there, but she treasured the sounds of India so much more. Her heart was full of love for the vibrant excitement of life that she could see on the streets below.

There were people everywhere. With no pavements to keep them safe, they walked on the road alongside cars, buses, lorries and rickshaws, all carefully avoiding each other more by luck than better judgement. There were children in abundance, playing in the streets, or just sitting watching the world go by. Street workmen were laying tarmac amongst the hubbub, the noise of their pneumatic drills lost in the din of everyday life. Beside them, dogs were lying prone in the heat, and the obligatory cow would amble by, looking for something to eat. The traffic stopped for the cow, or swerved round to the shop fronts to avoid bumping into the sacred animal. No one paid attention to anyone else, so inured were they to life on the busy streets around them.

Suman closed the window, reducing the pitch of the traffic to a hum. Inside her home, a roomy, modern flat on the twelfth floor of the attractive Florentine Apartments in Amrapali, she quickly tidied her bedroom and began to dry the dishes she had used for breakfast. Expecting a visit very soon from Vada, she was keeping one ear out for the buzzer. Her sister was visiting to return Suman's scooter, which was kept in the underground car park of the building.

About ten minutes later she heard the buzz she was listening for and hurried to let Vada in. Struggling with a number of bags, Vada was relieved to deposit them all in a corner of the hall and turned to hug Suman enthusiastically.

"Have you come for a week?" asked Suman with a smile.

Vada giggled. "No, that's just my washing. There's been a problem at the Nurses' Home and we've got no water, and I desperately need my washing done." She looked at Suman with a question in her eyes. Five minutes later the first wash was on, purring away in the kitchen, and the sisters sat down to enjoy a coffee and catch up with all their news.

"Great having a washing machine, isn't it?" Vada asked. "Bit of a difference from when we were young and had to walk all the way to the river to wash our clothes. Although, I have to admit, I used to love going there and the fun we had with our friends. Do you remember everyone doing their washing and making the river full of bubbles? And getting a bath in the river, too."

Suman stared into space as the memories of the river near their home came flooding back. "Gosh, yes. I remember. Going there every day to fill our water carriers and hoisting them up on our backs. It was a really long walk home, too."

Vada agreed. "I didn't do it as often as you did, though. Not long after you left, the villagers got some water taps put in at the bottom of the hill. I had to go and fill the carrier at the tap, which was so much easier. But we weren't allowed to wash our clothes there, it was just for drinking."

"Do you miss the village and all the family, Vada?"

"Sometimes, yes, especially Amma. I miss her like mad. I remember when she received the honour of sitting on the village council before she left to live with Hira. Did she tell you?"

"Yes, she did. I was amazed. She used to be so quiet – so insecure when our father was alive."

Vada nodded in agreement. "She became more so when you left, thinking she'd never see you again. She became depressed and angry. But once he died, she changed into a different person. Not so shy, much bolder and able to cope. I can see why they asked her to be on the council."

Vada turned to face her older sister. "Do you miss the village, Suman? I can't begin to imagine what it must have been like for you, being taken away the way you were, and all the things you had to go through."

"Well, don't try to imagine it, Vada. It's in the past, and look at the good life we have now, all of us, including Ai; we've been very lucky. And all the things that happened brought Ellie and Geoff into my life and, without them, my life would have been so different."

Vada's face was pensive, her thoughts for a moment on Suman's abduction at the age of just eight. Thinking of this gave her thoughts a slightly different direction.

"I meant to ask you, what happened to the little girl that was brought into the hospital? The one you thought had been trafficked? Habi, was it?"

"Yes, Habi. She's moved in with Daivey and his family and they've all been enrolled in school. I'll visit them very soon to see how she's doing. She's still in her plaster cast. You can come with me if you're free. But I didn't tell you; I had an encounter with Habi's ex owner, or 'Madam', as she calls her."

"You met her?" Vada gazed in amazement at her sister. "How did that happen?"

"I didn't meet her, no, but Habi pointed her out to me at the hospital one afternoon and I gave chase but lost her. So I didn't get to speak to her. I've been trying to find out who she is and, if I'm right, it looks like she came to A&E with vaginal bleeding. I think she may be expecting a baby. But I can't find out any more, as she gave a false name and address to the hospital reception. I've no idea where to begin looking for her."

"What name did she give?"

"Mrs Hingorani, but I don't think that's her real name. According to the phone she dropped, her first name starts with the initial 'J'. I think that's really the only true clue I have."

"Well, I'm going back out into the district to do some ante-natal home visits soon, so I'll keep an eye out for a Mrs Hingorani or for someone whose name starts with a 'J'. Do you know anything else about her?"

"Nothing other than that she's a very beautiful lady and very well dressed. Oh, and I think she is from the Dalit caste."

"Not much to go on, but I'll keep it in mind. You never know."

"Well, don't get involved in any way if you do find someone you think could be her," Suman warned. "Trafficking is a huge industry and a very, very dangerous one."

"I won't get involved, don't worry. There's not much likelihood of me finding her if Hingorani isn't her real name. Anyway, you be careful too. Ellie won't be happy if you get involved with someone working for traffickers after what happened to you. What day do they arrive, by the way? Ellie and Geoff. You said it was soon."

"They'll be here next Sunday. I'm taking the day off and going to the airport to meet them. I'm really excited to see them again."

"They're staying with you, aren't they? Are you taking some of your holidays to spend time with them?"

"Yes, I've asked for two days off."

"Suman!" exclaimed her sister. "You rarely take time off and I don't think you've had much in the way of holidays since you started at the hospital. Just take a week or a fortnight off and enjoy having them here."

"I might do that. I'd like to take them to meet Bimla and her family; I've told Ellie all about Habi and she wants to meet her. And Ellie and Geoff want to see more of Kolkata while they're here. There's still a lot they haven't seen. I'm so, so looking forward to seeing them. It seems so long since they were last here. Telephone calls and emails are just not enough."

Suman's excitement at seeing Ellie and Geoff again grew more noticeable as the week progressed and Sam, working with her in theatre during the week, sensed the impending visit was coming closer. Hearing it was happening on Sunday, he offered to drive her to the airport and bring them all home again, an offer she was delighted to accept.

The following Sunday she was up at the crack of dawn and ready to set off at least an hour before Sam had arranged to pick her up. Bored with pacing the floor, fifteen minutes before the agreed time, she took the lift down to the ground floor and made her way out of the gated area around Florentine Apartments. Sitting on a low wall to await Sam's arrival, she constantly checked her watch. He was only ten minutes late, an amazing achievement in this huge city with the roads as congested as they were.

"Well done, Sam," she congratulated him as she climbed into the front seat of his car. "Knowing what the traffic is like around here, I thought we might be working on Indian Time and you'd be at least an hour late."

He laughed. "I know all the shortcuts to the hospital and on a good day I can do it in less than half an hour. There were a few hold ups, but not many, and with a bit of luck we'll get to the airport in plenty of time, so don't worry."

Sam's words proved true, and their arrival at the huge, modern glass-steel structure that was Kolkata Airport was well ahead of schedule. They sat down to have a coffee in one of the imposing restaurants while they waited for Ellie and Geoff's flight from Mumbai to arrive. Suman had thought they would be coming direct from Dubai, as this was the usual stopping point en route to India from the UK. However, Ellie had texted to say they would be coming via Mumbai instead. Enjoying her coffee, she was keeping one eye on the huge electronic notice board announcing arrivals and departures.

"There it is!" she cried excitedly. "Their flight has landed. Can we go to the Arrivals Hall?"

"They'll be at least half an hour, maybe more. You know how long it takes to get off the plane, get their luggage and come through customs. Are you sure you want to go through just now?"

She laughed. "I'm just desperate to see them after all this time. But I'll wait if you want to."

He stood up and pushed in his chair. "No," he answered, "I'm ready to go, if you're sure you want me there with you. I don't mind at all if you'd rather meet them by yourself."

"Sam, they'll be delighted you're here. They know you're doing the driving and will be really grateful. Please come with me." She linked her arm through his as she spoke, giving him no option but to accompany her.

They made their way into the Arrivals Hall, where there seemed to be hundreds of people milling about, waiting to meet relatives and friends coming off the planes. Suman managed to find a space behind a rope barrier. Surrounded by lots of couriers holding handwritten signs with their visitors' names, Suman jokingly said that she wished she had brought a sign with Ellie and Geoff's names on it to surprise them.

However, it wasn't Ellie and Geoff who got the surprise when they came through the double doors with their laden trolley; it was Suman. Expecting only the two of them, she could not believe her eyes when she saw a third person walking beside them. Still some way away, she could see Ellie was holding the lady's arm and Suman's heart began to race as she realised she was looking at her beloved mother, Kanya, or Ai, her nickname for her Amma.

On the other side of the barrier, Kanya's eyes were searching the crowds as well, but it was Ellie who spotted Suman first. She shouted Suman's name and pointed her out to Kanya, who stopped walking and stared at her daughter. Suman, by this time, was standing with her hands over her mouth, disbelieving what she was looking at, and Sam laughed as he nudged her out of her trance.

"Is that who I think it is, Suman?" he asked.

She turned to him, her eyes shining with joy.

"It's my mother, Sam, my beautiful mother. I haven't seen her for two years and I've no idea how they managed to get her onto a plane to come here. She's refused every time I've asked her. I can't believe it. It's Ai."

Getting hold of Sam's arm again, she pulled him along behind the crowd until they came to a break in the rope barrier. Geoff and the two ladies, at a slightly slower pace, were headed for the same spot, trying not to take their eyes off Suman and Sam. All over the arrival hall, people were joining up with their long-awaited visitors, but Suman was unaware of anyone else even being there. Not being able to stop herself, she let go of Sam's arm and ran forward to her mother, who opened her arms and hugged her daughter as tightly as she had when she was reunited with Suman after eight intolerably long years without her. Tears were on both women's cheeks and neither could speak, they could only hold each other.

At last they moved apart and Suman, still holding her mother's hand, turned to greet her other mother. She let go to put both her arms around Ellie as Ellie did the same and, again, tears were flowing as they hugged. Suman turned to Geoff next, whose eyes were also sparkling with tears, and flung herself into his arms. After hugging him for a moment, she stepped backwards and looked at him.

"Tears, Geoff? But men don't cry, do they, my darling?" Her eyes were twinkling, not just with her tears, but with the joy of seeing him again, and being able to tease him with the same words she had used once before, many years ago.

"Oh yes, we do, as you well know, Minx."

Happiness surrounded the group like a halo as they linked themselves together and Suman led them over to where Sam was waiting, watching and enjoying the very emotional reunion. He felt quite privileged that he had been a witness to it, and once he had been introduced to everyone, he joined Geoff in pushing the heavy trolley over to the main doors and out to the car park where they had left the car. A slight concern at the amount of luggage on the trolley was niggling at him, but he put it aside, relieved he'd decided on a large five-seater car last time he'd changed it. *At least I'll get all the people in*, he thought, *if not the luggage*. He opened the boot and was even more relieved when the cases, with a lot of pushing and shoving, managed to fit inside. Smaller bags came into the car to sit on knees and on the back window ledge and he could feel a big difference in the weight of the car when they set off for home.

Geoff sat in the front with Sam, as fascinated as always by the scenes they passed as they drove through the huge metropolitan area of Kolkata, so overcrowded now that it took twice as long to negotiate the roads, adding an extra half an hour to their journey. The ladies in the back saw nothing of Kolkata, being aware only of each other, with Suman holding on to their hands as if she couldn't let them go. She and Kanya were chattering in Marathi one minute, the next Suman switched to English to speak to Ellie, her head turning from one to the other as if she was watching a tennis match.

Eventually, having made it safely through the traffic, Sam stopped the car outside Florentine Apartments, where everyone climbed out from the confines of the car onto the pavement. Geoff and Sam unloaded the boot and the five of them managed to carry the luggage in one journey into the building and up in the lift to Suman's apartment. Sam said his goodbyes at this point, deaf to all entreaties by Suman to come in with them.

"No, Suman, you need this time with your family. I'll phone you and maybe meet up with you during the week if you'll let me take you all out for a meal. But, just now, enjoy being with them."

She shouted her thanks for all his help as he walked away and he turned to smile and wave.

"Nice guy," whispered Ellie in Suman's ear.

Suman smiled and nodded before turning to walk into the apartment, amused that Sam may have heard the loud whisper.

Being summoned by Suman by phone, Vada arrived about an hour later, full of apologies that she couldn't get away from her patients on the ward as quickly as she'd hoped. Expecting to be meeting only Ellie and Geoff, she too received a wonderful surprise on discovering her mother there. More tears were shed, more hugs exchanged, more cups of tea and chai appeared, and Parle biscuits for everyone.

A long time later, when the conversation had begun to slow down slightly, they could see that Kanya was beginning to look weary from the travelling, and the two sisters took their mother into Suman's lovely, brightly-coloured bedroom to help her unpack and settle her down on the bed. They pulled out some extra bedding and put a mat on the floor, as Suman had decided this is where she would sleep, happy to be so close to her mother once again.

It wasn't without an argument, of course, Kanya adamant that she wouldn't put Suman out of her bed and Suman adamant that she would be perfectly fine on the floor. It was Ellie who settled the argument, suggesting that if Suman was getting sore on the floor, she could climb into bed beside Kanya.

"That's what she did with me, when I took her home to Edinburgh with me," said Ellie. With Suman translating, Kanya laughed, then cried, then whispered, "And with me, sometimes."

Suman stepped across to her mother and cupped her face with her hands, using her thumbs to remove the droplets coming down her cheeks. "And I probably will again, Ai."

Problem solved, she went off to the kitchen to begin preparations for their evening meal. Not long afterward Ellie joined her.

"You look so well, Su, and it's so good to see you. The house is empty without you. Hamish misses you too. I've brought a letter from him, plus loads of photos he wanted you to have. He's getting so grown up now, I can't believe it. He's even got a girlfriend."

Suman turned quickly. "A girlfriend? No! I can't believe it. I'll have to come home to see him again soon." At Ellie's raised eyebrows, she continued, "I know, I never have time, but I will come soon, I promise! I can't have my little brother beating me to the altar, can I? Not without me checking the bride out. Is it serious? Is she nice?"

"Who knows if it's serious? He never tells me very much, speaks to Geoff all the time about things like that. But he's far too young to be thinking about marriage, so don't worry. And, yes, she's a lovely girl, you'd like her a lot."

Hamish was Geoff and Ellie's son, born eighteen years ago and sharing a good part of his early childhood with Suman, his adopted big sister. Now in his second year at the University of Edinburgh, he was hoping to follow in her footsteps by getting a medical degree in Scotland and then coming out to India to work. The country had always fascinated him, and he had accompanied his parents on a number of visits out to see Suman and had fallen in love with the intriguing culture of the Indian people.

"Your friend, Sam," Ellie continued. "He's a really nice person too. So nice of him to come and pick us up at the airport. You mention him a lot in your emails, so it looks like you're good friends."

Suman laughed. "I know where this is going, Ellie, and yes, we are good friends, but not in the way you're thinking. We're colleagues, and work closely together, but we're not a couple."

Her voice lost its laugh for a moment and she turned away from the cooker to look at Ellie with a serious face. "You know how I've always felt about this. Despite my joke earlier, you know I'm not the marrying kind. I'm just a dedicated doctor and that's all I ever want to be. I'll never have a husband."

Ellie took a long pause before answering. "Well, I'm happy that you've got a good friendship with Sam and a good working relationship with him too. I like him…I like him a lot. Good friends are very precious in our lives. But never say never, Su. Please, for me. Never say never."

Chapter Fifteen

JAN'S HOUSE, KOLKATA, INDIA

Jan's breakfast was set out on the dining room table as she entered the room. Realising that this was the second morning this week she had risen from bed minus the nausea that had plagued her, she decided she would try to eat some of the little idlis that Cook had made for her. Before falling pregnant she had loved the little steamed rice-dough pancakes and she hoped she could enjoy them again.

While eating, she thought again about Robert's attack in the shower a couple of days ago. The vivid mark on her face from the blow he had inflicted was still very visible and, although accustomed to being treated by him in this way, this felt worse than normal; more violent and hate-induced than any beating she had received in the past. The reason for this was playing on her mind. She asked herself some difficult questions. Why was he having her followed and watched at this time? Did he know about the baby? Had Kali said something to her own husband that got back to Robert? And why had he raped her?

Now that the bleeding had stopped, knowing that the baby was still inside her, alive and kicking, was almost a lovely feeling, marred only by the fact that she knew it would be taken away from her if she stayed here with Robert. If he already suspected that she was pregnant, she and the baby were at great risk if she waited around for very much longer.

That meant she should go, and go today. She had given this a lot of thought over the years. If she had to flee, where would she go, how would she do it and who would she ask for help? These were all things she had tried to plan, should things go badly wrong in her relationship with Robert. However, planning an escape and executing it were two different things. In a lot of ways, she had felt safe living here; at least, she had felt safe from everything outside. The biggest danger to her had only ever been Robert himself.

Even after all this time, she had difficulty reading his moods and thoughts; he could erupt at a moment's notice, usually over something very trivial, like a lost sock or the television being too loud in the house. His temper was unpredictable. Yet, over the years, she had learned to stay on top of things, most especially keeping his clothes and belongings in immaculate order, and ensuring nothing disturbed him while he worked. This new Nokara was one of the best ones he had given her, learning quickly what was required of her. In fact, Jan thought, where was her maid this morning? The child had been so kind to her after the attack, helping her to bed and putting balm on her wounds. She felt indebted to the young girl and began to consider if she should take Nokara with her when she fled, not wanting Robert to blame the child in any way for her disappearance.

Rising from the breakfast table, she realised she had eaten all the idlis in the basket while her mind had been very far away, but now she must focus on what she had to do. First was to find Nokara. She made her way through to the kitchen area. Cook was there, stirring a pot of curried vegetables. However, there was no sign of Nokara. Perhaps the child was making the beds and cleaning the bedrooms, she thought. She would find her later.

She gave a curt thank you to the cook for her breakfast, trying to give an appearance of normality. After a quick look round the kitchen to see that there was nothing of hers lying about, she then informed Cook she was going shopping. Nothing out of the ordinary there, she hoped.

Jan had gone around the house the previous evening, gathering any personal items she could find. She didn't want to make it obvious that her belongings were missing, so she left a number of things still lying about, including a gold chain and a pair of earrings that Robert had given her for her birthday last year. He knew how fond she was of these, so if he saw them lying on the dresser in the hall when he came in, he would assume she was in the house too and probably not bother looking in on her in her bedroom.

Her own bedroom was the last place she entered, expecting to see Nokara hard at work cleaning the room or sorting out the laundry. Yesterday's underwear still lay on the floor where she had left it and, for a moment, Jan experienced a wave of concern. The child was not in the house. *The only place I haven't looked is the laundry room,* she realised. She hurried back down the stairs and through to the rear of the house. She looked round the door of the laundry room, but again there was no sign of Nokara.

Seriously worried now, she raced around the house, searching in all the nooks and crannies before going back to the kitchen. Cook was still there and looked up with a question in her eyes as Jan entered.

"Have you seen Nokara?" asked Jan, peering out of the window to see if she was in the back garden.

"No, Madam. I haven't seen her all morning. She must be keeping busy in the house, just like she should be."

"I've been all through the house and can't find her. She's not outside either. When she comes back here, send her to me right away."

Cook nodded. "Yes, Madam."

Jan returned to the lounge and sat down heavily in the armchair, a huge furrowed line appearing above her eyebrows. *If I can't find the child*, she thought, *I won't be able to take her with me, and if she turns up here later and is questioned by Robert, he'll lose his temper when she isn't able to tell him anything.* This would be disastrous for Nokara. Sitting staring into nothing for a few moments, her stomach began to knot as she considered what to do.

After some time, resigned to carrying out her plans, she made her way back upstairs to the bedroom, where she put her shoes on and took her leather shoulder bag out of the large double door wardrobe. Kneeling down, she pushed her clothes aside and pulled out one of the shoeboxes stacked at the back of the wardrobe. Raising the lid, she took out a large, very full wallet and a little jewellery pouch which she quickly stuffed inside the shoulder bag. After closing the doors of the wardrobe, she took a last look round before leaving the bedroom. As she made her way down the stairs, she stopped suddenly, her hand gripping the rail in fear as a blood-curdling scream came from outside the house.

The scream lasted only seconds and was followed by loud weeping and cries. As fast as her feet would carry her, Jan hurtled down the rest of the stairs, through the kitchen and out of the back door in time to see Cook fall to her knees, her face covered by her hands and the weeping changing to a frightening wail. Jan ran to the woman and knelt beside her, one hand on her shoulder.

"Cook, what on earth is wrong? Cook, look at me. Stop the noise and tell me what's happened. Is it the child? Tell me." Using both hands to clasp the stricken woman, she shook her fiercely.

Cook's wails subsided a little and she dropped her hands from her face. "Oh, Madam," she cried. "It's Nokara. It's Nokara."

"Where is she, Cook? Tell me."

The kneeling woman extended one long arm and pointed to one of two outhouses at the bottom of the garden, the one where all the garden furniture was kept.

"She's in there?"

Cook nodded through the tears rolling down her face.

"What's happened to her?" Jan asked quickly. With no answer forthcoming, she rose to her feet. "Never mind, I'll go and see."

Cook's hands swiftly grabbed Jan's sari. "No, Madam, you mustn't go."

Jan shook off the hands and turned and ran across to the outhouse. She heard another wail from Cook as she reached the door, which was standing ajar.

Undeterred by Cook's alarming howls, she went inside. The child, Nokara, was lying face down on the floor, her body looking broken and her hair in wild disarray. There was blood on the floor, lots of it, and Jan caught her breath on a sob as she knelt down beside the child's prostrate body.

"What has he done to you, Nokara?" she whispered, very gently pulling the girl's unruly hair back from her face, but not daring to move her. She put her fingers on Nokara's neck, checking her pulse, just in case there was any sign of life left in the child.

At first she felt nothing, but suddenly she became aware of a very slow, very soft pulse.

"You're still alive," Jan whispered, checking Nokara's pulse at her wrist.

She moved swiftly, running to Cook, still kneeling on the stone slabs in the garden.

"Cook, you must help me. Come on, get up," she ordered, trying to help the heavy woman onto her feet. "Nokara is alive, but we must get help for her. She is badly injured and unconscious."

Cook was staring at Jan, incredulous, but allowed Jan to help her up, her sobs abating slightly. She hastily wiped her face on her apron and waited for instructions.

"We have to get her to a hospital."

Cook nodded.

"You go and phone for a taxi to come right away. Don't phone the normal taxis that we use. Do you hear? You must find another taxi company in the directory. It has to be one we don't normally use."

Again Cook nodded.

"I'll get a blanket of some kind to wrap her in. I don't know what injuries she has and don't want to make them worse, but I need to get her out of here and to a hospital, somewhere safe. Go and phone quickly." She pushed Cook into action.

Inside, Jan found a few blankets in the airing cupboard and ran back outside with them. In the outhouse, she spread them out on the dusty ground and as tenderly as possible she slid them under the child, trying to move Nokara as little as possible.

She was wrapping the soft blankets gently around the girl when Cook, a little calmer than before, appeared at the door. "The taxi is coming, Madam. He will be here in ten minutes."

"Thank you. I'll leave her here till it comes; the less she is moved the better. There is so much blood, but I can't see where it's coming from without moving her more than I want to. Her face is bleeding slightly, too, and I think she's unconscious from a blow to her head. There's a big swelling that's turning purple."

She stood up and faced Cook. "I'm going to need your help again, Cook. Can you come with me to the hospital and take her inside to see a doctor? I can't do this. I can't go into the hospital with her. Will you do this for me?"

Fear was written across Cook's face as she shook her head.

"No, Madam. I can't get involved in this. It's too dangerous." Her voice was shaky with emotion and the sobs rose to the surface once again.

"I know and I understand, but I really need your help. Please come with me."

Cook continued to shake her head as she cried.

"No, Madam. No. I can't. I have my family at home and I can't put them or myself at risk. Your husband is a very dangerous man and I cannot do this. I need to go home now. I'm so sorry."

She was backing away from the door of the outhouse as she spoke and Jan's heart sank. She totally understood Cook's fear and was experiencing fear herself, but realised that she had to stay strong until she got the child to safety. She owed this to Nokara.

"Okay. If you must go, just go. I would advise that you say absolutely nothing about this to anyone. If he discovers that you found the child, I don't know what will happen. We don't even know if it was him or one of his men who did this, so say nothing. Please stay safe and keep your family safe too. Will you come into work tomorrow? Keeping things normal will stop him from getting suspicious."

"I don't know, Madam. I just don't know. But I've got to go. I can't stay here."

With a very worried face, Jan watched her go. Uncertain of what she should do now about her own escape, Jan was sure of only one thing. This child needed to go to hospital and Jan was the only person who could take her.

Leaving Nokara for a moment, she went around to the front of the house to look for the taxi. She could see Cook making her way down the street, hurrying as much as her large frame would allow her. There was no sign of anyone close by, watching the house, either from a car or on foot, but Jan knew someone could be there, hidden from view. She just prayed that Robert had not set a watch on her today.

Going back and forth between Nokara and the front of the house, Jan at last saw the taxi pull up at the gate. She ran to it and opened the door, speaking to the taxi driver at the same time.

"I need to go to the nearest hospital, please," she said hurriedly. "I have a sick child. I'll go and get her."

"What's the matter with the child?" queried the taxi driver. "Is it something catching, like smallpox or something?"

"No, of course not," Jan replied very crossly. "She's had an accident, so I need an Accident and Emergency hospital."

She hurried away from the gate and round to the back, to carefully lift the child into her arms. The taxi driver was at the gate, holding it open for her when she returned.

"Do you have a private hospital that you go to?" he asked as she laid the child on the back seat. "The nearest hospital with A&E is many miles away, but there are quite a few private ones closer."

Jan thought for a moment of the money she had in her wallet. It was a lot, but maybe not enough to pay for any private treatment the child might need. Medical treatment was expensive in the private hospitals and it would be harder to give false information. They may also ask for proof of her identity.

"No, take me to the nearest A&E clinic that you know of, wherever it is. I can't use a private one."

Sitting in the back of the cab, Jan was precariously holding her bundle and, after a few moments, reached for the child's wrist, to check her pulse again. Relieved that she could feel the same fluttering movements from Nokara's wrist, she pulled back the blanket slightly to look at the child's face. Nokara's eyes showed a slight movement, as if she was coming round from unconsciousness, and Jan panicked slightly, in case the child woke and started to scream, or say something Jan didn't want her to say. She hoped the hospital would not be very far away.

"How long do you think this will take?" she asked the driver.

"Well, I can go to the People's Municipal Hospital, which would take about an hour, depending on traffic, or I could go to the Sister Irene, which is a bit closer, maybe twenty-five minutes. That's the one I'm heading for at the moment. Which one would you like to go to?"

Jan had caught her breath at the mention of the Sister Irene Mercy Hospital, remembering what happened to her there so recently. However, she also remembered the kindness of the doctors and nurses and how quickly they had acted to help her. It was a huge hospital, and she thought she would take a chance and go there, hoping very much that she wouldn't run into the other Nokara or the doctor who had been with her.

"Just go to the Sister Irene, please. I need to get there quickly."

The taxi driver was very helpful, driving quickly and with care, and helped her with Nokara as she was getting out of the cab. She paid him well for his help and turned to the main entrance of the hospital.

"God help me, and God help this child, please," she whispered as she climbed the three steps to the big double doors, the child in her arms.

Chapter Sixteen

SISTER IRENE MERCY HOSPITAL, KOLKATA

The wait at the A&E reception was not too long, and Sunita was soon examined by a couple of doctors. After she was informed of the young girl's critical condition, Jan decided to stay with her until she knew the outcome.

After further examination and tests, the early diagnosis was not good. They told her that Sunita had a serious head injury, a number of broken bones, and possible internal injuries, adding gently that the child might not survive the night. The day had then been filled with x-rays, more examinations, blood tests, and a CT scan. Suspecting a skull fracture, the doctors explained to Jan that they would be putting Sunita into an induced coma, to keep her as still as possible, and that Jan was welcome to stay by her side for as long as she wished.

The form-filling had nearly been her downfall, but claiming the girl had been knocked over by a hit and run driver had seemed to be accepted for the moment. Not using the same alias as the last time, she had fabricated a new character for herself and for the child, whose name she gave as Sunny. She told the nurses and doctors that Sunny was her niece staying with her while her parents were in America. Aware of the scepticism in their eyes, she tried very hard to keep up the facade in spite of this.

Early in the evening she was approached by a doctor who introduced himself as Dr Kumara, a neurologist at the hospital. Dr Kumara gave Jan an outline of the results of the various tests they had carried out, detailing that Sunny had a linear fracture in her skull which they hoped would heal itself. He said that this could take a month or longer to happen and, to this end, he was proposing that Sunny remain in hospital for at least a month, under the close observation of the medical team. This would also give time for the child's broken bones, lacerations, and bruises to heal.

"We're going to put Sunny into ICU for tonight where the nurses can watch all her vital signs and spot if there's any deterioration in her condition. Do you have somewhere you can go overnight? There's a women's hostel close by if you don't."

Seeing that Jan was confused and undecided, he assumed she was most likely still in shock with the child's diagnosis and added, "Please feel free to stay here with your niece while you decide what to do. I'm sorry we can't let you stay in the ICU with her, but we don't have the facility for this. Someone from the ICU will come down for her as soon as a bed is available. You can stay with her until then."

"Thank you, Doctor," she managed to reply, realising she would have to make plans for herself tonight and wondering if she would be safe if she booked into the hostel for one night. Knowing that Robert would most certainly have his men out looking for her very soon, if they had not already begun a search, she was unsure of her next move. Tiredness, fear and worry for herself as well as for Sunita coursed through her body. She hadn't eaten since breakfast, with the exception of a biscuit given to her by a nurse along with a cup of chai. Worried about her unborn baby, she made the decision to go along to the hostel, find some food and book in for a bed for the night. Meanwhile she would stay here with Sunita until they came to take her to the ICU. With the exhaustion she was experiencing, it wasn't long before she slumped down into the comfy chair, closed her eyes and fell fast asleep.

In another part of the hospital, Suman was making her way to the bed of one of her little patients, having received a phone call to say that the toddler had developed a very high temperature and the nurses on duty were concerned about him. She had left instructions that, even while on holiday, they should call her if there were any emergencies they felt she should be aware of.

The nurse apologised profusely to her, explaining that Dr Nath and the doctor on call had gone into theatre and it had been as a last resort that they had called her in. Suman assured her that she was more than happy to come in to see the toddler, knowing that all her visitors at home were well catered for and had Vada for company tonight.

Giving the little boy a thorough check over, she was extremely glad that she had been called in, his temperature being dangerously high; it was recording a level of 102.2 degrees Fahrenheit and she could see that he was running a fever. Concerned about the possibility of meningitis, Suman worked quickly to organise the child's removal up to the ICU department, where she tended to him for some time, applying cool cloths to his small body and giving him sips of water in between his bouts of crying. Checking his temperature again, she was thankful to see that it had dropped by one degree at last.

One of the nurses, taking over the toddler's care from Suman, explained to her, "I'll be here for some time, Dr Sudra, and will look after him if you want to go. We're really busy tonight, but we've called in some extra nurses. They're due in any time now. "

"That's good," Suman replied. "You certainly need help tonight."

The nurse nodded. "Yes. We've got another young patient coming in too. One of Dr Kumara's patients, a young girl that's been in an accident. She should have been here by now, but we've no porters to bring her up at the moment."

"Well, I could go down and get her and bring her up. That's no bother. Then I'll have another check on little Shaan here when I get back, and if he's still okay, I can leave you to it. Do you know the young girl's name and where she is?"

Given instructions, Suman left the hectic ICU department and made her way down in the lift to Dr Kumara's domain on the ground floor. Reaching his waiting room, she knocked gently on the door, but received no reply. Quietly, she opened the door and peered around it. From where she was she could see a child lying on a trolley in the room, hooked up to a drip into her vein, whilst in the corner she spotted what she thought was the child's mother, sound asleep on a large chair. She entered the room, intending to wake the mother, but paused for a moment as she looked at the woman's face.

This woman is so like Habi's 'Madam', Suman thought. She studied the lady's face in silence for a minute and then turned to the child on the bed. *Is this another Nokara?* she wondered. She looked again at the woman, her face, her hair, her clothes, and the more she stared, the more convinced she became that this was indeed the lady she had chased from the building a couple of weeks ago.

As if aware of Suman's close inspection, Jan's eyes began to flicker and eventually shot open to find a strange doctor staring down at her. She sat up quickly, not recognising Suman but very uneasy at the intensive look on the doctor's face.

"What is it?" she asked. "Has something happened? Is Sunny all right?" She looked over at the bed where Nokara lay, still in a coma.

Suman hesitated, slightly unsure how to handle this situation. What if she had made a mistake? She couldn't go making any accusations until she found out a bit more about the woman and about the child in the bed. She reached out an arm.

"Please don't panic. Sunny is fine. I've just come down from the ICU, as I've been asked to take her up there for tonight. I'm sorry I woke you; you were in such a deep sleep. Has it been a frantic day for you?"

Jan was still trying hard to collect her thoughts and looked suspiciously at Suman, afraid that this doctor was going to ask more questions. She had answered enough today and now just wanted to leave. She was about to stand, but Suman's words made her hesitate.

"Please don't get up. I can see you're exhausted. I'm a paediatrician here at the hospital and just need to check one or two things before I head upstairs with your..." She stopped. "Is Sunny your daughter?"

Jan's heart was pounding, her suspicion of Suman getting stronger by the moment.

"She's my niece," she replied curtly.

"And what happened to your niece? I was told she had been in an accident. What kind of an accident was it?"

"A car accident."

"Where did it happen?"

"Outside my house." Jan, now seriously alarmed by Suman and her questions, stood up abruptly from the chair. As nonchalantly as possible, Suman moved a few steps to stand between Jan and the door.

"I'm so sorry to hear that. It must have been frightening for you." She spoke as gently as possible, trying to calm the frightened woman in front of her.

Jan opened her mouth, but no sound came out. Staring at Suman, she began to realise that this was her adversary from two weeks ago, when Habi had identified Jan in the corridor of the main hall. She made a dart towards the exit, but Suman was too quick for her and moved to stand with her back to the door so that Jan was trapped.

"Move out of my way. Let me out. I need to leave."

"I'm so sorry, but please don't rush away. As her doctor, I really need you to tell me more about your niece. I need more information about what's happened to her. Please sit down for a few moments. I won't keep you long."

Jan was afraid and had no idea how to handle the situation. If this doctor was not recognising her, it would seem very suspicious if she was to push her way past and flee from the room. She moved back slightly from Suman, but did not sit down.

"What else do you need to know?" she asked.

"I need to know what Nokara's injuries are." Again Suman spoke gently, very much with her calm doctor's voice, but testing the waters by using the child's working name.

"I don't know anyone called Nokara. The child's name is Sunny."

"Can you tell me her second name?"

Jan's body seemed to slump into itself, as if she was feeling defeated by Suman's questions.

"Please let me out," she whispered, looking into Suman's face. "I need to go."

On the trolley bed, the child stirred, as if hearing Jan and Suman's voices. Both women looked across at the bed for a moment and then back at each other before Suman spoke.

"Please, for the child's sake, stay and talk to me. I just want to help you both. I think you need my help." She paused, then continued. "Am I right?"

Jan nodded, turning her face away from Suman, who posed another question in a very gentle voice.

"And is your name really Mrs Hingorani, or is it something else? Little Habi told me about you and I don't think that is your name."

At this, Suman saw Jan sway slightly, clutching at her stomach, and she stepped forward to hold on to Jan's arm.

"Come and sit down, please. I know this is really difficult for you, but I need to know who you are and who the little girl really is."

Helping Jan move backwards the few steps to her chair, she gently pressed her into it and drew up another chair for herself.

"Are you in pain? Can I get you some water?"

"Yes, please," Jan replied quickly, "I would like some water. I've been here most of the day and I'm so thirsty and hungry, and very tired. Please just ask your questions quickly and let me go. I beg of you," she added as Suman handed her a glass of cold water and sat opposite her, watching her closely.

"Will you tell me your real name?"

"I'm called Jan, but that's all I will tell you."

"And the child's real name?"

Jan shook her head. "I don't know for sure. I think it is Sunita, which is why I said she was called Sunny. I've no idea what her surname is."

"Ok. We'll leave that just now. What happened to Sunny? How did she get hurt?"

"I honestly don't know. All I know is that someone hurt her. I found her like this and brought her here."

"Was Sunny working for you, like Habi was?"

Jan nodded.

"Was she trafficked by someone and sold or given to you?"

Jan looked away, suddenly feeling nauseous and overcome by emotion. Her head drooped forward and she put her hands over her face. "I'm going to be sick," she told Suman.

Swiftly, Suman reached for a bowl on one of the trolleys in the room and handed it across. She watched as Jan retched a few times before leaning back in the chair. Suman walked over and knelt down beside Jan, putting a hand on her shoulder.

"I'm really sorry to be upsetting you like this. You're expecting a baby, aren't you? I know that's why you were here at the hospital the last time." She spoke softly and Jan nodded and further confirmed her query by clutching her stomach with one hand and holding the bowl near her face with the other.

"I thought the sickness had passed." Jan's words were just a whisper.

"It will have. This is probably just the stress you're going through at the moment. It'll pass again." She lifted Jan's glass, now empty. "Would you like more water or some tea before you go?"

"Water, please. But I haven't anywhere to go," Jan admitted. "I was going to try the women's hostel for the night, but I've no idea where it is or if I'm capable of walking to it."

Suman refilled the glass with water at the water dispenser and passed it to Jan.

"Well, I can help you with that, but first I must get this little girl into the ICU as quickly as I possibly can. Just sit here resting for a moment while I organise that and then I will try to help you too."

Jan sat quietly in her chair, feeling totally disconsolate as Suman made one or two calls, firstly to the porters' rooms to see if she could have Sunny moved. In this she was successful and a porter arrived very quickly with a patient trolley, assisting Suman to lift the child and all her attachments onto it before wheeling her off to the ICU. Suman gave the porter a message for the nurses that she would be along as soon as she possibly could be.

The second call was just as important. She needed back-up to handle the situation with Jan and thought she knew just the person to help.

"Sam," she said as the phone was answered, "it's Suman. I need your help, but only if you're free. I don't want to take you away from your patients."

"No, you're not taking me away from my patients; I finished surgery a while ago and I'm just having a coffee. Happy to help. Where are you and what can I do?"

Chapter Seventeen

SISTER IRENE MERCY HOSPITAL

Jan sat with the glass clutched in both hands, her pale face a picture of absolute misery and fear. Her exhausted body was slumped into the chair, her bag on the floor at her feet. Suman had gone outside the room to talk to someone and she could hear the low murmur of their voices. She closed her eyes as tears gently began to fall down her cheeks.

On the other side of the door, a little way down the corridor, Suman was talking quietly with Sam, explaining what had been happening and why she had called for his help. With no clear idea of what she wanted from him, she was finding the explanation difficult and confusing.

"Her name is Jan," she continued. "She has admitted the two girls were trafficked and given to her as maidservants, but I can't get any more than that out of her at the moment. I've no idea what to do next. My impression is that she is in danger, just as those girls are. I do not think she is a bad person, just that she is in a difficult, dangerous situation. Also, my questions are just upsetting her."

He scratched his chin, thinking carefully.

"Well, from what you've told me, I think you've only got two options. The first one is the most sensible; you call in the police and let them deal with her. The only drawback with this is that, if they suspect she's a trafficker, they may just lock her in jail and throw away the key for a while. Not good for someone in early pregnancy. And if she's in jail, then we will be left to deal with the problem of the little girl up in the ICU. If she survives, she'll most likely be put in one of the children's centres when she leaves here."

Suman shook her head. "Sorry, but no, I don't like that idea one little bit, Sam. What's the other option?"

"You let the woman go."

"No. No, I don't like that one either. Can't you come up with another idea?" She smiled apologetically.

"I can't think of anything else. We can't keep Jan, or whatever her name is, here in the hospital for very much longer. What do you want to happen?"

Suman sighed in frustration. "I don't know. If I'm honest, I want something very unrealistic. I'd like to help both of them, Jan and the child. I suspect Jan is as frightened by it all as the child will be when she wakes. I've no idea how I can help them, but I'm certainly not wanting Sunny to go into a rescue centre for trafficked children. That's definite."

She saw the question in his eyes, and answered. "I have experience of these places, Sam. I couldn't do this to her."

He kept watching her, his heart touched, his imagination running riot at what her words meant.

"Okay, then we'll just have to come up with something else for both of them. The child is in the ICU for now and will be here in hospital for a while, by the sound of it. So we don't have to worry about her at the moment. We only have to worry about Jan. Can we give her a bed here for tonight? And, if we do, will she stay once we leave her alone?"

"No, I don't think she would and, anyway, we can't use the hospital as if it's our own and put someone in a bed just because we want to. What about the women's hostel nearby? Could we take her there?" She paused only for a moment before continuing, "I'd have taken her home with me and locked the door, but, as you know, my house is very full at the moment."

He shook his head and grinned. "You'd take in every waif and stray you came across, Doctor Barnardo, wouldn't you? We should be calling you Sister Mercy, like the hospital. No, you can't do that."

"No …" she agreed, looking very thoughtful. "I can't do that, but I could ask Ellie for help, couldn't I? Ellie always knows what to do with waifs and strays."

Again, Sam was left wondering about the meaning behind her words.

"What could Ellie do?" he asked.

"No idea, but she never lets me down. I'll give her a phone and ask for her advice. It's still early; she won't be in bed."

He checked his watch. "Okay. Do you want me to stay?"

"I'd love you to stay, but only if you want to. I'm so sorry for getting you embroiled in all of this."

She looked worried as she spoke, but he reassured her. "No problem. I said I'd help in any way I can. I'll keep an eye on the prisoner till you've made your call."

Suman smiled as she watched him go back into the room where Jan was waiting.

Back in Suman's apartment, Ellie and Geoff were relaxing with a cup of tea. Kanya had retired to bed some time earlier, the heat of the day and the visits to the

Marble Palace and Mother Teresa's house having taken their toll. She wanted to be fully rested for the next day, as Suman had promised to take her to the huge flower market at Kolkata's Eden Gardens. A visit to Bimla's house was scheduled for Friday, to catch up with Habi and the boys. Thoroughly enjoying her trip to Kolkata, Kanya fell into a deep sleep moments after her head hit the pillow. Even the telephone ringing in the lounge failed to disturb her much-needed rest.

Ellie answered on the fourth ring. Yes, she and Geoff were both still up, she assured Suman. Suman then launched into a very graphic account of all that had happened and what the dilemma was.

At the start of the call, Ellie had clicked on the loudspeaker, making sure Geoff was aware of all that Suman was saying, and it was Geoff who gave his advice first.

"I think you should do what Sam suggested and let the woman go," he advised, to the disapproval of both Suman and Ellie, who turned to him with a fierce look.

"Nonsense. We have to help this lady, Geoff, and the child she's carrying. She's probably in danger, especially if she's a trafficked victim herself. We don't know her circumstances." Ellie was, as he had realised right away, very keen to help solve the dilemma of what to do with the woman in trouble. He sighed and resigned himself to what he suspected would turn into a major event during their visit, knowing he was up against two very strong women, both blessed with huge hearts.

"Could Vada maybe help tonight?" he asked. "Her roommate is away, so there's an empty bed in Vada's room.

She was telling us about this today, and also that she's taken a couple of days' holiday to spend time with us."

Ellie nodded, looking at Geoff.

"Yes. What a good idea. What do you think, Suman? Will we ring Vada? She might be able to help, if she's allowed visitors to stay with her overnight."

"Well, let's find out," Suman said, her eyes alight with hope.

Chapter Eighteen

STUDENT NURSES' HOME, SISTER IRENE MERCY HOSPITAL

Geoff's suggestion proved to be a good one and provided a temporary answer to the problem of accommodation for Jan for the night. Vada, though slightly taken aback by the request, was happy to help and, after requesting permission from the manager of the nurses' home to have a guest stay, decided to come across to the hospital to accompany Suman and Jan back to the hostel.

Meanwhile, Suman, having checked up on her little patients in the ICU and waved goodbye to Sam, began to walk slowly through the grounds of the hospital with Jan, explaining where they were going and why. Jan was quiet, not agreeing or disagreeing with what was happening, and Suman began to worry about the decision and the burden she was putting on her younger sister to look after this virtual stranger.

As they drew nearer to the hostel, she could see that Jan was slowing considerably and looking near to total exhaustion. She took the young woman's arm, feeling her wobbling a bit and fearing she was very soon going to drop to the ground. Vada, meeting up with them at this time, moved quickly to take Jan's other arm and helped her walk the last fifty yards to reach the door. Four stone steps led up to the entrance of the building and it was with difficulty that they helped her up these steps.

"I'm really concerned about her, Vada. Being in early pregnancy doesn't usually mean this level of fatigue." Suman spoke quietly in her native language of Marathi, not wanting Jan to know what she was saying. "I'll check her over once we …"

The next few words were lost, a sudden, very loud explosion ringing in her ear. She knew instantly what it was; Suman knew the sound of a gunshot. She also knew right away where the bullet had gone, as Jan's body had reacted violently, propelled forward with the force of it. A cry burst from her as she fell towards the ground.

Suman and Vada's hands tightened automatically to stop her from hitting the ground hard, but there was a moment of confusion, as they too were shaken by the impact, and both nearly lost their balance. They lowered Jan to the ground as gently as they could, Suman hissing to Vada as they did so, "Get down, Vada! Quickly, keep on the ground!"

"What is it? What's happened?" Vada's voice quivered as she lay on the ground. "Has she been shot?"

"Yes," replied Suman. "We need to get her inside. But keep your body as flat as you possibly can. The shooter will still be around."

As they tried to lift Jan, Suman's fears were realised and another shot rang out through the stillness of the night. The two sisters reacted immediately and fell prostrate on the ground as the bullet whizzed by with what sounded like a deafening crack, hitting the wall of the building with a massive thud.

"Quick, Vada! We need to get out of here!" Suman shouted to her sister.

Moving at speed, the two girls managed to grab Jan and pull her up a tiny bit to drag her into the building, still keeping their own bodies as low as they could. As the door shut behind them, Suman did a very fast crawl over to the light switches on the wall and turned them all off, plunging the hallway into darkness. The sisters then began to pull Jan round a corner, out of sight of anyone looking through the door.

"Where can we go?" asked Suman. "Is there somewhere we can hide if they follow us?"

As she spoke, a shaft of light appeared further along the corridor and a voice spoke.

"What's happening? Can I be of any help?" The voice was that of a student nurse who had come out of a room on the ground floor. "Did I hear a gun going off?" she whispered, instinctively realising something very dangerous was happening.

"Yes," replied Suman. "Can we come into your room? We need to hide."

The young nurse's eyes widened and her mouth opened. Then she answered, "Yes, of course. Come in."

Suman and Vada dragged a now unconscious Jan into the room and, as soon as the door was shut and locked behind them, they knelt down at Jan's side, pulling aside her blood-stained clothes. Suman could see that the bullet had entered Jan's body very close to her right shoulder. As she worked, she spoke in a whisper to the student nurse, looking on fearfully.

"Thank you for letting us in here. I'm Dr Sudra, from the hospital, and this is my sister Vada, a nurse here."

The nurse nodded. "I recognise Vada."

Suman continued. "This lady has been shot. We have to be really quiet in case the gunman comes looking for us." The nurse nodded. "How can I help?" she whispered.

"Do you have towels or cloths? I need to stop the bleeding." The nurse nodded and hurried towards her bathroom.

Turning to Vada, Suman spoke again, keeping her voice as low as she could.

"Get my phone out of my pocket, Vada, and phone 112 Emergency Services and ask for the police. Tell them where we are and that there's a gunman outside who has shot one of our patients. Tell them they must come immediately."

The student nurse returned with a number of towels in her hand and she knelt beside Suman as she handed them over.

"Thank you." Suman moved swiftly, making a large pad with two of the towels. "Now, can you hold your hand really firmly against this, to help stop the bleeding?"

"I'm Zoya," the nurse whispered as she did as Suman had asked, then realised she hadn't been heard, as Suman was busy checking the pulse on Jan's neck and wrist and leaning over to listen to her breathing.

"We need to get her back to the hospital as fast as we can." Suman looked up at Vada, who had come back over to them after making the phone call. "Vada, call Sam. His number is in my phone. Ask him to send an ambulance over here, pronto, and tell him what's happened and that it could be dangerous."

She looked back at the nurse. "Zoya, you're doing a great job. Keep up the pressure. Change the towels if they get too wet." The young girl nodded, pleased that Dr Sudra had heard her name after all.

"I've got a stethoscope if you need one," she volunteered. "My mother gave it to me when I began my training."

"Excellent. That's exactly what I need. I'll take over the pressure."

Zoya released her pressure on the wound, then ran to a cupboard, opening the door wide and rummaging for a moment before producing a stethoscope. It was put to use immediately. Listening for a wheeze in Jan's chest, Suman felt a bit more heartened. She knew the bullet had damaged the bones and surrounding tissue, but the heartbeat was strong and Jan's breathing was not as slow as she had thought it would be.

She felt a tap on her shoulder and looked at Zoya, who pointed to the window with its closed curtains.

"I hear a siren coming closer. It could be the police."

"Oh, good," said Vada. "I told them to hurry. Fingers crossed that means it should be safe outside when Sam arrives with the ambulance."

Suman breathed a sigh of relief. She had been terrified that the gunman or gunmen would find their way inside the building, which could mean more casualties by the time the police arrived. They hadn't heard any more shots, but that didn't mean their assailants had gone. Hopefully, having the police here meant it would soon be safe.

Things happened quickly after that, with the police making their presence known and coming inside around the same time as the strident sound of the ambulance could be heard. Going out to speak to the police, Suman left her patient in the capable hands of Vada and Zoya and, as succinctly as possible, told the police what had happened. There was no mention of Jan's circumstances, Suman portraying her as a friend for the moment.

Sam appeared at her side as she spoke to the officer in charge, and she excused herself to quickly arrange for Jan to be lifted into the ambulance and taken to the hospital for what she knew would be emergency surgery. She then left that side of things to Sam, knowing Jan was safe in his hands, and hurried back to the police, who were beginning to organise a search outside for anyone with a gun. It was some time before the officers came back to report they had searched both inside and outside in the surrounding garden and paved areas and found nothing suspicious.

Following the all clear signal, Suman and Vada were offered a lift in one of the police cars back to the hospital. Desperate to get back there, Suman accepted, but Vada chose to stay at the nurses' accommodation with Zoya for a cup of chai, feeling their new friend was in need of company until all the stress and worry of the incident had died down. Suman thanked them both for their help, promising to come back to see Zoya with an update on the patient when time permitted. She also told them that some of the police officers would be staying around until the morning, just in case there was any more trouble.

Back inside the hospital, she was really happy to see Sam waiting around beside the paediatric wards. He was talking to some students, but left them to come over to Suman.

"Am I relieved to see you!" he exclaimed, the worried look leaving his face. "Are you all right?"

"I'm fine. Just a bit shaken. Where is Jan?"

"In surgery. Sai Patel is doing the op; he was one of the surgeons on emergency duty tonight and we just caught him as he was coming out of another surgery. Shouldn't take too long; he's one of the best. Are you sticking around until she comes out?"

"Yes, I'd like to see how she is and if all is okay with her and the baby before I head home."

"I'll wait around too and then see you home. From what I can gather, someone was shooting at the three of you. Is that true?"

"Well, I think they were shooting at Jan and we were just getting in the way. But it was pretty scary. I was afraid for Vada; a bullet skimmed close by us and we could feel it passing and hear the noise. It was the noise that scared me most. Brought back memories."

"Suman ...?" he began.

"I know," she interrupted, turning to look at him. "I know. I will tell you more of my childhood one day, but not just now. Though you might be shocked by some of it," she added, in an afterthought.

He closed his eyes for a second or two, trying to control his emotions. He desperately wanted to take her into his arms, but knew that this wasn't what she would have liked. He was silent as she continued.

"It's why I get so involved with anyone who's been trafficked. I want to help get them away from it and I want to track down those responsible and stop them. All of them."

This last sentence was accompanied by a smile, and he couldn't help but grin back as he replied, "You can't change the whole world, Suman, but, knowing you, you'll have a blooming good crack at it. And you'll take all your friends and relatives with you when you're doing it."

She grinned back. "You know me well, Sam. Come on, buy me a coffee while we're waiting for word about Jan, and I'll tell you all my plans to find these particular degenerate ... nefarious ..." She scrambled about in her head, trying to think of even stronger words. "Scabby, bloody bassas!"

Sam lifted his eyebrows, his eyes alight. "And that's another phrase you picked up in Scotland, is it, Dr Sudra?"

She laughed. "It is, actually. And if you ever tell Ellie that I've used it, we're done being friends."

"My lips are sealed."

Chapter Nineteen

SISTER IRENE MERCY GOVERNMENT HOSPITAL, KOLKATA

It was almost three in the morning when Suman arrived home. Ellie had been listening for her, and got up to find out what had been happening since they had last heard an update on the shooting.

There wasn't much to tell, except that Jan had come safely through her operation to remove the bullet, which had entered the brachial plexus area. That was her right shoulder, Suman explained, where the bullet had caused some nerve and tissue damage and shattered a few bones. Quite a complicated operation, but Dr Patel was particularly skilled in bone damage, and once the bullet had been removed, he had worked to remove or repair some of the little broken bones of Jan's shoulder. With the right care and nursing, she was expected to make a good recovery.

Ellie was relieved, as much by seeing that Suman was still in one piece as by hearing the news of Jan.

"What about her baby? Is everything okay?" she asked.

"Baby's heart's still beating, no bleeding, and everything looks fine. We'll know more in the next few days. Trauma can have funny effects on people, especially pregnant ones. You shouldn't have got up for me, Ellie, you'll be tired tomorrow."

"I couldn't sleep. I like to know you're ok. Old habits and all that."

Suman hugged her tight. "Well, I'm off to bed. I'm shattered. Tomorrow we need to plan our day; we're supposed to be taking Ai to the flower market, but I'll have to see how it's going at the hospital first. Anyway, tomorrow is another day. Tonight, I need some sleep. And so do you. Goodnight, Ellie. I love you."

"Goodnight, Su. I love you too."

Breakfast was buffet-style the next morning, each of the residents enjoying a very different type of breakfast. By the time Vada joined them around eight thirty, she found chaos ensuing in the kitchen, with idlis being cooked by Kanya, cereal being eaten from a bowl by Suman, and Geoff and Ellie enjoying bacon and eggs with a splash of beans. The sink was piled high with dishes, and Vada immediately got stuck in with the washing up. The noisy chatter was centred around the events of the previous evening, with Kanya berating both her daughters for putting themselves at so much risk and worrying their poor mother to death. Between laughs, both her disobedient daughters teased her out of her worries and informed her she was going to see the flower market at Eden Gardens today, and they would buy her all the rosebuds and petals her heart desired. She was thrilled at the treat in store.

As everyone rushed off after breakfast to claim the shower and get ready for the day, Suman made her way quickly across to the hospital to check on her charges; first Sunny, then Shaan, the toddler at risk of developing meningitis, and finally, to say hello to Jan. Jan was doing as well as could be expected and was waiting to be taken for an ultrasound scan to check on the baby's progress. She was scared, both for the baby and herself, worrying that someone would enter the hospital to try to end her life again. Suman reported this to the security staff at the hospital, who assured her they would try to keep a check on the ICU that day. Jan had been put into a small secondary ward with only four beds, and she had requested the screens be kept closed around her bed all day. Still, Suman knew it would be a fraught day for her, and reassured her that she would visit again later in the evening to see how she was.

Sunny had recovered consciousness, but was sleeping a lot; the painkillers and medicines making her quite drowsy most of the time. Suman knew it would not be a quick recovery for the child, and made a mental note to check on her again this evening when she was visiting Jan. Sam was on duty, but very busy with clinics, so she didn't manage to speak to him before hurrying back across to her apartment to join the holiday-makers for their outing.

Kanya was in seventh heaven with the trip to the flower market, known locally as the Mullik Ghat Flower Market, one of the biggest of its kind in India. The smell of the flowers reached their noses as they approached the Howrah River and the large iron grid Howrah Bridge that towered over the market. Kanya clapped her hands in delight at the sea of yellow that met their eyes, with basket upon basket of the yellow and gold marigolds that she loved. They walked around the beautiful displays of leis, garlands and flower handcrafts being made and Kanya stood at one stall long enough to try her hand at learning how to craft a tower of roses. Armed with a bagful of petals over her shoulder, two bunches of flowers in one hand and Suman's arm through her other arm, Geoff teased that the smile never left her face that day.

A visit past the huge Victoria Memorial Hall, with a stop to take photos, capped the day; the only disappointment being that the palatial building was shut to visitors from five o'clock onwards and they couldn't get inside to see the treasures and the many works of art housed in the galleries. This didn't spoil the wonderful day, however, and after a wander around the gardens, the weary group at last made their way home as the sun was setting.

Suman left her relatives in the apartment getting ready to prepare the evening meal as she once again made her way back to the hospital, promising to be back in time to eat with them. Her mind was very much caught up with planning the next couple of days' activities, hoping that they would manage to fit in the promised visit to Habi and Bimla with her boys. Trying to work out the logistics of all this, she wasn't watching her footing carefully enough and tripped slightly over a broken paving stone jutting out of the road.

As she righted herself, slightly embarrassed in case anyone had seen her trip, she looked around and a man a little distance off caught her eye. It was only a fleeting look, but in that moment, she noticed how he stopped suddenly and swiftly turned to walk in another direction.

The thought that he had been following her entered her mind and took hold. Her footsteps quickened on the path. Reaching the hospital grounds, she decided to have another look and glanced behind very quickly. Sure enough, the man was still there and, whilst some distance away from her now, he was walking around the trees in the garden and not sticking to the main path. She was pretty sure now that he was following her and, in light of the shooting last night, she decided to try to lose him somehow.

Picking up her pace, she began to run and entered the very first door of the hospital that she came to and charged up a flight of stairs ahead of her. At the top, she entered a cupboard, pulled the door almost closed, and stood behind it, listening to see if anyone came in the door in her wake.

A couple of minutes later she heard the door at the bottom of the stairs open and the footsteps mounting the stairs she had just come up. She turned in the large cupboard, spotted an iron and carefully lifted it up. Better armed than not, she decided. However, the footsteps only hesitated for a second or two on the landing and then continued up to the next flight. She pushed the cupboard door open another inch to listen more carefully and heard the steps go on up a further flight of stairs.

She was unsure if it was her stalker or not, and therefore waited another moment or two before peeping out from behind the door. There was no one in sight, so she emerged silently from the cupboard and ran quickly down the stairs and out of the door. Still running, she followed the side of the building until she came to another main door on the opposite side of the hospital from where she had been. Slightly out of breath, she nevertheless kept running into the building and hurried to the ICU.

There were no security people around, just a few medical staff, nurses, auxiliaries and doctors as she made her way to Jan's bed in the little side ward. The curtains were still closed, and she slipped behind them, relieved to see Jan still there, and looking a bit better than she had this morning. She was hooked to two drips, one on each side of her.

Suman pulled in a chair. "How are you?" she asked.

Before Jan could answer, one of the curtains was pulled back suddenly and a nurse appeared, startling both Suman and Jan.

"Oh, it's you, Dr Sudra," the nurse exclaimed. "I saw someone enter and didn't know who it was. We've been keeping an eye on our patient here, as she's been feeling a bit jittery after what happened to her last night. As anyone would." The nurse smiled at Jan, who returned her smile.

As the nurse left, Suman turned back to Jan and tried again. "So, tell me how you are and if they have told you about what happened?"

Jan hesitated before replying.

"Yes, they told me some of it, and I'm doing all right, considering." She lifted her arms to highlight the two drips. "My shoulder is very sore, but they are keeping me topped up with painkillers. I hope these are safe for my baby." She looked at Suman, as if she had asked this as a question.

"I'm sure whatever they're giving you is safe. They know you're pregnant. Do you know how far along you are? How many weeks?"

"The doctor in gynaecology estimated I was eleven weeks at my scan and that was nearly three weeks ago. So I must be nearing fourteen weeks. How long do you think I'll be kept here, now I've had the bullet removed?"

"Well," Suman began, "I'm sure Dr Patel will have given you an estimate, but we would normally keep someone in for five or six days after an operation like yours. The bullet has done a good bit of damage, I believe, and you lost an awful lot of blood. Has anyone notified your husband?"

"No," she replied forcefully. "I don't want him notified. I don't want anyone notified."

"I guessed you were having some kind of trouble in your life, Jan ..." She hesitated. "Is it okay to call you Jan? Is that your real first name?"

"My name is actually Janetta, but most people shorten it to Jan. I don't mind if you call me that, but please don't tell anyone about me. I don't want anyone to know I'm here." There was a pause. "You're right, I am in trouble. I'm trying to get away from my husband and would have been well away if I hadn't had to bring Sunny into the hospital."

"Can you tell me why you're trying to get away from your husband?"

"No, I can't do that."

"I'd really like to help you if I can, and it would be much easier if you could tell me what you know and be honest with me." Suman spoke in a very gentle way, hoping that Jan would open up to her.

Jan turned her face away. "I can't see how you could possibly help me or why you would want to."

Suman leaned a fraction closer and spoke softly, not wanting anyone else in the small ward to be disturbed by their conversation.

"Jan, I know that Sunny was trafficked and I know that Habi was also trafficked. I know that they both worked for you for a while. You called them both Nokara – you know you did. But did you know that Habi was brought in here after being rescued from the Dhapa landfill site with many burns and a broken leg?"

"Dhapa? Oh my God!" Jan exclaimed, closing her eyes. "I knew she fell unconscious, but I thought they would take her to a hospital or doctor and just leave her there. I had no idea that's what happened to her. Why in heaven's name would they take a child to Dhapa and leave her there?"

"You really didn't know this?"

"No, I swear I didn't know. She was just taken away and replaced. How did she get to the hospital?"

"She was brought in by one of the rag pickers."

"Is she still here in the hospital?"

"No, she's in a safe place and is happy, for now."

Jan turned away to digest this as Suman continued.

"So, Habi was trafficked, and Sunny as well, who I presume was Habi's replacement?"

"Yes." The answer was a whisper.

"Why do you use these girls as maids? Do you buy them from someone?"

There was no answer this time, but Suman decided to keep going.

"Jan, I don't know your circumstances, but I suspect you are somehow involved in trafficking, either by choice or by force. If you're trying to leave your husband because he's involved too, and you want to be safe from the people who are trying to kill you, will you give me some information and I can pass this on to the right people? People who will keep you safe."

Again there was no answer, and Jan's body was rigid as she lay in the hospital bed.

"Jan ..." Suman began, but was interrupted.

177

"I don't want to answer any more questions. I can't tell you anything else." Jan's tear-filled voice broke as she spoke to Suman.

Suman pushed back her chair and rose, saying, "I'm so sorry. Please don't get distressed; I mean it when I say I'm trying to help you. But I won't ask anymore, as it's upsetting you. Just remember, though, you can ask for me anytime if you feel you'd like to talk to me."

"Thank you," Jan whispered, her brain a jumbled mass of thoughts, regrets, pain and sadness. She just wanted the world to swallow her up and make her disappear.

Suman left the ICU, upset that she was not able to help Jan in some way. *Maybe when she's stronger she'll open up to me and allow me to help,* she thought.

For a moment she had forgotten about being followed to the hospital, and it was only when she entered the now empty corridor that she remembered. She decided to head down to the children's ward and see if Sam was around. However, it wasn't proving to be a good night for Suman, as the staff on duty told her that he had gone into surgery and wouldn't be free for some time. Still worrying about her stalker, she decided to phone Geoff to ask if he would come over and walk back to the apartment with her.

"Give me ten minutes and I'll be with you," he replied to her request. "Where will I meet you?"

"I'll wait in the front hall, near reception, and watch for you coming. Thank you, Geoff."

"No worries."

Suman popped into her office to collect the numerous messages she suspected would be in her in-tray after this length of time away, and, finding about a dozen, stuffed them into her pocket, deciding to take them home to read there. She re-locked the cupboard where her in-tray was kept and left the office to make her way to the front hall to meet Geoff.

She was halfway along one of the corridors when she heard her name called. Turning to see who it was, she was suddenly grabbed by two assailants and a cloth was stuffed over her face and into her mouth. She panicked and struck out with her hands, trying to push her attackers away, but she was being held too tightly. Seconds later she felt a sharp prick in her left arm and again tried to lash out at whoever was holding her. She sensed suddenly that there was a third assailant, someone who was attempting to put some kind of cover over her head. Struggling for all she was worth became futile as she felt the strength ebbing away from her and her last feeling was that of falling down into someone's waiting arms as everything went black.

Downstairs, Geoff waited patiently for Suman. He didn't know which direction she would come from, so his eyes scanned the vast hall every so often. Only ten minutes had passed since he left the apartment, so he controlled his impatience, leaning back against a wall and resigning himself to wait a little longer. However, after twenty minutes had passed, what began as a very slight concern started growing. Five minutes later, he decided to try to find her.

He approached one of the receptionists and asked if she could page Dr Sudra for him.

After checking the directory, the receptionist began ringing Suman's pager, but after three attempts, the pager had not been answered.

"I'm sorry, sir. It is ringing, so she should be hearing it, but she's not answering. She's probably very busy at the moment. Would you like me to keep trying?"

"No. I'll go and see if I can find her. Can you tell me where she is likely to be?"

The receptionist shook her head. "I'm not sure. It's a very big hospital, she could be anywhere. Mainly she works in the children's ward, and that's where her office is."

He was given directions and set off to find the children's ward, hoping very much that he would find her en route, making her way to reception. However, there was no sign of her, and he reached the paediatric unit within a few minutes. As he tried to enter the ward, he was intercepted by a nurse who spoke to him in Bengali. He replied in English.

"Dr Sudra. I'm looking for Dr Sudra. Is she here?"

The nurse began to wave her arms about. "Eengleesh, na. Dr Sudra, na."

He tried a different tack. "Dr Nath? Is Dr Nath here?"

The nurse nodded and indicated for Geoff to wait while she hurried back into the ward. He watched through the window and saw her approach a group of three men in white coats at the far end of the ward. He saw her point over to him and watched with relief as Sam left the group to hurry towards him.

"I'm so sorry, Sam, for taking you away from your work. I can't find Suman and I'm really worried. She was to meet me in reception some time ago and hasn't turned up. I'm concerned something has happened to her."

"What makes you think that? You don't think she's just busy with her patients or she's had an emergency or something?"

Geoff drew his hand through his hair and answered Sam with a rueful frown.

"God, I hope it is that, Sam. But she was worried when she phoned me. I could tell. She asked me to come over to the hospital to walk her home. I just sensed something was wrong and said I'd come straight away. She would have come straight to meet me, I'm pretty sure of that."

"Okay, give me two minutes to sort myself out and I'll come and help you look. Stay here."

Sam hurried back into the ward but reappeared very quickly, having given his apologies to the two doctors he had been conferring with.

"Right, where have you looked?

"Only here. But reception tried paging her a few times with no answer."

Sam pulled out his pager and tried keying in Suman's number, waiting to see if she would answer. However, like reception, he got no sign that she was receiving the call although he knew it was ringing.

"Come on," Sam beckoned Geoff to follow him. "We'll have a quick run through the parts of the building she may be in. She's got a number of patients in the ICU, so we'll start there."

Their search took a good twenty minutes, ending up back in the vast entrance hall, at which time Geoff tried for a second time to phone Suman's personal mobile in case she had gone back to the apartment, being unable to find him. Again, no reply.

While he was making the call, he saw Sam being hailed by a couple of doctors. He strode across to within hearing distance of them and very quickly realised that Sam had asked them if they knew Suman's whereabouts. He couldn't understand the language, but suspected Sam was telling them of their search for Suman. One of the two doctors, a man Sam called Sai, looked thoughtful.

"Have you asked security?"

"No. Why?"

"We've just heard a strange story from one of the porters." Sai frowned. "Seemingly, an elderly lady visitor reported to security that she had seen one of the lady doctors being knocked down in a corridor and then being carried away by three men she didn't think were doctors. I don't think security believed her story and we didn't when we heard it. But if Dr Sudra is missing, it'd be a good idea to ask security for more information."

Shouting his thanks to Sai, Sam set off running, beckoning for Geoff to follow.

Reaching the security department, they burst into the room. Speaking quickly in Bengali, Sam asked them about the strange story. Geoff stood watching, but he could see that Sam didn't like the answers they were giving him, his face growing grimmer with every word. At last he turned to translate to Geoff.

"This doesn't sound good. What Sai said was correct. The old lady turned a corner and was confronted by three men in the corridor who looked as if they were grappling with a lady doctor. She was frightened and quickly hid back behind the corner, but said that she peeped out to see what was happening. Apparently, one of them stuck a needle in the doctor and put something on her face and the doctor fell to the floor, at which point the old lady fled and went straight to reception. They sent her to security. The security guys said they investigated the story but could find absolutely nothing, either in the corridor or in any of the rooms off the corridor and nothing outside the building either. So they didn't know if it was true or not."

"Oh my God, Sam. Do you think this has something to do with the shooting last night? It may be the same people. But why would they want to take Suman? I thought it was Suman's patient they were trying to shoot, I didn't really understand what it was all about."

"Yeah, I do think it has to do with that. We need to go and talk to Jan, the patient who got shot. She's in the ICU, but she may be able to tell us who shot her and why someone would want to get a hold of Suman."

They hurried quickly up to the ICU department.

"You'd better wait outside," Sam told Geoff. "Visitors are not allowed in the ICU. I'll see what I can find out. You keep phoning her - keep trying to contact her."

Sam entered the Intensive Care Unit as quietly as he could, explaining to staff on duty that he needed to see Jan, one of their patients, urgently. Pointing to the curtained area where Jan lay, they told him she was asleep.

"I need to wake her up," he informed them. "Is she comatose or just sleeping?"

"Oh, she's just sleeping," one of the nurses replied. "She's still recovering, but she's much better than she was yesterday. Just don't stay too long, if that's okay, Dr Nath."

"I won't. I'll only be a few minutes."

Sam walked across and looked down at the woman in the bed, hooked up to a couple of drips and heavily bandaged around her shoulder. He gave her other arm a light touch, which woke her with a start, and she turned quickly to look at him.

"Hello, Jan. It's Dr Nath. You remember I spoke to you yesterday" He pulled a nearby chair across to the bed as he spoke and sat down at her side.

"I remember you." Her voice was low.

Seeing how delicate the woman looked, he thought it best not to frighten her. He began gently. "How are you feeling?"

"I'm fine. Pretty sore, but also scared. The people that shot at me wanted me dead and I'm scared they will find out soon where I am and come in here to try again. Can you have me taken to somewhere safer?"

"I'll certainly make enquiries about taking you somewhere safe, but, for the moment, I think you really need to be here. You've just had surgery and your body has been through a good bit of trauma. Probably the best thing I could do is ask one of our security men, or even call in help from the police, to provide someone to sit outside the ICU and keep an eye out for anything suspicious. The ICU doesn't have open visiting, so they can't just walk in. I can also enquire about getting you taken to another hospital in a day or two, if this would help."

"No police. Don't involve the police." She sighed and turned her face away again, looking very disconsolate.

"I won't promise that, but right at this moment, I really need to talk to you about Dr Sudra. Your gun-toting friends appear to have kidnapped her and I desperately need to know who they are and how I can find them. Have you any idea who shot you? Is it people that you know?"

Keeping her face turned away, she replied, "I don't know who they are."

"I don't believe that's true, Jan. Dr Sudra is in deep trouble and you know she was only trying to help keep you safe by taking you across to the nurses' home. She saved your life while waiting for the ambulance. So I think you owe it to her to tell me what I need to know."

Jan's eyes moved slowly downward as she looked at her stomach, unconsciously clenching the fingers of her un-bandaged hand tightly. The movement did not go unnoticed by Sam.

"I know you're having a baby, and I want to keep you both as safe as possible. If you had reached the nurses' home without the shooting incident, Dr Sudra would have done everything to help you get away from whoever it is you're running away from. She saved you and your baby."

At last Jan turned towards him, tears appearing in her eyes.

"And if I tell you anything, do you swear that you will keep my baby and me safe after that?"

"I will certainly swear to do my absolute utmost to keep you safe."

With a trail of tears making its way down her face, Jan nodded.

"I'll tell you what I can."

Chapter Twenty

SOMEWHERE IN KOLKATA

Robert Gall Gupta sat at the head of the boardroom table leaning back against his chair, a ferocious scowl on his rounded face. He was smoking a cigar and looked as if he had just received some bad news, which, of course, he had. With a deep sigh, he raised his eyes to the ceiling before addressing the three men in front of him. Robert was English, but had lived in India for a good part of his life. He had changed his surname to Gupta for business purposes and learned the language of his adopted city, Kolkata. Normally he spoke in Bengali, but today his words were interspersed by clipped expletives in his native language.

"What the hell did you bring her here for? That wasn't what you were told to do. You've got the wrong person, the wrong place and the wrong time. This is a bloody eminent doctor, not the whore I told you to get rid of." He leaned forward, blowing the smoke from the cigar towards them as he looked around the table.

"Whose idea was this?" Four short words, but the menacing way they were pronounced was not lost on the three men.

No one replied.

"And what am I supposed to do with her?" He looked directly at one of the three and narrowed his eyes. "Why? Didn't you think I had enough problems on my plate?"

A deep furrow then appeared on his forehead. "Why didn't you just shoot her or slit her throat?"

"As you say, Boss, she's an eminent doctor. We thought you might want us to bring her in, maybe get information out of her in your own way. She's been protecting the person you wanted dead."

"So you grab her in a public place, drug her, and then bring her to me. Are you bloody fools? Do you know how many cameras there are in hospitals? Did anyone see you?"

"No, Boss. Definitely not."

Robert sighed. "Where is she?"

"Upstairs, in the small storeroom, trussed up like a chicken." The man answering stood up, indicating to the other two with a nod of his head that they were to come with him.

"Well, we'll leave it to you, Boss. If you need anything else, you know where we are."

The door shut quietly behind them. Robert groaned, lowering his head into his hands and remaining like this for several minutes. It was only when his phone rang that he moved, opening it to check who was calling. He didn't like what he saw and swiftly cut off the call, whacking his phone back down on the table with a thud.

Upstairs, in a small storeroom filled with pieces of surplus furniture, Suman was lying where the men had put her on the floor. She was conscious, but extremely dizzy and confused; a very sore head made her wince every few moments. She had tried to raise her head, but a wave of nausea hit her each time and she lay back down, keeping her eyes closed.

It was some time later before she risked opening her eyes a second time. Moving her head had made the headache worse, and the nausea again became a problem.

She could see that her hands and feet were bound with a heavy cord, but unable to think logically at the moment, she knew she'd have to wait until the haziness and the nausea passed before she could do anything about it. She kept as still as she could, and closed her eyes again.

Another ten minutes or so passed before she decided she had lain there long enough. Headache and nausea or not, she needed to do something. With a strong effort, she managed to twist herself around and get into a sitting position. She moved her head around to check out the room, which brought on another wave of nausea. This time, she found herself being sick on the floor. After wriggling away from the messy puddle and then sitting still for another few minutes, she thought perhaps this had actually improved how she was feeling.

She wondered what the men had injected her with. *Probably something like Propofol,* she thought, an anaesthetic used for short-term unconsciousness, although she couldn't be sure, being unaware of how long she had been here, asleep. And where was 'here'? A storage room in a hotel was her guess, noting all the obsolete furniture around her.

Well, wherever 'here' was, she knew she needed to get away. She looked around, hoping to spot something she could use as a weapon, but decided that the first thing she had to do was get the bindings off her hands and feet. She started on the cord round her ankles. The knot was as tight as a knot could possibly be, and it took some time to make any progress getting it loose. Dogged determination was all she had. Thankfully, she had this in abundance.

Twenty minutes of picking and pulling and teasing the cord and at last she could feel it begin to loosen. Another few minutes and the rope fell off, to lie at the side of her leg. Her feet were free and she stood up to flex them. The red sores where the rope had rubbed her skin were visible, but there was no bleeding.

She walked round the small storeroom, looking carefully for a weapon she could use, but could see nothing suitable. There was also nothing that looked sharp enough to cut the thick cord on her hands. Slightly dejected, she sat down heavily on one of the shabby chairs in the room.

How did I get into this? she asked herself, feeling frustrated and almost giving in to tears. It was hard to believe that this was happening to her for a second time in her life.

"Déjà vu." She said the words out loud. In her mind she said a silent prayer, *Please, God, let Ellie come and find me.*

She thought also of Geoff, knowing he would have waited in the hospital reception until he realised she wasn't coming. *What would he have done?* she questioned herself. *He won't have a clue where I am, but I know he'll try to find me, wherever I am.*

Realising she had no way of working out how long she had been unconscious, never mind where she was in relation to the hospital, she turned her mind instead to how she could possibly get out of this room.

Getting up, she began to examine every bit of the room, her dejection growing as flashbacks from her childhood in captivity began to rear their ugly heads. She tried to shake off her morbid thoughts and concentrate on finding a weapon of some kind, something sharp enough to cut the bindings on her hands, tied tightly in front of her.

Moving the pieces of furniture around, she was able to see clearly what was there. She had uncovered a small, blackened window behind the furniture, and hidden round there as well was an old dresser unit, with eight drawers and four small cupboards which she quickly began to open and shut. She found nothing at all and lowered herself down to kneel on the floor in order to see underneath the furniture.

She was down in front of the old dresser trying to feel if anything was there when suddenly, from outside the door, she heard a key being inserted into the lock. She froze and curled up tighter, knowing she was out of sight of the door. Her heart skipped a beat as the door opened with a soft creak and a man's voice said, "Please come out, Doctor. I know you're in here."

She didn't move.

The voice continued, "I'm here to release you from …" Abruptly it stopped.

"I was going to say, 'from your prison', but I see it's been turned into a sickroom. Please come out and let me get this mess cleaned up. The smell is most offensive."

Very mystified by the man's words and by his English accent, Suman stood up and appeared out from behind the dresser. Saying nothing, she found herself staring at him, taking in all the details of his appearance. A tall man, heavily built; the idea that came to her mind was that he was an actor stepping out of a TV or a theatrical set. His black glossy hair was quite long but immaculately styled, as were his clothes, which really caught her attention. His blue checked linen suit and matching waistcoat had been made to be noticed. His tie, flamboyantly knotted around his neck, was bright blue, and a small matching blue flower on his lapel was linked to a silver chain which dangled down into his breast pocket. Unlike his fellow countrymen, he would have looked quite at home on a London stage. She wondered who on earth he was and why he was dressed in such a way in Kolkata, where temperatures reached as high as 35 degrees Celcius most days.

As her eyes travelled down to his brown leather shoes and then back up to his face, she had to stifle a gasp. Where his appearance gave off a distinct aura of wealth and power, his icy, penetrating eyes were even more distinctive. She straightened up, involuntarily resolving not to be intimidated by this unusual man.

He pushed the door a little further open with his hand. "Come, I'm sure you'll be glad to get out of this room and have a little water after your ..." he looked over to where she had been sick, "... mishap."

Still hazy from the drug she had been given, Suman began to feel as if she had entered a surreal world. She followed the man, catching a glimpse of a gun tucked into the waistband of his trousers. She walked with him along the short hallway and down a flight of stairs, aware of his slow gait and his heavy breathing, as if each step he took was a bit of an ordeal. She surmised that if she got the opportunity to run, he most probably would not be able to catch her, even with the binding still on her wrists. However, having seen his gun, for the moment she waited, unsure of her surroundings and hoping that she would eventually be able to see a way out of both the building and the situation she was in.

They reached the bottom of the stairs, at which time he pointed to a door not far away.

"Please go in there, Doctor, and take a seat. I'll be with you in a moment."

Still feeling that everything had turned most bizarre, she walked through the door, finding herself inside a very comfortable, furnished sitting room. He came in behind her a few moments later and shut the door before making his way over to a cocktail cabinet, on top of which was a silver tray with decanters and glasses set out.

"I can offer you whisky or brandy, Doctor. Or would you rather have something else? I've got a very well-stocked drinks cabinet."

"Water will be fine, if you have it," she replied, beginning to wonder if perhaps she was still hallucinating.

She was handed a crystal glass with water and ice and held it in her cupped hands, still bound together. She sipped her drink slowly, grateful for the feel of the cool water in her mouth after being ill upstairs.

"Would you like to sit down?" he asked.

"No. I'd like to be taken back to the hospital. Please," she added sarcastically, "since we're being polite to each other."

He laughed.

"Well, I'm pleased to learn you have a sense of humour, Dr Sudra."

"I don't find anything remotely funny about this situation. And how do you know my name?"

"I make it my business to know things like that, Suman. May I call you Suman?"

"No, you may not. I repeat, how do you know my name?"

"I know a lot of things that would surprise you, Suman, and a lot of people. It's in my own interest to know about

192

the people that I come across, especially in my line of work."

"That being ...?"

He laughed again. "I said I like to know about people I come across; I didn't say they needed to know anything about me."

Suman opened her mouth to say that she knew he was a trafficker, but shut it again quickly, changing her mind. Perhaps it wasn't in her best interest to let him know that she had guessed who he was and therefore was well aware of his line of work.

He was watching her like a lion watched his prey, stealthily and silently through his narrow eyes, waiting to pounce as soon as he had the advantage.

"Well, Suman, or Dr Sudra, since you prefer that title," he backtracked, as Suman had frowned at the use of her first name. "I believe you have recently met an acquaintance of mine. A female acquaintance." He took a sip of whisky from his glass before continuing. "And I believe you have treated her in your hospital. You must have been a very excellent doctor for her to have returned to you for rescue when she was in trouble. May I know the nature of her treatment?"

"So you don't know everything about the people you come across."

She spoke with courage, fully aware that she was his prisoner but determined not to let him see that she was afraid of him. That fear grew as he narrowed his eyes even further.

"It will not pay you to cross me, Dr Sudra. I hold your freedom in my hands; in fact, I hold your life in my hands at this moment. Do you not value your life?"

She didn't answer his question, but asked a question of her own. "Am I to be set free to return to my life if I answer your questions?"

"I think I could see my way to setting you free if you gave me honest answers."

Suman waved her water glass in his direction, staring straight at him as she spoke.

"You see, that's a problem for me, giving honest answers to you. If you're set on asking me questions about my patients ..." She paused for only a second or two before continuing, "I will not give you answers. Being a qualified doctor of medicine, I have, of course, sworn the Hippocratic Oath to maintain the confidentiality of my patients. I'm unable to break that oath. Not even for you."

She could feel his fury even though he hadn't moved a muscle.

"So, Dr Sudra, my earlier question has been answered. You do not value your life, nor, I assume, your freedom."

"I certainly value both my freedom and my life." Suman spoke fiercely, her voice rising. "And my integrity. I certainly do not value your integrity, however. I don't believe you would ever let me go even if I were to answer every question you asked me."

He bowed.

"Well, now that we understand each other much better, I'm going to leave you for a while, to think things over. I believe that the storeroom upstairs will now have been cleared of the contents of your stomach, so my employee will take you back up there. I may, or may not, see you later, Dr Sudra."

He laid down his glass and made for the door. As he exited, she heard the words, "Oh, and my employee is armed and very dangerous, just like me."

"I bet he is," Suman said angrily as the door shut behind the obnoxious, chuckling man.

Chapter Twenty-One

SUMAN'S APARTMENT

The clock in Suman's apartment struck four a.m. as Geoff let himself in. Closing the door as quietly as he could, he re-locked it and used the security chain to double lock it before entering the lounge. Ellie came out of their bedroom, hurriedly pulling on her dressing gown as she ran to hug him.

"I've been listening out for you for hours and heard you opening the door. Where is she, Geoff? Did you find her?"

He held his wife tightly as he replied.

"No, we haven't found her yet, but we've managed to get quite a bit of information from Jan. That's the woman she was trying to protect, the one who was shot."

"Was she able to tell you where Suman is?"

"No, unfortunately not. She told us of two places they could have taken Suman, but we've been to both with no luck."

The pair sat down on the sofa as they spoke, keeping their voices low so as not to wake Kanya and Vada.

Geoff continued.

"Sam has been great, but before Jan would tell him anything she made him promise to keep her safe. So he had to organise a transfer to another hospital; all cloak and dagger stuff getting her out of the Sister Irene and into an ambulance. She's positive the gunmen will come back looking for her, which would put everyone in the hospital in danger, so he got her sent to a private clinic on the other side of town. It's run by a friend of his and he's organised a couple of bodyguards from a security company to try to keep her safe. That was part of his deal with Jan.

Until then she would say nothing. We followed her ambulance in his car and, once she was settled, she gave him some information on where Suman is likely to be. That was around one o'clock in the morning. She then told us that she herself had been trafficked when she was younger, and had been bought by the man she now lives with. He owns her; he's not married to her. He seems to be a man with quite a number of businesses, including a few shops on MG Road, which were the first places we looked for Suman. MG Road was relatively quiet; no shoppers, but that meant there was no one around to ask where his shops were. It took us a while to find them. Then, between us, we broke into each one; there were five, but they were all empty. We had to break windows to get in, but thankfully the roads were still busy with traffic, so no one heard us or stopped us. God knows how anyone living around there gets any sleep."

When he paused for a moment, Ellie urged him on, "So where else did you try?"

"The second place was a massive factory. I'm not exactly sure where it is, but I know it was north of Dhapa. It's an area called Bidhannagar, quite near the Eastern Railway line; we could hear the trains in the distance. The factory was going like a fayre, with people coming and going, obviously working the night shift.It seemed like there were hundreds of workers. We went around the outside of the building, but it was very tightly secured, each door padlocked, and most had entry systems. Sam tried to get inside by joining a few workers and walking in with them, but there were guards inside the entrance who were checking each individual person. They all had special passes, so we had to abandon that. The hard thing is, Suman could easily be in there, but without the police or someone in authority I don't think we'd manage to get in."

"Then we should get the police."

"I suggested this, but Sam thinks it would be useless, and I think he might be right. You and I both know the corruption that goes on in the trafficking industry. If that factory is linked to trafficking, the police will probably know about it and not interfere. No, if we want in, we'll have to find another way. But first, we're going back to see Jan again, to find out more. It's torture, knowing Suman's in their hands and not being able to find her quickly."

"I know. I'm coming with you."

"No, Ellie, it's too dangerous at the moment. You wait here. Sam's gone back to the hospital; he got beeped to check on someone, so I thought I'd come and see that you were all okay."

"We're fine, don't worry about us. But I won't wait here. I need to come and help you find her. I can't bear the thought of her being in the hands of traffickers for a second time. We got her away the first time, and we'll do it again ..." Ellie's voice cracked and Geoff quickly jumped in.

"We'll find her, Ellie. She's the bravest person we know, and if anyone can get away from them, it's Suman. And she knows we'll be looking for her. She knows we'll do everything in our power to find her. Sadly, Jan's the only person who can help us at the moment."

"Maybe not. Vada was telling me how Suman came across Jan in the hospital a couple of weeks ago, and about how Jan dropped her phone when she ran away. Suman picked it up and had been trying to find Jan by phoning the two numbers in the contact list. One of the numbers belonged to a lady called Kali, and there were texts back and forth from her. She could be one of Jan's close friends. Maybe if we could find this woman, she might be able to help."

"And you've got the phone?"

"It's here, let's have a look." Ellie turned to a table beside the sofa, lifted a small mobile phone and opened it up. "The number's in the contact list."

She quickly called the number listed as belonging to Kali. It rang five times before cutting to a voice speaking in a language she presumed was Bengali. Ellie guessed that she was being told to leave a message, so when she heard the beep she began speaking.

"Kali, I'm a doctor from the Sister Irene Hospital. I have a message from your friend Jan. I'm using Jan's phone, as she has been admitted to the hospital and really needs your help. She's asking for you. Can you please contact me on this number? It's very urgent."

Ellie pressed the off button, but kept hold of the phone.

"Pray she speaks English and understands what I've just said. And pray she calls me back quickly. Now I'll just go and throw some clothes on. Wait for me."

"No, Ellie. I need you to stay here. I'm going back to the hospital now to get Sam and I'm not sure what's going to happen after that. I'm not taking you with me. I'll contact you as soon as I know anything. If we need you,

you can come. But, right now, we've no idea of how dangerous this is going to be."

A brief, tight hug and he was gone, leaving Ellie feeling angry, upset and helpless. She walked to the door and locked it with a deep sigh. Shoving her hands deep into her dressing gown pockets, she strode over to the window and stood for a moment, staring out at the streetlights and the car headlights still illuminating the darkness of the roads of Kolkata. Her mind began to recollect the frantic journey she had taken with Suman, the eight-year-old child she had rescued from traffickers so long ago. How unthinkable and disastrous that she had been captured again and was once more in the hands of people who think nothing of the evil they do! And how unthinkable and despicable that Geoff had not allowed her to get out there and rescue Suman again!

She sighed deeply, wishing with all her heart that she could once again rush to the rescue of the girl she loved so much.

There is a saying from one of Aesop's fables, 'be careful what you wish for lest it come true', which sprang to Ellie's mind when the phone in her hand began to ring.

"Hello?" she questioned hesitantly, her heart beating like a train pounding down the tracks.

"Hello," the caller replied very softly, in English, but with a very marked Indian accent. "Can I speak to the doctor? She called me a short time ago."

"I'm the doctor. Who's speaking?"

There was a long pause and then a reply. "I'm Kali, a friend of Jan. Is Jan alive? Is she okay? You said she needs my help urgently."

A huge feeling of relief flooded through Ellie's body; relief that Kali had replied to their call and that she was speaking in excellent English.

She quickly replied.

"Yes, she's alive, but she's very ill. Unfortunately, she was shot."

"Shot? With a gun? Is she going to survive?"

"We hope so. But we believe that whoever shot her might come back and try again. We also believe they have taken a doctor who saved her and was looking after her. We need to know where they may have taken this doctor. Do you know anything about these people? Who they might be and where they are?"

There was another long pause before Kali replied.

"By talking to you I'm putting myself in a lot of danger. My husband isn't here at the moment, but if he returns, I could be shot too." She stopped, as if considering what to say next. Her next words were hesitant.

"My friend, Jan, do you know if ..." she hesitated a moment. "Is Jan still... Has she lost...." The question was blurted out.

"You mean her baby. No, she hasn't lost her baby. But to keep both her and the baby safe we need information about the people who did this to her. Do you know who they are?"

"I'm sorry, I can't say any more. I must go before my husband returns."

Ellie silently waited, hoping Kali would speak again. She wasn't disappointed.

"You should check out the Soohor Chemical and Textile Company. Also check the Reterron Apparel Company."

Kali switched the phone off immediately when she had finished speaking, and Ellie speedily grabbed a pen and paper to write down the two names. Not knowing the correct spelling, she wrote them phonetically, hoping she was near the mark. Using her own phone, she searched for the names, but found scant information about them online. Neither company had a website she could check out. However, she was relieved to see addresses for both organisations amongst the search results. She scribbled the addresses beside the names and, seeing one of them, realised it was the same company that Geoff had mentioned, the Reterron Apparel Company in Bidhannagar.

A plan had started circulating in Ellie's head, so she immediately crossed to the room where Vada was sleeping and knocked, at first gently, then a little louder. There was no sound from inside, so she opened the door and peeped inside.

Vada's sleepy voice could be heard from the bed. "Is that you, Suman? Is something wrong?"

"No, it's Ellie. Can I come in and talk to you?"

Vada struggled up to a sitting position and beckoned. "Of course, come in."

Sitting on Vada's bed, talking in hushed tones, Ellie very hastily caught Vada up with what was happening to Suman and then outlined her idea of what they could perhaps do to rescue Suman. At first Vada recoiled.

"Try to sneak into a factory to search it?" she squeaked. "Ellie, we'll end up in jail or dead, and then we'll never be able to find Suman. This can't be the only way. And just you and me? We need the men."

"No, we don't. Geoff and Sam are not here, so it's got to be you and me. For all I know they may be going there too, but they are going to see Jan first, and they have another place to check out as well. So you and me it is. And, to be honest, I'm going to stick out like a sore thumb with my white skin, not to mention the fact that I don't speak the language. So you may have to do it on your own. We'll keep our phones on and I'll stay outside and be ready to rush in to rescue you if there's a problem. Come on, Vada, Suman's in trouble. Get your clothes on, something very plain, not noticeable, and let's try to find her. Oh, and I need some of your darkest make-up, dark kohl for my eyes and a Punjabi suit, please, and maybe a long dupattà to cover my head and face."

As Ellie rushed out of the room to go and get herself ready, she glanced back fleetingly at Vada to check that she was obeying her instructions. She shouldn't have worried. Vada's legs were already over the side of the bed and on her face there was a look of fierce determination.

Chapter Twenty-Two

BIDHANNAGAR, KOLKATA

Arriving at the car park of the Reterron Apparel Company's factory in Bidhannagar, Ellie and Vada dismounted Suman's scooter and switched off the engine. Ellie pocketed the key, padlocked the scooter, wound the long dupattà shawl around her head and over her mouth and nose, and then turned to Vada to put phase two of her plan into place.

Their journey had taken around thirty minutes, longer than it had looked on the map. Both being unfamiliar with the area of Bidhannagar, they had got lost a couple of times and had to stop and ask for directions. It was just after five o'clock, but Kolkata was a city that woke up early, with many workers already on the streets, so there were plenty of people around to help. *A good and bad thing*, thought Ellie, who had hoped for darkness to make them less noticeable when trying to enter the factory.

For a few moments, they stood and looked at one another, Ellie chewing furiously on her bottom lip, an old nervous habit from when she was younger. She turned around to watch the small but growing stream of workers heading towards a huge door at the side of the vast building.

The workers consisted of both men and women. Some looked very young, and Ellie began to wonder if this was one of the sweatshops that she had read about, employing children and young people who had been trafficked. The men seemed to walk in pairs as they headed to work, while the women arranged themselves into little groups of five or six as they approached the door. Watching, Ellie realised that they were entering through different doors, one for men and one for women.

She beckoned Vada to follow her closer to the building. They stopped at a bicycle park where some of the workers were securing their bikes to poles. Vada turned to Ellie.

"They're carrying passes," she whispered. "Looks like I'll need one to get in. How do I do that?"

For a moment Ellie was annoyed with herself. "I forgot Geoff mentioned that. We're going to have to get hold of one somehow, even if we have to steal it. Let me think."

After a few minutes watching the workers make their way to the doors, she came up with an idea which she quickly explained to Vada.

"It might work, we can only try," she ended. "Come on."

They made a detour back towards the car park and stood waiting at a gate as a number of people approached. One group seemed quite animated, the six or seven girls all chattering happily amongst themselves. At a sign from Ellie, Vada moved in front of the group, where she was sure they could all see her. A moment later, with their attention on her, she did a beautiful job of tripping over her own foot and went down with a wail and a clatter to the ground. She sat up, began to groan and clutched her foot. Ellie, with everyone's attention now on Vada, closed in to the girls at the back, as if she also wanted to see what was going on.

Two of the girls had rushed over to Vada and were trying to help her back onto her feet again. Vada, following Ellie's instructions, explained through sobs that she had twisted her ankle. The other girls were watching the proceedings, making sympathetic comments. This gave Ellie the opportunity she had prayed for. She had spotted a work pass peeping out of someone's shoulder bag and now, with a lightning move, she pulled it out and pocketed it. Immediately after, she moved away from the group, praying that no one had noticed.

By this time, Vada was standing, but limping badly. She told the girls that she would sit for a while before coming in to work, and thanked them for their help. Knowing they were on a time limit to clock in at work, the girls wished Vada well and moved away. Once they were nearly out of sight and had stopped turning to see that she was all right, Vada began running to the gate of the car park, where Ellie was hiding behind a bush.

"Well done, Vada. I'm really impressed. You'd make a good actress."

Vada smiled. "But did you get a pass?" she asked.

"I did. Put it in your pocket. Your name is now Divya Laghari. Here, put my scarf around your head and keep your face half hidden. You don't want these girls to recognise you if you see them again. You're going to have to hurry to get in with the rest of the people and not be late for this shift. Run all the way and just copy what everyone else does to clock in. Then you know what to do after that. Memorise the inside of the building, the bits you're able to see. And, if you can, text me to let me know you're safe. Good luck, Vada. If you're not back out in about forty minutes, I'm coming in to get you."

Suitably disguised by the dupattà, Vada set off at a fast trot, reaching the door just as one of the guards was coming forward to close it. There were a number of people in front of her and she watched closely as they held their security passes against a screen on the wall. She did the same, relieved when 'Pass Accepted' appeared on the screen. She was in.

Following others along a corridor, she could hear the sound of machinery getting louder as they approached a doorway into the main factory floor. Going through the door in the wake of everyone else, she found herself in the biggest room she had ever seen, stretching for what seemed like the size of a cricket field. The room was full of sewing machines on tables, the whirring sound of the hundreds of machines filling her ears with their deafening sound. She looked around, spotting clusters of machines with no one sitting at them.

Making her way towards one of them, she glanced at some of the workers she was passing, shocked to see a number of very young children amongst the adults, all preparing to begin work on their sewing machines, or already started, their heads bent low over the tables. Some of the children she judged to be around the age of six or seven, and although they seemed to be very adept at using their machines, she was shaken to see so many. Casting her eyes around the back of the huge room, she could see other children working on huge industrial machines which she thought were looms. Near these machines were a group of elderly men and women, dipping fabrics and stirring them in big circular tubs of dye. In another area of the factory people were working on industrial pressing machines. She realised she had entered what seemed like an immense production line churning out denim jeans, beginning from the creation of the material itself right down to the finished product. *This is massive,* she thought, a real sweatshop like those she had read about in magazines.

One or two people she passed looked up, but no one said good morning or acknowledged her in any way. Supervisors, wearing grey uniforms, patrolled among the aisles. Becoming aware that one was coming her way, she quickly slipped into a chair and picked up a pair of denims, half sewn, from a huge pile on her table.

Keeping her head down, and thanking her lucky stars that she knew how to use a sewing machine, she saw with relief that the supervisor passed by, barely noticing her. She thought it safest, in case he came back, or in case someone else was watching, to act as though she knew what she was doing and, trying to look confident, she slid one of the legs of the trousers into the machine and began to sew.

Outside, still in the car park, Ellie was feeling most uncomfortable; with the dupattà gone she was nervous and hyper-aware of her blue eyes and fairer skin. Sitting astride Suman's scooter, she kept her eyes lowered and her bare arms crossed in the hope that no one would stare and wonder what she was doing there. The long stream of workers had gone and she surmised that the early morning shift had begun, with only a few latecomers scurrying by to get to work.

She glanced at her watch. Twenty minutes had passed and in another twenty minutes she was going to have to try to enter the building to find Vada if she had not returned. What had seemed like a good plan now felt totally flawed. Just how she would be able to get Vada out was a mystery to her and she decided that, for the moment, she would investigate the outside of the vast building. Her idea was to find out where all the entrances, exits and security cameras were situated.

Before setting off around the building, she felt the need to cover her face, not wanting to stand out in any way. She had nothing on hand that she could use. However, looking down at the Punjabi suit she was wearing, the one Vada had given her, she decided to tear off the bottom part of the tunic. It was quite a long tunic, stretching down well past her knees, so there was plenty of material to spare. She ripped it carefully, trying not to have too much fraying. Folding the material, she wrapped it around her head and covered her mouth and nose, leaving only her eyes showing. She re-mounted the scooter and was looking down to turn on the engine when a loud voice behind her made her almost jump out of her skin.

"My good Punjabi! That's the last time I give you any of my clothes!"

"God, Vada. You scared the living daylights out of me." She jumped off the scooter and ran quickly to Vada to give her a hug.

"I was starting to panic. It was so wrong of me to send you in like that on your own. We might never have seen you again. What happened? Did they spot you? Did you manage to look around?"

"So many questions! No, Ellie. I couldn't get anywhere at all except onto the factory floor and into the ladies' toilets. I had to pretend to be a seamstress on one of the sewing machines, but I could see where the other parts of the building were, mainly at the very back, where there were six big doors. When I went to the toilet, I checked the doors and could see that they were all heavily padlocked. There was nowhere else to go; there were security guards everywhere and, you'll never believe this, some of them were carrying guns. Guns! In a textile factory! That's not good, is it? I think it must be a dangerous place for all these women and kids to be working. It's a total sweatshop and I'd bet that they've all been trafficked."

"That's horrific, but we knew it might be a dangerous place when we came and you've just confirmed it. Heaven knows how, but we've got to try to get into the back of the building to see if Suman is there. You didn't manage to see if there were doors round there when you were coming back, did you?"

"I could only see this side of the building when I was walking back. There were quite a lot of windows, but all of them were blackened and heavily barred. To keep folk out and workers in, I expect, and to stop anyone looking in. But no doors that I could see except the two the workers use."

"Hmm. If we can't see in the windows, it would be pointless to take a run around the building on the scooter, as I was about to do. We've got to get into the back of that building." Ellie frowned deeply as she spoke.

"Ellie," Vada said quietly, coming closer. "I don't want to worry you, but there's a car that's been circling around outside the car park for a few minutes. I can't see the driver from here, but it's creeping me out a bit, the way they've been circling around and then coming back, as if they're checking us out. Do you think we should maybe get out of here?"

"Where is it? Where's the car?" Ellie tried to peer over the hedges around them.

"It's gone into that clearing over there and stopped. They could be watching us. If it's security men and they've got guns, we should go."

Ellie nodded. "You're right. Get on," she commanded, climbing back onto the front of the scooter. "And hold on tight."

The scooter took a leap forward as she accelerated the engine and turned the front wheel to aim for the gate close by. As they exited at speed, Vada risked a glance over to where the car was.

"It's moving, Ellie. I think it's going to follow us. Drive fast."

Ellie increased the speed a little, not wanting to lose control of the scooter. More used to driving her car in Edinburgh, she was not unfamiliar with driving a scooter, but it had been some years since she had been on one.

After a moment, she shouted to Vada, "Is it still there? Is it following us?"

Vada turned her head to look and shouted back, "Yes, and it's gaining on us! Can we go faster?"

Ellie again increased the speed until it felt as if they were flying along the road. However, the driver of the car was increasing his speed as well and reducing the distance between them. It didn't take them very long to catch up with the scooter and, to Ellie's dismay, the driver of the car began to pull out to overtake. Ellie slowed down quickly, manoeuvring the scooter up onto the banking at the side of the road with the intention of turning back the way they had come.

The car braked fast as well, drawing to a stop in front of them. A moment later, Ellie and Vada were headed back down the long straight road in the direction of the factory. Vada craned her neck around to look at the car.

"It's turning! Hurry, hurry!"

For a second time, the car was racing after them, and this time it seemed to catch up to them even quicker. Despite other vehicles being on the road, Ellie could see in her mirror that the car was again going to try to overtake them, and tried the same tactic as before. She slowed the scooter down quickly and turned to her left to pull off the road. This was a much bigger banking than before, and, unfortunately, it had a hidden ditch halfway up. Inevitably, she reached the ditch before she saw it and the scooter fell over on its side as the front wheel caught the edge. The two of them yelled in fear as they tipped over, landing with a clatter on the grassy bank, and watching in horror as the car screeched to a halt on the road beside them.

The doors of the car shot open and two men leapt out, abandoning the car to rush towards Ellie and Vada. The expression on the girls' faces changed dramatically as they saw who their potential assailants were.

Geoff spoke first.

"What in the name of God were you doing, trying to do a turn in a ditch? And why were you trying to get away from us?"

As he spoke, he helped Ellie to stand as Sam hurried to Vada's side.

"How were we supposed to know it was you two?" Ellie replied angrily. She winced as she put one foot down on the ground. "We just saw a car following us. How could we have known it was you?"

"Okay, well, sit down and let me look at that ankle. Where is it sore?"

"I'm fine, don't worry." She dismissed him and pushed his hand away. Then, looking at his face, she realised how worried he looked. "Sorry, Geoff, I should have realised it was you, but I didn't recognise Sam's car."

By this time, Vada was back on her feet. Her right arm was very sore, but she was pretty sure it wasn't broken. She tested it by lifting it high, grateful to feel no great pain; it seemed to be intact. She turned to Sam.

"How did you know we were here? And why didn't you phone us to say you were coming to help?"

He shook his head ruefully. "We didn't know you were here. We just got some information from Jan that this might be the place where they've brought Suman, so we thought we'd come and check it out properly. Did you manage to find anything, any signs of Suman?"

Ellie answered. "Vada got inside and had a look around the factory. It's a huge sweatshop making denim jeans. But so far we haven't found any way into the back of the building. We think that, if she's here, that's where she might be held." She moved over to Vada as she spoke.

"Are you sure you're all right, Vada? I'm so sorry I overturned and threw you off the scooter."

"I'm okay, thanks. Just a bit sore. What about you?"

"Just my ankle," Ellie replied. "The scooter came down on top of it."

Sam moved forward. "Sit down and I'll have a look at it."

Ellie obeyed and took off her shoe. He examined the ankle, turning it this way and that and asking a few questions before giving his diagnosis.

"I think you've been lucky, Ellie. No apparent breaks; I think it's just had a knock from the scooter. It'll probably get sorer as the day goes on. I could bind it up with your scarf, if you like, though I don't think it'll make a big difference."

"No, Sam. I'm fine, thanks for looking at it." She turned to Geoff. "We really want to get back into that building. Now that you've come, can you think of a way we can do this? If Suman's in there, we need to get her out PDQ."

Geoff nodded in agreement, resigned to the fact that his wife was now back in charge.

The other two looked questioningly at Ellie.

"PDQ?" they both asked at the same time.

Ellie smiled. "Means pretty damn quick."

Chapter Twenty-Three

BIDHANNAGAR, KOLKATA

Inside the storeroom, Suman was feeling the heat of the day seeping into her bones, causing a lethargy in her body she didn't want to give in to. *This is no time to sleep,* she thought, rubbing her face with her hands and stomping around the confines of the small room. Frustration was showing on her face as she thought back to her encounter with the flamboyantly-dressed man she suspected was Jan's husband, coming to the conclusion that she had not handled him correctly. Maybe she should have tried harder to escape his clutches instead of holding a polite conversation with him. She had to try to escape; she had to get out of here. Her mind, still not fully recovered from being drugged, was playing tricks with her, taking her back to her previous experiences of being kept in captivity, and she was trying hard not to give in to despair.

She crossed to the small blackened window, feeling the need for some air. It was too small for her to squeeze out of, so she began to think about how she could break the glass. Using a piece of furniture to smash it looked like the only way.

She had no sense of where in the building she was, having seen only the inside of the sitting room downstairs, the storeroom she was in now, and the stairway she had climbed to get back here. That hadn't been a pleasant experience, with a henchman shoving a gun into her back,

215

causing pain in her ribs. She had tried to push the gun away, but received a thrust forward that had caused her to fall into the steps and hurt her leg. With her hands still bound, there was nothing to grab to keep her balance. Knowing it was too risky to try to get away from this man and too foolhardy to try to get the gun away from him, she had allowed herself to be locked into the storeroom again.

A big metal plant pot caught her attention. The plant inside was long dead and she discarded it onto the floor. Pleased that it was a good, sturdy pot, she approached the window, holding the pot by the rim, its base facing the window. It was heavy, and she hoped it would do the job of breaking the window on the first try.

She was in luck. With a very loud crash, the darkened glass shattered on the first attempt, bits of it falling outside but leaving many shards of glass. Using one of these, she managed to cut into the rope around her wrists until her hands were free. She rubbed them, relieved that her shackles had gone.

Through the hole she had made in the window, she could see a couple of metal bars on the other side of the glass. *So I wouldn't have been able to climb out even if it had been a bigger window*, she thought, again wondering what type of building needed bars on its windows.

Lifting the metal plant pot again, she smashed more of the window, and heard a tinkling noise as the glass fell to the ground outside. She leaned in close, breathing deeply, and, although the air outside was almost as warm as the air inside, she was pleased to be breathing fresh, cleaner air.

Unfortunately, the noise of the breaking glass had caught the attention of guards outside and the incident brought a flurry of people going up and down on the stairs outside the storeroom. She stayed quiet as she listened to try to hear what they were saying, but their voices were too muted.

Eventually the voices died away. However, not long after that, she again heard the key being inserted into the lock and the lock being turned. Quick as a wink she picked up the ropes from the floor and wound them around her wrists again. A shard of glass caught her eye and she grabbed it quickly, closing her hand around it softly so as not to cut herself. She was just in time. The man who strode slowly into the room was the same man as earlier, his ostentatious clothes as immaculate as before, his eyes showing the same icy coldness and intimidating stare.

"Well, Doctor," he spoke softly. "So you decided to break one of my windows. That was not very sociable of you. What end did you hope to achieve with this? I fear the window is too small for you to escape through."

Suman didn't reply, but watched the tall man closely. For a second time, she thought she detected a slight breathlessness as he spoke and for a second time the thought that she could outrun him flitted into her head. She glanced behind him at the door, which was lying open.

"Oh, yes, my dear, I've left the door open. But there's no escape that way; my men are just outside, and armed, as you know."

Suman's heart sank though no expression crossed her face as he continued.

"In any case, I'm not intending to keep you here for very much longer, pretty though you are. I would like to get to know you much more intimately, Dr Sudra, but time does not permit. Your fate was sealed when you refused my amicable request to tell me where my whore was."

He raised his very bushy eyebrows as Suman looked quickly at him.

"Oh, you don't like that? But she is a whore, Doctor. There is no other word I can think of to describe her. Except that she is, of course, my whore. I own Jan, you know, body and soul. I own a lot of people, an awful lot of people, and I'm very proud of my achievements in my line of work. This factory is full of people downstairs and I own every one of them, as I now own you - to do with as I will."

"You do not, and never will, own me." Suman's voice was as sharp as a needle.

He laughed. "Well, we'll not quibble about that one. Let's just admit, I have you in my power, alongside thousands of others. Yes, thousands, all ages, all mine. Each one has ... let us say, come into my possession. Some have come and gone, and some I have decided to keep."

His voice became less frivolous and more malicious. "I will keep Jan, Dr Sudra. She will never, ever escape me. Just like you. I'm sorry to be putting an end to your existence, just the same. I like pretty things. Sometimes, I like to ... get to know them fully before I bring them to an end."

Suman's fists clenched tightly, but she said nothing, just watched him as he turned to close the door and then turned back to face her, a condescending smile on his face.

"Will you tell me where she is, my dear? Give yourself a little chance, at least."

Suman stared, the aura in the room so full of evil she felt like she was breathing it in. Her eyes never left the predator in front of her; she was watching him and listening so fixedly that she again heard his breathlessness as he moved. She stayed motionless, like a deer caught in the headlights, startled but alert.

Robert took two slow paces towards her, a malicious smile on his face. Suman's heart pounded and her breath stopped, another sudden flashback of past horrors coming into her mind. She acted without thought, the piece of glass in her hand coming forward in a flash as his fingers reached out to her neck. It caught the side of his hand and stopped him in his tracks. He brought his hands back and looked at the gash on his left hand, where blood was coming from the sharp wound. She lifted the glass again, holding it as a weapon. Their eyes met and held, his full of hatred and hers full of determination.

After a few moments she blinked, still staring at him and realising that something was happening to her tormentor. His face, in slow motion, began to twist itself gruesomely into a contorted grimace. His hands shot up to try to reach his face, blood dripping furiously from the wound, but stopped at chest level, his body beginning to buckle beneath him.

Suman watched as his mouth opened and his eyes narrowed. The next moment, his whole body collapsed with a massive thud on to the floor in front of her.

Instantaneously, her instinct and her medical training took over and she shot forward to kneel on the floor beside him. Hauling him around onto his back, she could see that he appeared to have suffered either a seizure or a massive stroke, the right-hand side of his face now twisted beyond recognition and drool beginning to come from his mouth. His body was starting to spasm and she rapidly began to loosen the tight clothing around his neck, check his breathing and feel for a pulse.

While she worked on Robert, her mind assessed how best to deal with this situation, given the circumstances she was in. Aware that she was a prisoner in the building, with armed men nearby, she had to consider the possibility that they may harm her if she was to call for help. However, she knew she had to take the risk. Putting the patient first as she had been trained to do, she stood up quickly and rushed over to the door and began to shout. One of the guards at the bottom of the stairs ran up, his gun in his hand. She pointed into the room as she tried to explain that his boss needed an ambulance or, as she knew ambulances were exceptionally scarce in Kolkata, someone to take him to hospital immediately. Without taking stock of the situation, the guard grabbed hold of Suman and shoved the gun into her neck.

"What did you do to him?" he yelled in her face.

"Nothing!" she shouted back, trying to free herself from his tight grip. "He is having a seizure and needs immediate help. You need to get transport for him, now!"

The guard released his grip for a second, but Suman was taken aback when he gave her a swinging blow to her face with the back of his hand. She fell backwards, holding her cheek and looking at him.

She tried again.

"Can't you see how urgent this is? Your boss is dying. Get him to hospital!" As she spat the words out to him, she crawled backwards to where Robert lay and knelt back down beside him, reaching for his pulse again.

The man waved his gun about.

"No ambulances are allowed to come here. They bring the police with them. You deal with him. You're a doctor."

After he uttered these words, he hurried out through the door, slamming it shut and locking it, before she heard his footsteps pounding down the stairs.

Assuming there was no help coming, Suman turned all her attention to Robert. His breath was now coming in noisy rasps, and his pulse had slowed considerably. As she placed him in the recovery position, she again heard footsteps clattering on the stairs and looked over as the lock rattled and the door flew open.

The guard was back, accompanied by a second man. He continued waving his gun about as he pointed to Robert and Suman, speaking in a dialect that Suman had never heard before. The second man approached Suman.

"What has happened?" he asked in Bengali, a language she did understand.

"He's had a seizure, a massive one. He's unconscious and needs to go to hospital immediately. Can you get an ambulance or a car?"

"No, I can't do that."

"Why not?"

His answer was just a shrug of his shoulders. "You must look after him yourself and save him."

"Don't be ridiculous. I haven't got any equipment or medicine here. I can't save him on my own. He needs to be taken to hospital. Can you get me a defibrillator?"

The man looked perplexed.

"We could get medicine for you, but we can't get an ambulance here or let him be taken to hospital. These are his orders."

"Medicine is not going to save his life. This man is dying as we speak."

"So be it, Doctor. That's how it must be. You must do your best."

"I need a defibrillator. He could go into cardiac arrest at any moment."

The man shook his head. "It's not possible. We don't have one and I don't know anyone who would have one."

Suman was almost at her wits' end. Her fingers were still on Robert's pulse and she knew he was slipping away. His death seemed inevitable, but still she seemed unable to give up on saving this wicked man's life. She was bending forward to listen to his breathing one more time when, suddenly, the door burst open again and four more men appeared in the room. One of them advanced menacingly towards Suman and forcefully moved her out of the way. With him directing operations, the other men encircled Robert and slid their arms underneath him. The order was given to lift, and once up, with great effort, they slowly stepped towards the door, holding on tightly to their boss.

"Where are you taking him?" Suman asked, wondering what was happening.

Every one of the men ignored her and continued their exit with Robert in their arms, now totally unconscious. As Suman tried to follow them, the man with the gun shouted, "Keep her in there! Lock the door."

"No!" she screamed, looking for somewhere to run. One of the men dashed towards her, leaving the others to hold on to Robert. He grabbed her and very roughly thrust her back through the door, where she lost her footing and fell. The man shut the door quickly. The lock was turned before she had time to reach for the knob. Frustrated and angry, she banged loudly on the door.

"Let me out of here! Let me out!"

As she expected, no one answered her plea.

Chapter Twenty-Four

BIDHANNAGAR, KOLKATA

The world outside was in darkness. Dusk had fallen early and, as the night crept in, the grounds around the building were starting to come alive with the songs of the insects hiding in the grasses and bushes. The cicadas, with their high-pitched singing, competed with the musical chirping of the crickets; and the male katydids called out loudly in their search for a mate.

Suman sat at the broken window listening to their calls, the orchestral rhythm of the insects keeping her spirits up and her mind off the growing thirst and hunger she was experiencing. The afternoon had been long and silent, with no one approaching the door with water or food and no one coming to her rescue. Her thoughts were remorseful. She knew that, to save herself, she should have taken the opportunity to run instead of trying to save Robert's life. But a second voice in her head reminded her she was a doctor, committed to saving lives and alleviating pain and suffering. She knew it was only that instinct which had kept her by Robert's side. Regret was pushed to the back of her thoughts.

She wasn't giving up yet. She had faith in those who loved her and knew they would be searching for her. She would just have to wait. Peering at her watch in the moonlight, she could see it was after eight o'clock in the evening and she was resigning herself to a night in the storeroom, hoping that sleep would come and help to pass the hours till daylight. She began to think of her foster mother, Ellie, and the bond that had formed between them over the years she lived in Scotland.

She had been fifteen when she was reunited with her family in Maharashtra. She loved Kanya, her real mother, dearly; the woman who had given birth to her in their village home in India. Yet she loved Ellie just as much - loved her as a mother who had fed her, nursed her when she was sick, dried her tears and held her through the dark hours when homesickness for Kanya and her family was keeping her awake. She remembered those bad times, the night terrors in particular, dreaming she was back in the hands of her traffickers.

She was remembering a story that had been lying dormant in her head. Ellie, comforting her and holding her tight, first created the story when Suman was only nine years old. That same story was told many times over the years, whenever the blackness of her memories took over.

The story was that of a mouse - a tiny harvest mouse born in a farmer's field along with its brothers and sisters. One day, a huge tractor came into their field, driving closer and closer to the family of mice. The mother acted quickly, taking the mouse baby in her mouth and moving her out of the way of the big tractor, and then went back for the rest of her babies. Disastrously, the rest of the family was wiped out, the tractor doing its worst that night.

Mouse baby, safe, but left on her own, was terrified, crying out for her mother again and again. No-one came near the tiny mouse, and over the next few days, mouse baby had to dig very deeply within herself to find the courage to go and forage for food, to survive. One day, while looking for food, she met another mouse, a mother, who asked mouse baby to come and live with her and her family, not worrying that it was another mouth to feed. She only knew that this little mouse needed her help. So, mouse baby grew up with love, growing stronger within herself, and helping to care for all the other baby mice that came along. She learned to listen out for the big tractor, and, when it came, helped to move all the family to a safe place so they could survive too.

Nine-year-old Suman had loved this story, often imagining herself in it. She was the little mouse, helping all the other mice that she could. And nine-year-old Suman had grown up knowing that she would somehow give back to other people the love and care she had received. Today, twenty years later, she thought of the story once again and knew that Ellie would be trying to find her for a second time. She just had to wait.

She began to hum quietly to herself, her fear subsiding as she waited. One day, she vowed, she'd tell Sam how that story had seen her through the difficult times; to help him understand what her motivation in life was. She had been sitting at the window for what seemed like a long time before moving to the chair to doze. Eventually, she gave up on her fitful attempts at sleep and moved back to the window, knowing it must be the middle of the night. As she began thinking about the story again, a sound outside the window reached her through the noise of the night insects.

She stayed still and listened carefully. Yes, she was right; something or someone was treading on the broken glass underneath the window. She started to sing softly, a song from her childhood, not wanting to call out in case it was her captors outside. Her heart began thumping like a drum and almost leapt out of her chest as someone below began singing quietly along with her. She stood up and gripped the sides of the window, putting her face up close to the broken glass.

"Ellie," she whispered as loudly as she dared. "Is that you?"

"Yes, it's me." The soft voice was excited, relieved and tearful all rolled into one, and so very welcome to Suman. "Are you all right, my darling?"

"I'm great now you've come for me. I knew you would. Can you get me out?"

"We will but we don't know how to get in. Where's the door?"

"I don't know. I woke up inside this room, which is locked, and I don't know what the building looks like or where the doors are."

"It's a clothes factory. It's massive and your window is at the back of it." Geoff's voice was also soft, but she knew it straight away.

Geoff continued quickly. "We'll keep looking, but we've been almost right around the building, so the doors must be well camouflaged. We'll get to you soon, honey. Keep singing."

"Sam and I are here too, Suman," whispered Vada, and Suman's heart swelled knowing they were all out there, looking for her. She spoke again into the little broken window, trying to help them.

"This room is up a flight of stairs, above a big, old-fashioned lounge, like it's inside a house. I'm locked in, so you'll need to find the key; it's a mortice lock. Someone has it, but I don't know who. Please, please be careful. There are lots of guards and they all carry guns."

Ellie's voice answered. "We'll get you out, Su. Just hold on in there. We're going to search for a way in now."

"Be careful, all of you. I love you so much."

Ellie's voice was the last she heard, saying, "We love you too." The footsteps moved away.

The night song of the cicadas, the crickets and the katydids returned slowly to her consciousness.

Four figures moved stealthily in the semi-darkness through the undergrowth around the building. They had split up into pairs and begun to circle the vast building again, checking each nook and cranny they came across for access. Every so often, security lights would come on and the figures would fall into the bushes to wait until the lights went off again.

It was a good while later and after much searching that Sam and Vada realised that one of the walls at the very back of the building was made of metal instead of concrete and they saw what looked like the faint outline of a door. Both of them began to feel all around the door and along the metal wall for something that would open it. It was Vada who found it, a button at the far end of the wall, down at foot level, almost hidden by the long grasses growing around the wall. When she pressed the button, the door quietly clicked open and she grabbed Sam's arm, whispering that she would go and find Ellie and Geoff and that Sam must wait for them to return before entering. He agreed, though reluctantly, desperate to get in and find Suman.

While she went off to find the other two, he looked around the undergrowth for some type of weapon, successfully finding a decent-sized stick. It wouldn't be much use against a gun, he knew, but it was better than nothing.

Vada wasn't long in returning, and the four huddled in a spot away from the building, behind a large banyan tree whose branches and enormous roots gave coverage from anyone passing by. They spoke in whispers, working out a plan for when they were inside.

"Someone should stay behind and go and get the car so we can make a quick getaway when we come out," Ellie suggested.

"Good idea," agreed Geoff. "Sam, unfortunately it has to be you, as Ellie and I don't have Indian driving licences. I'd rather have had you inside helping us. We've no idea what we're facing in there."

Sam's face was a picture of misery as Geoff spoke. He wanted to go inside the building to help get Suman out.

Vada interrupted with a solution. "I've got a learner's licence, as well as my MC one for the scooter. I can go and get the car and be the driver as long as Sam is beside me when I'm driving on the main roads."

"I can do that. Thank you, Vada." Sam was grateful for this offer and vowed to himself that he would give Vada some more driving lessons if they all got out of this unharmed. "Just keep the car out of sight until you see us coming out, then drive over to pick us up. Stay safe and don't come looking for us, no matter what happens."

"Okay. Are we all ready? Let's get going." Ellie was back in her role as leader and desperate to get the job done.

As Sam handed over the car keys to Vada and gave her a hug, Ellie was already heading over to the door standing ajar, Geoff hot on her heels. Sam caught up with them and, seconds later, the three of them were standing inside the building.

Through the gloom, they could see that they were standing in what looked like a large office, with a glass partition on one side through which they could see a battered desk and a toppled, broken chair. Dotted around the office were some old, rusty filing cabinets. The space looked unused, with no paperwork in evidence and only a thick layer of dust on top of the desk. Even the glass partition was cracked in a number of places, giving an abandoned look to the place. However, it was clear to all of them that the huge office they were in had not been abandoned altogether. Against each of the walls were piles of identical brown cardboard boxes, all neatly stacked and covered in labels, and looking as if they were waiting to be collected. Geoff went closer to have a look at them, sniffing the air as he approached. Sam and Ellie were right behind him, and when he imitated smoking a cigarette, they nodded in agreement. All of them knew what cocaine and opium smelled like and all of them knew they had entered a drugs' den, and a big one, judging by the volume of boxes and the strong smell pervading the air.

"Now we know why it was so hard to get into this place," whispered Ellie. "Let's do this quickly and get out of here."

Keeping close to the walls, they headed to an open door, with darkness behind. Peeping through, Geoff signalled to the other two to follow him. Fortune seemed to be with them, as there appeared to be no one around. Sam switched on the torch on his mobile phone but kept the light covered as much as possible.

They had entered a long corridor with more doors, but this time the doors had signs on them. Ellie led the way, borrowing Sam's torch to illuminate the signs until they came to one marked with the word 'Chaambiyaan'.

"Keys," Sam whispered, and tried the door. Good fortune was still on their side, as they found it unlocked. It was dark and dingy inside, but, with the torch, there was enough light for them to see hooks at the back and a number of keys hanging on them. Quickly and quietly, they all began to fill their pockets with every mortice key they could find. Closing the cupboard door, they started to look for a way out of the corridor. Right at the very end they turned a corner and spotted a set of stairs. With Sam in the lead, they crept towards the stairs as silently as possible.

As they got closer, they heard the sound of voices coming from inside a room behind the stairs. Instantly, Sam turned the torch off and pocketed his phone. Behind the closed door, they could hear men's voices, some raised, all angry; it was obvious they were having a very heated discussion. Ellie pointed upwards and they hurried up the stairs away from the voices as fast as they could. Upstairs they found the floor was carpeted, making their footsteps silent.

"Someone seems to be ill or dying," Sam whispered, as they headed for a bend. "That's what they're arguing about."

He saw Ellie's eyes widen in fear and quickly added, "Not Suman. They're saying 'he'. Don't panic."

Around the bend, they spotted a door with a mortice lock. They approached it and listened carefully but heard no sound. Sam bent down to see if he could see through the keyhole.

The view was very limited, showing only a small part of the wall at the opposite side of the room. He turned back to the other two and shook his head.

"Can't see," he whispered.

Ellie had a look through the lock too, but, like Sam, saw no sign of Suman. There were no guarantees that Suman was in this room, but Ellie realised that they did not have time to hang around to see if she appeared. She didn't want to knock; the room could have someone in it they really didn't want to meet, but she bent down and blew through the lock with a very soft whistle. Suman, over at the window, heard the tiny sound and flew over to the door to peer through the lock from her side. She saw an eye peering back at her and grinned.

"Ellie?" The word was barely a whisper, but Ellie heard it.

"Yes!"

Suman pulled her face back from the door, but kept watching through the empty lock from a few feet away. She watched as key after key was inserted and withdrawn. Minutes passed until, finally, she heard the noise she had been praying for, a key that turned the lock.

Within seconds, all three rescuers had entered the room and shut the door quietly behind them. Suman was in Ellie's arms for a moment, then Geoff's, and then ran over into Sam's, elated and relieved to see them.

In whispers, they told her that there were other people in the near vicinity; men arguing in the room below the stairs. Sam then opened the door and slipped out first. He crept along to the bend in the corridor, peered around it, and gave a thumbs up to the others. Ellie and Suman fell in behind him, with Geoff bringing up the rear as they tiptoed down the stairs.

As they neared the bottom, they noticed there appeared to have been no let up in the argument taking place in the room downstairs, and it was with massive relief that they got out of range of the angry voices and arrived at the derelict office, heading for the way out. As they hurried towards the door, Geoff inadvertently bumped into Suman, whose footsteps had slowed. She was staring at the boxes around the walls and sniffing the air, beginning to realise what the smell was. He grabbed her hand and held it tightly, forcing her to hurry again, although she found time to mouth the word 'cocaine?' to him as they ran. He nodded.

It was when they reached the metal wall that they found their good fortune had run out. The door they had left pulled to, but not fully closed, was now shut tight and, after a quick panicky search, the means to open the door from the inside could not be found.

Chapter Twenty-Five

SISTER IRENE MERCY GOVERNMENT HOSPITAL

The duty nurse held up her clipboard. "I've been paging Dr Nath a number of times and he's not answering. It's not like him to be late. He's booked for surgery in just half an hour and he's got a few patients waiting to see him first."

The sister in the paediatric ward looked at her with a frown. "No, I agree, it's not like him, but he'll have a good enough reason when he comes in. I expect he's had some kind of emergency to attend. Don't worry, I'm certain he'll show up very soon. Please continue with your duties."

With those encouraging words, Sister Sett turned her back, not wanting the nurse to see the worried look in her eyes. She, too, had heard the rumours circulating about a female doctor being attacked in the hospital last night and taken away by her attackers. Some of the rumours had mentioned Dr Sudra by name and also that Dr Nath had gone off in a hurry with one of Suman's relatives. Now, with him not turning up for work today, she wondered if the rumours were indeed true and something nasty had happened to one or both of them. She certainly was worried, but didn't want a panic to break out by showing this.

In the meantime, she thought it prudent to make it known to the other doctors on duty in the surgical wards that Dr Nath was not at work and to see if they could make arrangements for other doctors to cover his surgeries.

She was on her way to do this when her phone rang.

"Hello, Sister Sett speaking."

"Sister, it's the ICU, Dr Chanda here. We have a little problem up here and I wondered if you could possibly spare the time to come and help sort it out."

"What kind of problem?" she asked snappily, feeling she had enough problems this morning already.

"Erm ... it's difficult to describe, but it's to do with Dr Nath. Could you come, do you think?"

"I'm on my way." Many thoughts were flying around her head and she hoped very much she wasn't going to get bad news. In her own reticent way, she was very fond of Sam and would not like anything to have happened to either him or Suman. She hurried up to the ICU as hastily as she could.

"Dr Chanda. You said you had a problem."

"Ah, Sister Sett, thank you for coming so quickly. I didn't know who else to turn to."

He took hold of her arm and gently propelled her out of the ICU ward and along the corridor as far as the waiting room, where she noticed an attractive young Indian lady sitting very straight in her chair.

Before they entered, Dr Chanda explained.

"I'm going to introduce you to Mrs Hossain. She has come to see a patient, Mrs Gupta, who I believe was one of Dr Nath's patients. Unfortunately, Mrs Gupta is not here anymore and no one seems to know where she's gone. Mrs Hossain is saying she's going to wait here until someone tells her where her friend is. I've searched, but there's no record of where she's been transferred to."

Sister nodded. "I believe Mrs Gupta is the lady who was shot, is that not the case?"

"Yes, she is. Dr Patel did her operation and then passed the case to Dr Nath, who organised her transfer to somewhere she would be safe, in case the person who shot her came back to the hospital. To finish the job," he added, as an afterthought.

Sister Sett wrinkled her brow. "I see. Well, this is a most irregular situation. You've absolutely no idea where she was taken?"

"No, Sister, and, to be honest, I wouldn't tell this lady if I did know. She may have come from the people who did the shooting."

"Oh, that would not be good at all; you did the right thing by not saying anything. Unfortunately, we also have the problem that Dr Nath is nowhere to be found either. He hasn't turned up for duty today and there's no word from him. I'm very concerned about it all."

She took a deep breath in and thought for a moment.

"Well, I think we just have to tell this visitor that Mrs Gupta has been discharged and to contact her friend at her home. And that it's against the rules to have her sitting here for any length of time. We must get her out of here, and quickly."

Dr Chanda almost smiled at the drama in her voice, but he knew that Sister Sett was only talking out of fear for the patients in the ICU and told her, with a very serious face, that he would attend to this immediately and see the lady off the premises. He entered the waiting room and crossed over to Mrs Hossain, thinking that, although he had become used to unusual things happening within the hospital, this one was winning the prize for being the nearest to a scene from a Bollywood movie.

Politely explaining to Mrs Hossain that her friend had most likely gone home, having been discharged from the hospital, he could see how worried she was and felt quite sorry for her. He was gently dismissive and kind at the same time, and eventually Mrs Hossain left him to make her way back down to the entrance hall, feeling very worried about Jan and wondering where in Heaven's name she had gone. Had Robert or his men taken her out of the ward or had she perhaps discharged herself to find a hiding place from Robert?

So deep in speculation was she that Kali reached the door without being aware of her surroundings, in particular a couple of men whose faces she knew very well standing around outside, watching her come out. Outside the gates, she looked around for her taxi and found it close by. The driver nodded to her and opened the back door for Kali to get in.

Once in, just as she was adjusting her sari, she was startled by the door being pulled open again. Her surprise turned to fear as someone climbed in beside her, hastily pushing her along to the middle of the back seat. On her other side, a second man climbed in too, trapping her there, unable to get out or even move very much, so tightly did they pin her in. She knew at once who they were, but as she opened her mouth to shout for help from the cab driver, she felt a dig in her ribs and looked down to see the nose of a gun pointing straight at her body. She changed her mind and said nothing. Robert's men were not to be disobeyed.

The man on her left gave instructions to the driver and they set off down the hill into the very busy traffic at the bottom, taking a right turn at the first set of lights they came to. Knowing this was not the way home, Kali was terrified. Where were they taking her?

The drive took a good forty-five minutes, the roads being as congested as ever. Yet it seemed too quick for Kali. When the taxi pulled into the back of Robert's factory and business headquarters in Bidhannagar, she knew exactly where she was. Being very familiar with the Reterron Apparel Company building, her heart sank. This was where she had been taken to work when she was twelve, no more than a child, having been sold down through a line of traffickers, and made to sew garments each day from dawn to dusk. There was no time off, no holidays, very little food, sleep or comforts, and a very heinous form of punishment should she fall asleep at her machine, or disobey the factory bosses. The punishments were whatever the boss decided on and often took the form of severe whippings or sexual acts, abuse that would be imprinted in her mind forever.

She was seventeen the day she caught the eye of Asheesh, one of Robert's closest friends, starting on his first day as one of the managers in the factory. As time went on, she realised he was a bit different from the other managers. He hadn't beaten or abused her in the same way as the others, but had taken a liking to her and, eventually, made a financial offer to Robert to buy Kali out of the control of his empire and into Asheesh's own control. He, like Robert with Jan, had offered Kali a domestic relationship: no marriage certificate or formal vows, just a life of servitude to her new owner. However, there was no violence used against her, something she appreciated very much. Since Asheesh had plenty of money and was happy to spend it on her, the relationship worked for both of them. It gave her an illusion of independence that enabled her to live as happily as she could under such an arrangement.

She accepted that he was a trafficker, and turned a blind eye to anything about the business that she saw or heard. This was what kept her safe from harm, or so she had thought; something had obviously changed. Her heart skipped a beat as she wondered why she had been brought here and why a gun was nudging at her side.

As the men paid the taxi driver and she watched him drive away, her fear increased. The gunman never left her side; neither did the gun as they led her round the side of the building and up to a metal wall, to gain access into the factory. She watched the second man press a button behind the tall grasses and a hidden door opened. Not having been in this end of the vast building before, she was surprised it was so different from the sewing factory, with its entry security measures and guards on the doors. *What is going on in here?* she asked herself.

Once inside, she knew the answer. Like the others, Kali recognised the smell of the drugs that were stored in the boxes. Robert's empire was obviously bigger than she had thought, which made her immediately wonder if Asheesh was aware of all this. *Of course he is; he is up to his eyes in it*, she realised. She knew in her heart that this was true and that it was highly possible he would not be able to get her out of the danger she was now in.

As she stood thinking about it all, the gun still pressed against her side, she noticed the other man hurry over to a glass partition. Through it, she watched carefully as he made for the broken desk, bent down and did something she couldn't see; press a button, maybe, or a switch. She then watched as the large metal door behind her closed on its own volition. She heard the click and swallowed, looking round at the grim face of the gunman, also watching the door as it shut.

"Shiva," she prayed silently to her god, as they moved on, "help me, please."

Back in the dilapidated office, there was silence for a few minutes, after which a face peeped out from behind one of the high stacks of cocaine boxes, piled six high. Seeing that the coast was clear, Ellie emerged, signalling to the others that it seemed safe to come out. Geoff, Sam and Suman then clambered out, warily and silently. All three walked cautiously over to the broken desk to see if they could find what the man had pressed to close the door. Geoff knelt down to look underneath. There it was: the button that had closed the door from inside the building. Would it open the door as well? He pressed it, watching closely. All four faces broke into smiles as the door opened inward and stood waiting like a friend to welcome them to the outside world and freedom.

The four ran as fast as they could, through all the bushes and trees, searching for the car they hoped would still be there. Holding Suman's hand, Sam stopped suddenly.

"Over there," he motioned, keeping his voice low and pointing to a small shed not too far away.

Vada was looking out from the side of the shed and gesturing to them as they ran towards her. Before they got there, she had already opened all the doors and was back in the driver's seat buckling her seat belt. Sam climbed in the front beside her, with Suman, Ellie and Geoff scrambling into the back. The car was moving as they shut the doors, accelerating faster and faster as Vada drove like a maniac, trying to escape from the grounds of the factory. At last she shot through the gates of the car park, almost taking one of the iron railings with her, and it wasn't until they were at least half a mile away that she began to slow down.

Suman, in the back, was clinging to Ellie for dear life. Geoff, grasping the back of the driver's seat with one hand, had his other hand on Ellie's arm. No-one spoke a word until they were a good distance away, going at a slightly healthier pace and having checked that no-one was following. Even then, nobody seemed to have anything to say.

It was Vada who broke the silence.

"That was the worst night of my life, you guys. I've been sick with worry. You took so long to come out!" Her voice broke on the last words.

Ellie leaned over and patted her on her back.

"Vada, everybody's here; don't cry. They're safe now, honey."

Suman leaned forward, too and put her hands on Vada's shoulders.

"We are, Vada. We really are safe now. You mustn't cry; you'll set us all off if you do that."

Vada managed to turn round to her sister and give her a teary smile. "I was just so frightened."

"I know, but you managed to wait for us to come out. Thank you. We just couldn't get to you. Nobody had a phone signal, so we couldn't even let you know what was happening."

"Tell me what happened," Vada asked, glancing again at her sister in the back.

Ellie answered. "Not now, honey. You just concentrate on your driving. Give Suman time to recover. She's been through an ordeal. We'll talk later."

Suman looked at Ellie. "Thank you," she mouthed silently. Ellie nodded and moved her eyes back to the front window, watching Vada negotiate the road which was getting busier the nearer they got to the centre of the city.

Vada was struggling. Having had only a few driving lessons, she was having problems anticipating what drivers were going to do next. Adrenaline was still coursing through her body, so her speed was faster than she was used to on straight roads. However, at busy points, she slowed to a crawl, meaning that they were frequently overtaken on both sides, with drivers cutting in front of her and tooting their horns to say they were coming into the lane whether she liked it or not. At traffic lights it seemed to be a free-for-all, everyone edging forward to make their getaway as soon as the lights began to change, some even sneaking through before they changed. After a number of crunching gear changes and frequent near misses, Ellie had had enough.

In her thick Scottish accent she blurted out, "My God, Vada! I love you so much, but this is almost as scary as what we went through earlier! Sam, why on earth are you not driving? Please, let Sam drive, Vada. Please." The shouts of agreement and laughter from everyone else in the car set Vada laughing too; a relief of tension for each and every one of them in the car.

"Well said, Ellie," Suman shouted through the hilarity. "Somebody had to say it. We're even going the wrong way!"

Chapter Twenty-Six

SUMAN'S APARTMENT

Peace reigned in Suman's flat on the twelfth floor of Florentine Apartments, all explanations, discussions and opinions finished for the moment. Kanya, shedding tears of relief when her two daughters arrived home safely, had been given a shortened version of events, minus some of the dangers. Her relief that they were safe was palpable, and the three women hugged and cried together.

Knowing how independent Vada had become in recent years, Kanya resisted the temptation to try to talk her daughter into coming back to Maharashtra with her, where she could be looked after and, so Kanya thought, be kept out of harm's way. With Suman it was different. The thought that she would ever be able to look after Suman again did not even enter her head, knowing that this young, beautiful, highly-qualified doctor would never again return to Maharashtra to live with her mother. She had come to terms with this, and was proud of her daughter and the person she had become.

Both Sam and Suman had been over to the hospital. The visit mostly comprised apologies and explanations to worried staff and patients about their absence. Sister Sett was probably the most relieved person to see them, having been shocked when they told her the story of Suman's abduction within the hospital building.

"Well, you're back now and we're glad to see you safe and sound." She spoke rather sharply, not prepared to reveal her real feelings in public. It was back to business for the wards and clinics as far as she was concerned, and she speedily brought them up to date with the patients' notes and the surgeries that had taken place over the last twenty-four hours.

She told them, too, about Kali's visit, referring to her as Mrs Hossain, a name Suman suspected was not Kali's real surname. It had crossed Suman's mind back in the dilapidated office that the woman they had seen coming in with two men might have been Kali, and she hoped very much that Jan's friend was safe and not being held against her will as she herself had been.

The visit to the hospital would have gone on all afternoon and evening if they had allowed it, but Sam was adamant that Suman should return home and spend the rest of the day with her mother. He even managed to convince her that the following day should be a day off, her holiday not really having materialised into what it should have been.

"I can manage here," Sam assured her. "Spend time with Kanya. Once she's gone home you probably won't see her again for a while. Visit Habi and Bimla; your mother was hoping she might be able to meet them."

"Yes, I think I will do that," Suman agreed. "And I'd love to see how Habi is doing. Thank you, Sam. Unless something drastic happens here to any of my patients, I'll do as you say. I'll hire a car to get there."

"No, take mine. I won't need it tomorrow. It just sits in the car park all day."

She paused, looking at him long and hard. "Sam, you've no idea how grateful I am for what you've done, and..."

He interrupted. "Aye, right! I'm no needing yer thanks!"

A laugh broke from her, her eyes dancing with delight.

"You've been learning Scottish, you devil. Aye, right, indeed! Who taught you to say that?"

He laughed too, a good, hearty chuckle. "Well, to be honest, I wasn't taught it. I heard Ellie say it to Geoff and tucked it away in my head so I could say it at some point!"

Laughing along with him, the temptation to touch him, to have his arm around her shoulders again or hold his hand was immense. She was staggered, never having thought that at any time she would experience an overwhelming feeling like this. She thought she was immune to it, immune to any feelings of this kind. She thought that this side of her had been destroyed all those long years ago.

Maybe, just maybe, she was wrong.

In Suman's apartment the next morning, breakfast was slow and leisurely, the two ladies and Geoff sitting around the table in their dressing gowns, enjoying being together. Kanya was at the cooker, delighted to be making the food, her daughter translating some of the conversation for her, to keep her in the loop. Not all of it; some of the most dangerous incidents were left untranslated. At times the discussion was very serious: what to do about all the unfinished business of the abduction of Suman, and whether the dangers were still around or not. These items also remained un-translated for Kanya. Geoff and Ellie were adamant that they would not be going home until they knew Suman was in no more danger from the traffickers.

There were also the problems of Jan, Kali and, of course, Sunny, the child recovering from her serious injuries, to be discussed at great length. Decisions had to be made about these issues. However, laughs and light-hearted moments were included in the conversation, too, and Ellie listened and watched her beloved foster daughter, becoming aware of a huge change in her. She had picked up very quickly that within Suman's conversations, the name 'Sam' was cropping up every few minutes.

She leaned back in her chair and asked, "So, Sam's going to cover for you today and tomorrow?" Suman nodded and Ellie continued. "That's really good of him. And we'll have to thank him for lending us his car. He's such a lovely man. Will we see him today?"

Suman's eyes were alight as she looked at Ellie. "Well, I will. I'll have to give him back his car keys later."

"Why don't you ask him to come for his evening meal tonight and I'll cook something special?"

"Oh, I think he's busy tonight. Maybe another night."

"Tomorrow, then? Ask him to come tomorrow."

"No, he's busy tomorrow, too. He told me he's going out with his girlfriend tomorrow."

Ellie's face fell. "His girlfriend? He's got a girlfriend?"

Geoff, oblivious to the undercurrents at the table, replied to this. "Don't think so. He's never mentioned a girl to me."

Suman, looking innocent, continued. "She's a nurse. I think she's American. He calls her Sweet Adeline."

Ellie's huge smile spread quickly across her face. "Suman, you wee fibber! Stop telling all these lies."

Suman leaned back in her chair and crossed her arms.

"Well ... you stop matchmaking and I'll stop telling lies. Deal?"

"Deal," agreed Ellie, thrilled to bits with this conversation. She reached across the table to shake hands with Suman.

Geoff paused in the act of buttering his toast, looking puzzled.

"So ... has he got a girlfriend or not?"

Chapter Twenty-Seven

SCHAANAPUR, NEAR DHAPA LANDFILL SITE

It was around two o'clock in the afternoon when they arrived at Bimla's smallholding in Schaanapur, past Tiffin time, as Suman did not want to put Bimla out by arriving at a time when lunch was being served.

They found Bimla alone, Daivey being out on the Dhapa landfill site, and Raja and Habi still at school. It was good to have Bimla to chat to, with no distractions from the children, although Suman was looking forward to them coming home. It had been a good while since she had seen them.

Instead of being put out by her unexpected guests, Bimla was delighted, most especially by having the honour of entertaining Suman's mother in her little house. Able to converse well, each with a good knowledge of the Hindu language as well as their own dialects, Kanya and Bimla were soon firm friends, Kanya at ease and very complimentary about Bimla's work out in the gardens and her son's recycling work on the big landfill site.

After a tour around the house, to see the new bedroom, all finished and furnished, and the garden with its lush vegetables, Bimla insisted on providing refreshments for her guests. The hospitality of Indian people was second nature to them all; it would have been taken as a snub if they had refused. She served chai, enjoyed by most of the ladies. Ellie wasn't too keen, but drank it politely, and a bottle of Indian beer was given to Geoff. Little home-made ginger biscuits accompanied the drinks, and Bimla beamed as she looked around at her very welcome visitors.

"How is school going for the children?" Suman asked her.

"Oh, very well. Daivey is top of the class, such a clever boy. I'm very proud of him. He has caught up with the rest of the class so well. They want him to go to high school soon, but he says the teachers there won't let him leave class to carry on his business, so he wants to stay where he is. He had to stay off school today; he didn't want to miss a huge delivery of good plastics coming in from Bihar. His friends told him it was coming."

Suman thought for a moment before commenting on this, worried how to phrase what she wanted to say. "It might be that they feel school is very important for him, Bimla. If he's clever, they will want him to do well, which will be good for him and his business. Do you not think it would be good for him? Does he like school?"

Bimla stared. "He loves school and stays late when he is there, to catch up, and he does his homework every night. But his business is very important to him, Suman. He's kept the family together and fed us for many years. We can't ask him to stop. He says it is his life's business and the school work he is learning will help him with this when he is older."

Suman smiled at Bimla and nodded, trying to make amends for upsetting her friend. She did realise the importance of Daivey's work to the family and knew that she shouldn't interfere with this, at least not at the moment. She decided to say no more for the present and perhaps tackle it next year when Daivey's classmates were all going up to high school and leaving him behind.

"I'm sure it will, Bimla. As long as he is going to school and learning, he must continue his business too. What about Raja? Is he liking school?"

"Raja loves it too. He's not as clever as his brother, but he likes being with the other boys. They play games, cricket and football, and he loves them. The teacher says his reading is excellent. He brings home lots of books and reads them to us."

"That's wonderful, Bimla. He'll have to read to us, too, when he comes home from school. And Habi? Is she good at reading?"

Bimla started to chortle, a very infectious sound.

"Oh, Habi. Our little one. Learning like a sponge, the teacher says, and everyone loves Habi, so funny and so pretty. She is a little mother hen, always trying to look after everyone else except herself. She keeps us right, making us eat our food, and giving the boys chores to do in the house." She laughed again. "And they do it! If Habi tells them to stop fighting, they stop; if she says go to bed, they go. They won't do it for me, but for Habi, anything!"

Suman was laughing along with her by this time. "Sounds as if I've given you a real handful. But seriously, is this arrangement of ours working out for you? You must tell me the truth. Habi might be with you for a very long time, and it's only good if it's working for you. Tell me the truth."

Bimla moved her chair over to Suman's side and sat down again, taking Suman's hand.

"Suman, bhalobashi, I love Habi so much, as if she was my very own. And the boys adore her. You would destroy us as a family if you took her away. She has made our family complete. Ask the boys yourself when they come in; they will tell you the same. Please, never take her away from us."

Suman did ask the boys when they returned. Speaking to each of them and watching the dynamics of the little family, she was moved by the love and happiness in the house. Habi, now wearing a smaller cast and able to hobble about, took to Kanya, too, sitting on her lap to tell her all about school and describing all her friends. She was shy at first with Ellie and Geoff, but when Ellie suggested some fun games, it wasn't long before Habi got everyone down on the floor to join in, even Kanya, and the ice was soon broken.

After the games, Habi went across to Ellie, touching her blonde hair and staring into her bright blue eyes. She fingered the earrings Ellie was wearing and, when Ellie took them off and gave them to the child, Habi was silenced, unable to speak for happiness. Bimla, there and then, pierced Habi's ears for her, with only a small yelp from Habi as she did so, and the little girl proudly put her new earrings on. Bimla cried, too, when gifts were handed to everyone, her own being a beautiful rug for the floor of her bedroom.

"No, no," she said through her tears. "This is too good for a bedroom. It must go in this room so that everyone can come and see it. I won't let them walk on it, but they will come to see it."

Habi was also given a little bracelet, which she showed off to everyone in the room, and the boys were delighted with pencil cases and geometry sets each, and a real cricket set between them. It wasn't long before the whole household ended up outside playing cricket, with all the neighbours coming out to join in or watch and cheer them on.

Waving goodbye was an emotional time, with everyone exchanging many hugs and tears. Once home, Suman dropped Kanya and Ellie off at the apartment block, intending to take Sam's car back to him before coming back for the evening meal with them all.

"I'll come back over to the hospital with you," Geoff volunteered, an offer gratefully accepted by Suman. Geoff had been like a father to her since she was small, and Suman felt safe and secure with the man who had protected her for so many years.

Parking in the car park of the hospital, they walked inside and through to the paediatric ward, where she hoped Sam would be. He was just leaving the ward as they arrived, and, delighted to see them, he ushered them into his office for a chat before they returned home.

"Habi okay?" he asked, perching on the back of his chair and pocketing the car key Suman had handed to him.

"Habi is wonderful," Suman replied. "So are the family. I made the best choice there, Sam. Such a happy family."

"That's good. Well, I'm pleased you came in just now. I got a phone call today that I thought you needed to know about."

"From a patient?"

"Sort of." He looked across at Geoff. "This concerns all of us. I got a message today, asking me to phone a mobile number belonging to someone called Jan Gupta, so I phoned and spoke to her. That's Jan's real name, by the way; not sure if you knew that. She was phoning from the private clinic I had sent her to, and she sounded very concerned. It wasn't her husband she was concerned about, it was her friend, Kali. She's convinced Kali is missing.

I didn't know what to say to her, so I said nothing. But she wants us to go and visit her tomorrow, so that she can tell us more and maybe start a search for her friend."

He looked at them both.

"What do you think? The woman we saw coming into the factory yesterday could have been Kali. So it might be a dangerous thing for us to do, to go searching for her."

Suman was very quiet for a moment, reflecting on all that had happened yesterday and the day before, and mulling over a question she'd been asking herself ever since. How far did she want her involvement in this to go? Did she want to go after these traffickers; try to do something to end the criminal operation they were running, along with their drugs empire? She thought of the effect trafficking had on little girls like Habi and Sunny. Could she live with herself if she didn't try to put a stop to this immoral operation?

Chapter Twenty-Eight

BHOJWANI SANITORIUM, PURULIA, KOLKATA

The car pulled into the car park of the Bhojwani Sanitarium in the district of Purulia, West Kolkata. The satnav had failed to help them find the exact location they were looking for, but pedestrians on the busy streets gave them better directions. It had been a lengthy journey, the heavily congested streets hard to navigate.

Being quite accustomed to the congestion, Sam wasn't fazed by this, or by finding the district of Purulia; it was just locating the sanitarium that had tested his good nature to the limit. It really was well hidden, and he made a mental note to thank the driver of the ambulance that had carried Jan to her destination a few days ago. He wondered how long it had taken him to locate the little clinic and then to find his way home again out of the maze of narrow streets. Each road Sam drove along was a one-way street crowded with pedestrians, each area an amalgamation of old-world charm and the new, modern face of the city.

Parked neatly in the car park at last, he turned off the ignition, breathed a heavy sigh and turned to face Suman, sitting beside him in the front.

"Okay. Still sure you want to come in with me?"

Suman nodded. "I am. More than sure. I think I need to be there." She laughed. "Ellie wasn't happy, though, was she?"

He grinned. "No, not happy at all. She wanted to come with us. Strong lady, your foster mother."

She turned a serious face to him, speaking in a quiet tone. "I wouldn't be here if it wasn't for her, Sam."

Sam leaned forward, never before having had such a strong desire to hold her face in his hands and kiss her. He hesitated, not knowing why, just knowing it wasn't the right time. Not here, not at this moment.

Suman leaned forward slightly too, a smile appearing. "She wasn't happy when I asked her to take Kanya to the market for some food for dinner, was she? But we couldn't have presented ourselves as a foursome to Jan. Too many people. That would not have worked."

He said nothing, disconcerting Suman, who leaned even further in and almost rubbed noses with him. "Would it?"

"Not on your Nellie!"

Suman's laugh could be heard two streets away even with the car windows shut.

"You don't even know what that means, Sami Nath," she accused.

He was laughing too as they climbed out of the car, but the laughter disappeared as they remembered the serious visit they were about to pay with Jan. They walked up the path that led to the entrance of the building, a modern, elegant two-storey structure. Built to mimic the more traditional buildings still seen in parts of the city, it had green-shuttered windows with small balconies in front. The sign showing the name had a simple classiness, and seemed to them to be in keeping with the upmarket building, with just the words 'Welcome to Bhojwani Sanitorium' on it. *Not too shabby*, thought Suman as they approached the door and rang the bell on the speaker system.

"Suprabhata, good morning," a pleasant voice said.

"Good morning," Sam replied in Bengali. "My name is Dr Nath from the Sister Irene Mercy Hospital. I have Dr Sudra with me. We have an appointment to see Mrs Jan Gupta."

Replying in the local language, the voice requested, "Please wait a moment."

Suman looked at Sam, her brow lifting slightly.

"It'll be all right," he assured her.

After a few minutes, the voice came back.

"I'm sorry, Dr Nath. I'm not allowed to give you access."

The machine switched off.

Sam re-pressed the button. "Are you sure? We phoned earlier to make the appointment and were told that this would be permitted. Mrs Gupta has given her permission for our visit as well as your superintendent."

"One moment, please."

Suman took a deep breath in and let it out again. This time, the voice returned much quicker.

"My apologies. I will let you in. Please push the door when you hear the buzzer."

Standing inside the reception area of the building, the two of them looked at the pristine walls, ceilings and stairs. Everything was painted pure white except the reception desk, which was a deep ebony, making it somewhat incongruous. The woman behind the desk came round and put her hand out to greet the visitors.

"I apologise again, Doctors. We were given instructions not to let anyone in to visit Mrs Gupta, and I didn't realise that this rule was to be ignored for you. Please follow me and I'll take you to her."

The woman led them up the marble stairway and along a corridor with rows of doors, some open, allowing a glimpse inside the room, and some shut tight. Halfway along she stopped outside one of the closed doors with the number 36 on the wall at the side. Unlike the other doors, there was a chair at either side of this one, and a guard sitting on one of them. He stood as they approached, a huge, burly man in a black T-shirt, his muscular body filling the shirt to capacity. He had a fierce expression as he looked at them, causing Suman to unconsciously move closer to Sam as they walked to the door.

The woman addressed the guard. "It's okay. These visitors are allowed in."

Without a word, the guard drew a key from his pocket and unlocked the door, standing back to let them all in.

The receptionist led the way. "Mrs Gupta is in here."

She then turned to the visitors and addressed them in stilted English. "Can I offer you a cup of coffee, lemon tea, or chai?" Suman opened her mouth, but no sound came out. Sam jumped in quickly. "Coffee would be lovely, thank you very much." He grinned at Suman and whispered as the door closed behind the receptionist, "Do you think we should start a new trend at the Sister Irene and offer refreshments to all our visitors?"

She smiled back. "I think the nurses would go on strike if we did!"

Collecting a chair each from over beside the window, they sat down around the bed, Suman greeting Jan with a warm hello. Jan, propped up slightly on her fluffy white pillows, an embroidered cotton nightdress peaking above the stiff white sheets, returned the greeting, though anxiety was written all over her face.

Suman spoke gently, wondering why she looked so on edge with them. "So how are you feeling, Jan? You haven't got your drip in now and you're certainly looking so much better."

"Yes, I do feel much better." Then, almost rudely, Jan turned round to face Sam and said, accusingly, "You told me Dr Sudra had been captured by Robert's men. Was that just lies to get information from me?"

"No, Jan." he replied swiftly. "I would never do that. Dr Sudra will tell you herself; she was forcibly taken from the hospital and held, tied up, for quite some time. But we managed to get her away. We don't know who they were, but it could well have been your husband's men."

"No, it couldn't have been Robert; she'd never have come out alive. He never lets anyone get away. That's why I just know he'll come and put another bullet into me. He'll never let me go, alive."

Sam looked at the frightened woman with tears in her eyes, his doctor's bedside manner coming to the fore.

"Please try not to worry, Jan. You're here to recover and get well again. That guard on the door will take care of anyone who shouldn't be here. He really didn't want to let us in. And neither did the receptionist."

He smiled. "So, tell me how you are. They must be looking after you well, and I'm assuming all is well with the baby?"

Jan relaxed slightly, her hand moving to its usual place, on the sheets above her stomach. "Yes, the baby is fine, they tell me. I'm getting looked after very well. Thank you for sending me here. It's a nice place, but I'm worried that I can't afford to pay for it."

"We won't be asking you for money to pay for it," he assured her. "Not something for you to think about. But you wanted to see me. You're worried about your friend."

"Yes, as I said on the phone, I wanted to ask you about my friend, Kali." Jan sighed, relaxing her face and leaning back into her pillows. "The staff here have been phoning her for me since I arrived; I've lost my own phone somewhere." She glanced at Suman before continuing. "But Kali's phone has never been answered. This is not like her, so I've been worrying about her. More so when I heard that you were missing, Dr Sudra. Where did they take you?"

"I'm afraid to say I was drugged and taken to a very large textile factory, with offices and living accommodation attached. The factory had an awful lot of people working there. The men who captured me just wanted to know where you were, but I promise you, I didn't tell them anything."

"Did they hurt you to try to get information out of you?" Jan didn't wait for an answer to this. She already knew the answer. "I'm so sorry. I really am. Where was this factory?"

"In a place called Bidhannagar in west Kolkata."

Jan closed her eyes for a second, her hand clutching at the bedsheets in front of her.

"That's definitely Robert's place. So it was him and his men. We're all in danger, Dr Nath. He'll come and shoot us all."

Suman, closest to the bed, took hold of the agitated lady's hand.

"Don't panic, Jan. You're safe. They have very tight security here and there's no reason why they should know where you are."

"You don't know what they're like. He can …"

Jan stopped abruptly and shrank under the covers in fear as the door opened. Suman squeezed her hand.

"It's only the tea trolley, Jan. Come on now, sit up and have some chai with us. You're safe here. This won't be doing your baby any good." Her quiet, authoritative voice had a calming effect on Jan, and she sat up again. The auxiliary nurse with the trolley helped Suman to make her comfortable again before handing out the drinks to everyone and leaving the room.

Jan's panic had been diffused and, for the moment, she took refuge in her cup of chai, sipping slowly and breathing deeply. The visitors remained quiet, allowing her time to regain her self-control. It was Suman who began the conversation again, talking softly and calmly.

"Jan, if what you're saying is correct and it was your husband's premises I was kept in, I'd like to ask you one or two questions about him." She waited, looking to see Jan's reaction to this.

Her answer was wary. "You can ask, but I'm not sure if I can answer."

"Okay, well, my first question is nice and easy. Can you first of all tell me what your husband looks like? I obviously don't know him and I'm wondering if I met him."

Jan looked straight into Suman's eyes. "If you'd met him, you'd remember him."

"Why, Jan?"

"He's ... different. What he looks like and how he dresses."

"How is he different? What does he look like and how does he dress?"

The scared look was back on her face. "You would see right away how he's different. His skin is whiter than ours. He says he's British and he's very proud of that."

"What else?" Suman probed.

"He's big, he's strong. But he's also very frightening. He likes to be noticed and likes people to be afraid of him, you know ... likes people to do what he says. He wears weird clothes because he believes this makes him better than others."

"What kind of clothes?"

"Different. He gets them sent in from abroad."

"Describe them to me."

Jan's brow puckered. "Why?"

"I'll tell you in a minute. It would help me if you described the clothes."

"Well, he normally wears a suit. But never a plain suit, always patterned, like a check, and always a bright colour. And a waistcoat, a shirt and a tie. A red or yellow tie, or something he calls a cravat."

"Jewellery?"

"No jewellery as such, but he picks a fresh flower from the garden and sticks it in his buttonhole. Oh, I suppose he does wear jewellery of a sort; he has a watch with a long chain which probably looks like jewellery. He's never seen without it. I can't remember the name he gives it." She hesitated before adding, "He's an evil man. That chain can be used to ..." She stopped abruptly.

"To what, Jan?" Sam gently probed.

"Kali once told me that he ..." Time stood still while she plucked up the courage to say the words. "... strangled someone with it. I don't know if this is true, but I know he's perfectly capable of it. And..." She turned from side to side, looking at both of them, panic showing in her eyes.

"And I'd rather that my baby and I were dead before we put ourselves in his hands again!"

Suman leaned forward and grasped the hand that was waving about.

"It's okay, Jan. I don't think you're going to have to worry about that again." Jan stared at her hard. "How can you say that?"

Suman continued. "Your husband. Robert, I think you called him; I did meet him. And yes, it was him who was holding me captive in the factory. When I met him, he was dressed just as you described."

"And ...?"

"And, unfortunately, Robert had a very bad turn, a seizure of some kind. I was there at the time and, even though I'm a doctor, I'm afraid to say I wasn't able to do very much for him."

Jan sat bolt upright in the bed, staring at Suman.

"A seizure. You mean he's dead?"

"Well, I didn't actually see him die, but he was definitely in a very bad way when his men took him away. I don't think he would have lasted very long."

Jan's eyes were miles away as Suman watched for her reaction. Sinking back onto the pillows, her body slid back down into the covers and her eyes moved upwards as she stared at a spot above the door. They waited a moment before asking her if she was all right.

The words brought her out of her trance. "If he's dead, then yes, I might be all right." As she spoke, the tears began to flow like an avalanche straight down her cheeks onto the quilt. "Dr Sudra, maybe, if the gods have answered my prayers, then I just maybe ... I might be ... free." She laid her hands on her stomach. "We ... my baby and me, we might be free from him ... free from his ... cruel ... cruel ..."

Suman enfolded the sobbing woman in her arms.

Chapter Twenty-Nine

SUMAN'S APARTMENT

Suman lay on her back on the bed, alone in her room with the curtains drawn to block out the late afternoon sun. She wasn't asleep; sleep was something that was going to elude her for a little while. It had been a strange day, some of it spent with Jan in her room at the sanitarium and some, in the afternoon, spent with Sam discussing the revelations that had been made by Jan over more coffee and chai in the private hospital's ward.

After a few sentences from Jan, Sam had stopped her from saying any more and had gone to get a notebook and pen from the receptionist. From then on, he had taken many notes of Jan's memories of her time in the hands of Robert, the man who was not her husband, but her owner. Information on the businesses that Robert owned followed her own account of a horrendous life of violence and fear and her knowledge of his trafficking operations over the last decade made unendurable listening for Suman.

The numbers were unthinkable, if what she was telling them was correct. Her words made it sound as if hundreds, if not thousands of men, women and children had been sold into his hands, which Suman found sickening. Most had been put to work in his three huge factories and some had been sold into the sex industry in Kolkata. Others, like Habi and Sunita, had been sold into domestic servitude in many homes through the area and beyond. Forced marriages were discussed as well, where young girls, not yet into their teens, had been taken hundreds of miles from their homes and married for a payment to men old enough to be their fathers and grandfathers, never allowed to return to their own homes again.

For Suman, it was all too close to home. Lying on her bed with her arms behind her head, her own memories had resurrected themselves slowly but surely. She was back in the lorry, being pummelled about, trying to hang on to a bar on the wall, not knowing where she and her two friends from the village were being taken. She only knew it was a long way away from the only home and family she had ever known, the lorry not stopping for hour upon terrifying hour. No toilet stops for the little girls who had cried as they wet themselves in a corner of the lorry. No stops as one of her friends was sick in the back, petrified as the sickness came, time and again.

Into Suman's mind came the memories of the beatings they endured at the end of the journey, and their captors making them clean up their messes. Yet those beatings were only the tip of the iceberg. More beatings followed, and burnings, rapes, abuse, violence, fear, and screaming... All these memories were rising fast, and she couldn't stop them. It was too much, and she turned over on the bed, burying her face into the pillow. They had lain dormant in her head for so long, she knew she couldn't have them reappearing now. Not now! her mind shouted. No more memories!

But they wouldn't go away. Her past had awakened from a deep sleep and she found herself back in the little room in Amsterdam, high up above a den of vice that was masquerading as a nightclub. Taken out of the room and downstairs, to where the nefarious business of the 'nightclub' was happening, she had discovered all kinds of nightmares that a child of nine should know nothing about; nightmares of pain and degradation. Added to this were the loneliness, the homesickness and the heartache, day after day after day.

I can't do it, she thought. *I can't allow my thoughts to drive me mad.* Suman's pillow was drenched with her tears, the bedcover soaked with her sweat. She was fighting so hard to stop the memories, but she had lost the battle.

"Ellie!" she screamed at the top of her voice. "Ellie! Ellie! Help me!"

Her bedroom door was thrown open and slammed shut with a bang as Ellie flew across the bedroom and gathered Suman in her arms. Just as she had done twenty years ago with the little girl in the bedroom of their house in Edinburgh, she lay on the bed with Suman, crying with her, rocking her, holding her close until the heart-rending sobs eventually subsided.

Together they sat up, still holding each other close, and together they wiped their tears. Together they sat in silence until the noises from outside the bedroom heralded the arrival of Vada and Kanya, home from another day of sightseeing. Kanya was like a child, talking nineteen to the dozen with excitement, keen to tell everyone all about her experience of entering Mother Teresa's house and seeing where her great idol had lived and worked.

Suman and Ellie rose, wiped their faces and tidied their hair. No words were exchanged; there were no words. Together they left the room with smiles on their faces, and welcomed Kanya and Vada home from their exciting outing. The chatter and the laughter coming from the kitchen as the women prepared the evening meal together gave no hint of the pain and sadness left behind in the bedroom, behind the closed door.

Only Geoff knew, having been left behind in the sitting room when Ellie had flown to Suman's side. Only he had heard the weeping of his daughter and his wife, and he had wept, too, knowing what the weeping was for. Suman had crossed to his side when she left the bedroom and sat close to him on the sofa. Her face was smiling as they listened to the events of the day, but her hand was tucked in his, holding on with a tight grip.

The following morning was the start of Kanya's last day in Kolkata, and Suman wanted no interruptions to the time they would spend together. Kanya had requested a nice, leisurely day spent in and around the apartment with her two daughters. They made an early start, strolling over to the hospital as soon as they had finished breakfast. Kanya asked to see where the girls worked and what they did. So a visit to the paediatric wards and Suman's clinic came first, followed by a tour around the nurses' home where Vada lived, and into the vast college where she studied.

Kanya's heart swelled as she realised the valuable work and the dedication shown by both her girls; she met a number of patients who testified to this and was a very proud mother. A light lunch in Vada's canteen followed, with the girls introducing their mother to her very first self-service cafeteria. Afraid to help herself to the food on display, Kanya needed coaxing to fill her plate.

After lunch, they ambled round the extensive gardens of the hospital, sat at the fountains and watched the magic waters dance and bounce in the pools beneath them. Wandering home around four, Kanya wanted to spend some time packing her small bag, her possessions being few but precious. She was taken aback by Suman and Vada, who presented her with a larger, brand new suitcase, stuffed with gifts for each and every member of their family. There were gifts for Kanya, too, including a large framed photograph, taken by Geoff without her knowledge and enlarged professionally to fit the beautiful frame. The photo showed Suman, Kanya and Vada side by side on Suman's sofa, their heads together and deep in conversation. Kanya loved it, touching it over and over again; a photograph of her was a very rare thing, and showing her with her two daughters was the icing on the cake.

Suman's mother's possessions were removed from the small bag and placed in the larger suitcase. The small bag was then filled with goodies for Kanya to enjoy on the long flight across India to Mumbai. Hira, Suman's eldest brother, was collecting her at the airport on her return tomorrow to take her home to his house, where Kanya now lived with him and his growing family.

Bags all packed and placed ready at the front door to be picked up early the next day, Kanya asked for the rest of her time at Suman's home to be spent in the company of the people she loved. There were six people sitting around the table for their meal that evening. Underneath the vast array of colourful decorations, fairy lights and garlands of flowers which had been strung up on the ceiling and the walls, Kanya had pride of place at the top of the table, with a daughter on each side of her. Geoff was beside Suman and opposite him sat Sam. Sam wasn't there at Kanya's request; he was there at her insistence. Facing Kanya was Ellie, the woman Kanya loved as much as her daughters; the woman who had brought Suman back to her when she had thought her daughter was dead.

Prior to the food being served, Kanya had asked her daughters if she could perform Aarti, a Hindu devotional ritual consisting of prayers, candles and blessings. Especially for this occasion, Kanya had prepared a small shrine. Surrounded by flowers, a pooja thali set took centre stage on the table and the rich smell of incense and perfumed candles filled Suman's sitting room and beyond. Her daughters were aware of just how important this ceremony was to their mother, with all the family and friends there, and everyone took part in the rituals as Kanya blessed each one of them in turn.

The meal was long and languorous, the food delicious, course upon course until Kanya professed herself 'as fat as the Great Indian Elephant that roams the forests of Kerala'. The laughter rang out at this, but stopped hurriedly as Kanya stood up, holding up a hand to let everyone know she wanted to speak. This was such an unexpected thing that Suman and Vada stared at her in wonder, interested to see what she was going to say. What was even more surprising was that Kanya's little speech to her family was spoken in English.

"Geoff, Ellie, Sam, Suman and Vada," she began. "Thank you for my holiday. For looking after me and feeding me well." She patted her tummy to much laughter around the table.

"Most importantly, I love you with my heart." Her hand went to her heart.

Looking directly at Suman, she continued, "Suman, majhi mulagi, my first daughter, I love you." She then looked directly at Vada. "Vada, majhi mulagi, my second daughter, I love you."

At this she sat down on her chair and looked at Ellie.

"Ellie ... okay?"

Ellie rose quickly to embrace her. "Very, very okay, Kanya. You did it beautifully."

Suman and Vada were at Ellie's back, trying to hug their mother too. Chaos reigned for a few minutes, until Kanya pointed to the chairs in the sitting room and everyone filed through, wondering what was going to happen next. Once they were all seated, with the two men on the floor, Kanya led them in a family singing session, her daughters and Sam joining in at the top of their voices with some beautiful, traditional Indian folk songs.

In the darkness that night, Suman lay in her bed thinking over the events of the evening, happy and full of love for her family. The terrors that had returned to torment her earlier were once more dormant, where she hoped they would stay for a long time to come.

Chapter Thirty

SUMAN'S APARTMENT

It was another early start the next morning, with everyone getting up and ready for Sam, who was coming to pick them up. Once again, he was giving the use of his car and his time to drive Kanya, Suman and Vada to the airport. Geoff and Ellie were staying on for another week and, after many hugs, kisses and waves, the car drove out of sight.

They made the journey with plenty of time to spare, and Sam stayed with the car while Kanya and her daughters entered the airport to help with the check-in process. The girls were tearful, Kanya more so, but at last, goodbyes over, they waved their beloved mother off on her journey.

"I'll come and visit you really soon, Ai," Suman had told Kanya. "I promise. I won't leave it too long this time."

She meant to keep her promise, and made a mental note to book some time off work for the Festival of Holi, in a couple of months' time. She felt such a strong need to see Kanya again soon, and to catch up with the rest of her growing family.

Coming home in the car with Sam, the conversation turned very quickly to the information on the traffickers that Jan had given them. All agreed this needed to be put into the right hands, although there were differing opinions about whose hands were the right hands. The discussion continued right up until they arrived at Suman's apartment, and Sam, wanting to get decisions made, phoned across to the hospital to get a stand-in doctor to take his clinic.

"This is urgent," he told Suman and Vada. "We have to do something quickly; we can't just sit on it while all these hundreds of people are being kept in bonded labour at the factory, and many more working for Robert's different companies. There's all the drug smuggling that's going on, too."

Suman and Vada agreed wholeheartedly, and the three entered the apartment, much to the delight of Ellie and Geoff, who were having a lazy morning in the flat and drinking a newly made pot of coffee.

"Come sit with us at the table," Suman told them. "You can help us decide what to do."

Around the dining room table, the discussion began in earnest, with Sam putting forward his view that the Ministry of Home Affairs should be contacted, as they were the official body responsible for human trafficking problems. When Suman suggested the local anti human trafficking unit in Kolkata might be a point to start with, Sam shook his head.

"I'm worried they may not follow up our suspicions. They're such a busy organisation. I think we should start right at the top." He took out his phone and brought up a website he had been looking at last night. He translated a sentence from the published report.

"'Too many times the laws and those enforcing them fail the victims, with a lack of protection for the victims. Some trafficking victims can remain in state-run shelters for years due to lengthy or non-existent repatriation methods.' We don't really want that, do we?"

"No, absolutely not." Suman was vehement in her agreement.

"Have you any thoughts about the CID, the Criminal Investigation Department?" suggested Geoff. "I've had dealings with them in Britain and in Europe, and found them excellent."

All ideas were discussed at length, but after three quarters of an hour, no decisions had yet been made. Finally, Sam put forward an idea with which everyone was in full agreement.

"I think that, before we do anything at all, I should speak to one of my brothers. He's a lawyer in Delhi, and I'm sure he'll be able to give us good advice about who to go to with all this information we've been given. I'll tell him it's urgent and that we can't sit on it for very long. I'm sure he'll help."

"Sam, that sounds brilliant." Suman smiled at him. "I didn't know you had brothers. What's his name?"

"Devesh. You'd like him; he's very well respected in his job. I'll do it tonight after work and, if it's not too late at night, I'll come visit you and tell you what he advises. You're sure that's okay for everybody?"

Assurance came from everyone.

"Okay. Well, I'll leave you just now and get back to work."

It was well after nine o'clock that night when Sam returned. Working late to catch up with some of his patients, he did not leave the hospital until eight, and then spent a good forty five minutes at home on the phone to his brother. He was hungry and tired, but he was keen to get back to Suman's apartment to let the others know how the phone call had gone.

Entering the flat, the delicious smell of food met his nostrils and his stomach rumbled. Geoff and Vada were sitting in the lounge, but the only person he saw was Suman, who appeared out of the kitchen holding a very tempting plate full of bhapaa aloo, a dish she knew he loved, made from pieces of potato tossed in panch phoron, coconut paste and mustard oil. He looked surprised.

Seeing this, Suman stopped. "You haven't already eaten, have you?"

"No. So that's for me? How did you know I wouldn't have eaten?"

"I knew you wouldn't have time to cook anything. Sit down and have this before you say a word."

"Ah, Suman, I love you." Embarrassed at what he had just said, he sat down hard on the chair she had pointed to and looked at her with a wry smile. "I love your cooking so much, especially when I'm so hungry."

She laughed at this, noticing his embarrassment and wondering about it.

"I knew you'd be hungry, but it's Ellie you should be declaring your love to. She cooked it, with just a tiny bit of instruction from me."

He lifted his head from the plate and shouted, "I love you, Ellie! Thank you so much."

"Love you too, Sam!" she shouted back from the kitchen.

He ate quickly, enjoying the chatter of the others. Geoff poured him a beer and joined him, relishing the thirst-quenching drink. Sometimes the heat of India was a bit much for him, and he often enjoyed a long glass of cold beer in the evenings.

Sam's meal was finished quickly, and the group joined him at the table to hear what he had to say about the phone call to his brother, hoping it was going to be good advice that they could take on board and get the job done. Suman in particular wanted to follow it right to the end, to try to get the traffickers arrested and stopped from carrying out their criminal activities, as well as prosecuted for the things they had done. Everyone listened carefully.

"I'll start with the good news," he began.

"My brother assures me that he would be glad to help us, and he's sure his firm will be interested in taking us on. Dev listened to the notes I took when speaking with Jan, and asked us not to do anything for the moment. He wants us to wait until he finds the right people to do the investigations and follow them through. He agrees we need to stop the traffickers in their tracks and then try to get them prosecuted, though he warned that's a rare event. It seems it's an extremely difficult road to go down, but well worth the effort if we're successful."

He paused for a moment to allow the others to ask questions, and then tried his best to answer them.

"Yes, Dev says he'd be happy to handle a lot of it personally. I know he lives in Delhi, but they have an office in Kolkata, with a good number of lawyers working here, so he can liaise with them. He needs to talk to his bosses to verify all this, but he's quite convinced they will be delighted to take it on. And yes, Jan will probably have to become their client, but that's a lot further down the line."

Suman was desperate to ask another question. "How soon will he be able to tell us which organisation we should contact to get it all investigated?"

"Dev knows the urgency and says he'll talk to his bosses tomorrow. We may not get all the answers we want straight away, but he'll get back to us tomorrow with an update. He'll at least tell us his bosses' reaction to it."

"And is there anything we can do in the meantime?"

"He implied our job was to keep Jan as safe as we possibly can, as she'll be the most important witness if the whole thing ever gets as far as court. And we've to try to get even more information from her, and to try to find Kali. I did tell him of our fears for Kali, so he warned we must keep ourselves safe. He's had experience of trying to bring traffickers to court before, and warns that they're usually extremely dangerous people."

"What are you thinking about all this, Suman?" He asked this because he had noticed her head down, her eyes miles away.

She looked up quickly. "I'm thinking that if we can stay safe whilst helping the police take this group of traffickers off the streets of Kolkata, it will be fantastic. It will also be great to have your brother, and maybe even his whole law firm, on our side. And I agree with what you say about Kali. I think we carry on looking for her, but don't take any chances. Does everyone else agree?"

There were nods and agreements all round.

Ellie spoke. "We certainly do agree, but the law firm will probably only be involved at a later date, once any arrests are made. At this moment, the first thing we need to do is get the right people to carry out the investigation.

If we botch it up at the start, it may not get anywhere at all, and we could just be putting ourselves at risk."

Sam assured them that he had raised the same point with his brother and that Dev understood the dangers they all could be in if it wasn't handled correctly. There was an awful lot more that his brother had said to him about these dangers and advice that had been given, but he felt he had said enough for now.

He knew it was going to be a difficult, uncertain road, risky for them all if anything went wrong. He also knew he was going to be there, at Suman's side, during the whole journey, no matter how long it took.

Chapter Thirty-One

LALIT GREAT EASTERN HOTEL, KOLKATA

It was Wednesday, two days before Geoff and Ellie were due to fly home. On the Tuesday, Yash Singh, Deputy Inspector General of Kolkata CID, had phoned to invite them all to a meeting with him and his associate, Detective Constable Arin Shan. These were the two names Dev had given Sam, assuring him they were trustworthy, honest members of the CID. The meeting was to be held the next day in a boardroom in the five-star Lalit Great Eastern Hotel in the city.

The five of them piled into Sam's car, Geoff in the front beside him, and Suman, Ellie and Vada squeezing into the back. It was with a certain amount of apprehension that they set off on the journey, all of them highly conscious of the seriousness of this meeting and the consequences should it not go well. Singh had asked if it would be possible to have Jan present at the meeting, but a call to the private clinic had informed Sam that she was not quite well enough to be taken out for the evening. However, the clinician he spoke to softened this blow by inviting Sam and the CID men to visit the clinic to speak to Jan in her room at any time over the next couple of days.

Upon arrival at the hotel, Sam's car was taken away to be parked and the group soon found themselves being ushered into a very smart boardroom on the fourteenth floor. Introducing themselves individually to the two men already there, they took their seats around the vast table, hoping against hope that these two policemen would be able to work magic and put an end to the trafficking empire built by Robert Gupta.

Pleasantries over and their glasses filled with water, the meeting began. Yash Singh took control, his colleague doing the note-taking. They began by explaining that they were acting on behalf of both the CID and the law firm, who were very interested in taking on any work that resulted from this meeting.

"I believe Devesh Nath is your brother, Dr Nath?" The Deputy Inspector General leaned forward in his seat and looked directly at Sam.

"Yes, my elder brother. Do you know him?"

Yash smiled. "I certainly do; we were at university together. Thankfully, we both survived the experience with each other's help and have stayed in touch ever since."

Sam returned his smile with a grin and felt a surge of optimism, confident now that they were speaking to someone who would help them. It wasn't long before they were all on first name terms and at ease, allowing the conversation to feel more like an informal chat than an interrogation.

Nevertheless, an interrogation it was, with every fact given by the group and every note that Sam had on his pad being recorded and discussed at length. The information Jan had given them about her husband was proving of great interest to the two CID men, and the questions were coming thick and fast.

It came as no surprise to any of them when Yash dropped into the conversation that Robert Gupta's two main businesses, the Reterron Apparel Company's factory in Bidhannagar and the Soohor Chemical and Textile Company, were currently under investigation by their staff and had been for some time. He also made it clear that the CID had long suspected that Robert was running a huge human trafficking racket and a drugs empire. Yash took the time to explain to them how he had never been able to get the necessary evidence to arrest the man. He outlined the intricacies and difficulties of producing a strong enough case against businesses like Robert's.

"Prosecutions for trafficking rarely happen in India," he explained. "It's much more likely that we can arrest them for several minor crimes, but, unfortunately, they pay their fines and carry on with their main criminal activities regardless. We need some infallible evidence to get them where we want them. And I'm beginning to believe you may have this evidence, given what you've already told us. Do you think Gupta's wife, Jan, would be willing to work with us, to give us the evidence and to stand up in court and testify against him?"

Suman answered this one. "Well, we don't really know her that well, but he's made one or two attempts on her life recently, and we know he's been subjecting her to physical abuse for many years. So I think that, with the right kind of support, and finding a way to keep her safe, she might well do it. It would be in her own interests to help you."

She paused and drew a breath before continuing.

"Also, as I mentioned earlier, there's a strong possibility that Robert has passed away and is no longer a threat to her. From what I saw, he was all but dead when his men took him from me. And from what Sam and Geoff overheard, they believe he could be dead, too."

Yash stroked his chin thoughtfully.

"Well, we'll certainly investigate that right away, and also try to find the whereabouts of Jan's friend, Kali Dutta. If she's alive, she sounds as if she'd be an excellent witness alongside Jan."

Ellie came into the conversation at this point.

"Will you be able to tell us the outcome of these investigations, Yash? It's very important for Jan to know if her husband is alive or dead before she attempts to go home. And it's vital that Suman knows she's safe to walk the streets and do her job at the hospital without having to watch her back. So, they both need to know if someone has taken Robert's place in the businesses to know if they're safe or if they should go into hiding when Jan comes out of hospital."

He nodded. "I understand. However, I'm going to have to speak to Jan myself and get my team to investigate her involvement in the business. I'd appreciate it if you didn't tell her this; it could hamper our investigation."

Each of the five responded with a nod.

"Then, yes, the answer to your question is that I am willing to tell you if we find out anything about Mr Gupta and Kali; you all need to know you're safe, too. You're very exposed at the moment, and I'm afraid you may be for some time to come, until we get our investigations going and possible arrests made. But that won't be overnight. Could I offer you some protection in the meantime? I could put you in a safe house for a spell."

Yash's last comment seemed to have stirred up quite a dilemma for the five, Geoff and Ellie explaining that they were returning home to the UK in two days' time, and Sam, Suman and Vada putting forward a strong argument that they needed to be in their posts at the hospital and could not afford to disappear, even for a short time.

Yash listened carefully to all their comments, finally suggesting that, instead of a safe house, he could put some of his plain-clothes men on surveillance of their homes and their work places. With slight reluctance, they agreed to this.

Yash leaned forward, his face solemn.

"This investigation is going to be a very serious one, and very thorough. It will most likely be dangerous, depending on what we find. But it would be a very pointless exercise if anything was to happen to any of you. You are all heavily involved as witnesses and very necessary to the whole investigation. And, with a lot of luck, will be needed at any legal proceedings we manage to take against the criminals."

He addressed Geoff and Ellie.

"My men will look after you for the next two days and, all being well, we'll allow you to return home to Scotland. However, we need your assurance that you'll remain in contact with us electronically, and that you will return at any time if we deem it necessary. This will most likely be if we manage to get to court. Can I have your guarantee on this?"

Geoff and Ellie agreed to this, and he continued. "We'll have statements written up from this meeting; personal statements which we'll need you to confirm are correct, and we'll get you to sign them. We'll do this before you go."

He then turned to Sam, Suman and Vada. "Okay. I understand your need to get back to your posts at the hospital. But, before you do, could I ask that you give me, say, five days, to get the investigation underway and to make some arrests if I possibly can? I think if I do this, it will be a whole lot safer for you to return to the hospital. I'll put security in place for Mrs Gupta, too. Would you agree to this?"

The three exchanged glances; five days seemed a long time to not be at work. Yet each realised the importance of staying safe and thinking about the safety of others in the hospital, too. Any threats or violence towards Sam, Suman or Vada whilst on duty could put their patients and colleagues in jeopardy as well.

As they debated the ins and outs of this and decided to agree in full to all of Yash's security arrangements, no-one around the boardroom table that evening could possibly have foreseen the unexpected and totally catastrophic happenings two days later.

Chapter Thirty-Two

KOLKATA

It was Sam who heard it first, on the local radio station. Sitting at lunch in his kitchen, he was only half aware that the music on the radio had stopped and the hourly news bulletin had begun. The newsreader was making the announcement in a level, expressionless voice, and Sam's ears did not pick anything up until the word 'Bidhannagar' was mentioned. At that he paused and sat very still to hear the rest of the announcement.

"The horrifying incident took place inside the factory itself," the voice intoned. "So far, eleven bodies have been recovered from the building, but this figure may rise. It's known that more than five hundred people are employed at the textile factory, and more than fifty percent of them were present at the time of the incident.

It appears from first reports that some type of fracas broke out in the rear of the building, with shots first being heard around ten this morning. Armed police were called out, arriving to find what they called 'a war zone'. Fire trucks also attended, two fires in the building having been reported by the staff. A mass evacuation of all workers took place and we are told they have been taken to one of the secondary schools in the area, closed at the moment due to school holidays. We have no information yet on any injuries incurred by the workers during the shootings or the fires.

The whole area has been cordoned off and police are requesting that people stay well away from the factory while they are conducting their inquiries into the shocking incidents."

The rest of the news was lost on Sam as he quickly rang Suman's mobile. She answered immediately.

"Suman, it's Sam. Have you heard the two o'clock news?"

"No, we don't have the radio or TV on. What's happened?"

"I think, although I'm not positive, that there's been some kind of shooting incident at the Reterron factory in Bidhannagar, Robert's factory, although the name of the factory wasn't mentioned in the report. I didn't catch it all, but there seems to have been fires there as well. Do you think I should call the CID and try to speak to Yash?"

"Yes, you should try, but if it is the Reterron factory, I imagine he'll be up to his ears in whatever's going on. When did it happen?"

"I think it must have been this morning. I didn't hear the beginning of the report, so I don't know the full story. I desperately want to get out of my flat and go and investigate to see what's happening."

She answered quickly. "No, you mustn't. You know we've been told to stay in our homes. I've got a security guy sitting outside my apartment. If you've got one too, ask him if he has any news, but please, don't leave the building."

"Okay, I won't leave. But I'll certainly speak to the guard outside and then I'll ring Yash. You never know, he might answer. I'll phone you back shortly. Are you all keeping safe?"

"Yes, we're all here. Vada is staying with us at the moment, until it's safe to go back to the nurses' home. Ellie and Geoff are just doing some packing for tomorrow. I'll go and switch on the radio so we don't miss the next bulletin. Keep me updated, Sam. And keep yourself safe."

Suman had no sooner switched off her phone than it rang again. This time it was Jan, calling from the clinic.

"Suman, something's happened at the factory. The staff here are all talking about it, but no one will tell me anything. Do you know what happened?"

"I've only just heard about it myself, and don't know any details. It seems to have been some kind of a shooting incident, and possibly a fire. The police are dealing with it. Don't go worrying about it until we find out more; it might be nothing much at all. How are you feeling?"

"I'm fine. I'm just worrying about Kali, not knowing where she is. They're talking about letting me out of here in a few days' time, but I've nowhere to go and I don't know if it's safe for me to go home. Can you ask Dr Nath to get in touch with me? And will you promise to let me know what's happening at the factory once you find out?"

"Yes, I will. Please don't worry."

Suman understood how on edge Jan was about this turn of events. She turned back into the room from the window to find Ellie, Geoff and Vada standing expectantly behind her. They had obviously overheard bits of the conversations she had just had, so she quickly brought them up to speed.

Ellie addressed Suman.

"We should stay a few more days. Something serious is obviously happening, and I don't want to leave you and

Vada on your own." Turning to Geoff, she asked, "Can we get our flights changed?"

He smiled. "Ellie, you haven't changed in all the years I've known you. If you get even a whiff of trouble, you want to be in the thick of it." As he said this, he put his arm around her shoulders and pulled her in close.

"That's a yes, then," she said to the others with a smile. "So, if Suman allows us to stay here, we can try to postpone our flights. What do you say, Su? It's your decision."

"Well, just get on that phone as quickly as you can and get your flights changed!" She grinned as she turned to Ellie to add, "That was a daft question to ask me when you already knew the answer."

Later in the afternoon, settled down on the sofas with their chai, they listened to the four o'clock news. The last report, at three, had told them nothing new except to verify that it was indeed the Reterron factory where the incident had happened. They had hoped the next report, at four, would contain some new information, but were disappointed. The report was almost word for word the same as the previous one. Suman had tried a couple of times to get Sam on the phone, but had been unsuccessful.

He's so frustrating, she thought. *He must know I'm worrying about him; the least he could do is answer his phone.*

As if she had read Suman's thoughts, Ellie leaned over. "He'll call as soon as he's got any news. Don't worry."

However, it wasn't until nearly seven o'clock in the evening that Suman received the call she'd been desperately waiting for. She answered it on its second ring.

"Sam, are you okay? Do you have any news?"

"Yes to both questions. But, can I come over to see you? And before you say I'm not allowed out, I've been given permission to visit you. My guard is going to bring me over in his car. There's quite a lot to tell you."

"We'll see you shortly, then."

Within twenty minutes, the doorbell rang and Vada rushed to answer it, letting Sam in with a hug.

"We're so pleased to see you, Sam. Suman's been climbing the walls worrying about you."

"Has she?" he asked, delighted by Vada's comment. "No need. I'm quite safe."

Handed a coffee as he came into the lounge, he was soon sitting down, surrounded by four eager faces, all desperate to hear the latest news. He certainly had a lot to tell, and began by explaining that Yash had phoned him in the early afternoon, requesting his help at the factory. Apparently they needed a doctor to attend to one of the injured, someone who had refused help from all the police doctors.

"Who was it?" Suman asked.

"It was a woman called Kali," he announced. "She was adamant she wouldn't let any doctor near her except Dr Nath from the Sister Irene."

"Kali?" asked Vada. "Jan's friend, Kali?"

"Yes. They found her locked up in one of the rooms in the factory, beaten about a bit, but alive and kicking. She's one feisty lady. I had to dress her wounds and stitch her up a bit. She demanded food and water from the police, saying that she had been practically starved to death while she'd been locked up and that, if they wanted her to help with their enquiries, they would have to feed her. So they sent out for sandwiches!" He laughed.

"When they got her calmed down a bit, she asked what had been happening, having heard all the gunshots and the sirens from the fire engines."

"Must have been scary for her," Vada said.

"She's a really strong lady. When Yash asked if she could help him by identifying some of the people who had been killed and the ones who were injured, she said yes straight away. And volunteered to tell him all about the set-up; who did what in the businesses and things like that. Yash thinks he's got another great witness if this all gets to trial."

"So did you stay around while she identified people?" Suman was curious to know.

"I did. I got the job of helping the police doctors to examine the bodies, basically to confirm death and any obvious cause of death if there was one, and a rough timing of when death occurred. All very informal; it was just as a favour to Yash to help with his investigation of the scene. The coroners and the forensic guys will all do the official work. They arrived before I left."

Geoff asked the question everyone was wanting to ask.

"So, who was killed? Can you give us any names, or tell us anything about them? Why were they all fighting and killing each other?"

"I can tell you some of the people Kali identified and how they died. But you've got to remember, this is all highly confidential at the moment. I did ask Yash if it would be all right to tell you the names and he agreed I could, but said I had to stress how hush-hush it all was."

"We understand this, Sam." Geoff said quietly. "We'll keep it all quiet until it becomes public knowledge."

"Thanks, Geoff." He looked at everyone in turn before beginning.

"Well, I'm sure it'll be no surprise that one of the bodies was the British man, Robert. And, like you thought, Suman, he didn't die of bullet wounds or any injuries. It was clear the man had suffered a massive stroke, and I'm sure the pathologists will find his heart just gave out."

Suman nodded. "Yes, I thought so. I'd noticed he was really short of breath before it all happened."

"Another body Kali identified was her own husband, a guy called Asheesh Dutta, if I remember right. He'd been shot in the stomach."

"How did she cope with finding her own husband dead?"

He looked over at Suman to answer her question. "Surprisingly well. She told Yash that Asheesh had been Gupta's right-hand man, and also that he'd been in the group that had locked her in the room. She thought he was going to allow them to kill her. They'd been interrogating her to find out where Jan was and he had stood back and watched as they tried to beat it out of her. So I don't think she was feeling as upset as she might have been, finding out he'd been shot.

Kali identified a few more of the bodies, all men who were part of the main trafficking team. Some of them had bad injuries consistent with fighting, and they all had bullet wounds. Strangely, they found only two guns at the scene, but these hadn't been used."

"So, they're thinking the ones who did the shooting have escaped?" Geoff asked.

"I'm not sure what they're thinking, but that's certainly what I thought. Hopefully, once all the evidence is gathered they'll know the answer to that."

Geoff asked another question. "What about all the people working in the factory and who caused the fires? Did you find out anything about them?"

"The people in the factory were taken away, presumably to somewhere safe. I think it was to a school building. Yash told me there was a huge number of youngsters working in the factory, some as young as six. And from what I overheard, the police are certain that most of the workers were all trafficked victims and were being forced to work in the factory. I heard them mention bonded labour. Let's hope they all get freed now and get to go home. I got no information on the fires and saw no sign of the damage. There was only a strong smell of smoke hanging about."

Suman asked, "So, what were the reasons for all the shooting and fighting?"

"It's just speculation at the moment, but the police seem to think that once Gupta died, the men were fighting to see who was going to take his place as head of the organisation. Kali agreed with this, saying that there was always unrest amongst the men; Robert seems to have been a pretty unpopular boss."

Suman sighed. "A bit of a sadist, as far as I could see. Are we allowed to pass any of this information on to Jan? She has the right to know that Robert's dead."

"I agree, but we should wait for permission before we tell her. Yash is going to attend to all that. Kali was badgering him about visiting Jan, and he's going to take her to the clinic in due course. Once he's been there and spoken to Jan, then we can visit, before she gets discharged."

Ellie sighed. "Well, let's hope life gets a lot better for her when she comes out of the clinic. Poor lady."

She turned to Geoff.

"Bet you're glad now that we changed our flights, eh? We'd have missed all this."

Geoff shook his head, looking around the room. "What did I tell you? Any kind of trouble and she's got to be in the thick of it!"

Ellie got her wish and was most certainly 'in the thick of it' for the next few days, as more and more information came out about the shootings. However, within a week, their flights had been re-booked and, with reluctance, she and Geoff had to say goodbye to everyone and wend their way home to Scotland, where the wind, rain and a hint of snow met them as they descended from the plane in Edinburgh.

"Back to auld claes and parritch, Geoff. I'm going to miss them so much, and the sun too!" she complained on the drive home.

"Oh, I wouldn't worry too much. I think we'll be back again before you know it, either for the trial, or maybe even for a wedding?"

She perked up quickly. "A wedding? So you think that's going to happen too, do you?"

"Oh," he replied, "I'd put my money on it."

Ellie grinned. "Me too!"

However, five thousand miles away, in the heat of Kolkata, nothing was further from the minds of Suman and Sam. Life at the busy hospital carried on as normal, and the doctors, badly missed during their recent time off, were in great demand for surgeries, clinics and ward rounds. A new intake of students had just arrived, and they found their time taken up with new teaching duties as well.

So it was back to auld claes and parritch for them, too!

Chapter Thirty-Three

SISTER IRENE MERCY HOSPITAL, KOLKATA
SIX MONTHS LATER

The children's clinic was bustling all morning, and Suman gladly accepted the coffee she was handed after the last patient had disappeared. She sat down at her desk, a huge pile of medical files in front of her, all waiting to be updated with the morning's activities before she could start her rounds on the children's wards. She sighed and, opening the first file, turned to her computer.

Just over an hour later, she was done and the last files were back in the cupboard. As she turned the lock and pocketed the key, there was a light knock on the door.

"Come in," she called. The door opened and a very pregnant lady entered.

"Are you busy? Have you time for a chat?"

"Jan, how lovely to see you! Come and sit down. I've always got time for a chat. You're looking well, in fact, I'd say you're glowing."

Jan laughed as she waddled over to the chair and lowered herself into it. "That glow is probably just sweat. I'm exhausted, and this heat is too much for me. The sooner the monsoons begin, the better, and the sooner this baby comes, the better, too."

"Yes, you've got quite a bump there. When's baby due?"

"My due date is next Friday, so it could be any time. I've just been at the antenatal clinic and they're very pleased with me. So, apart from the heat, everything's going well. But I wanted to have a chat with you before this little girl appears."

"Sure. What's bothering you?"

"Well, you know how nervous I am about having the baby, so I wondered ... Is it possible, could you maybe deliver my baby for me? Or even just be with the midwife during the delivery?"

"Gosh, I'm very flattered, but that's not my job, Jan." She watched the disappointment on Jan's face and relented.

"However," she began with a smile. "I'll most certainly try to pop in and see you. I can't interfere with what the experts are doing. I'll just come and hold your hand for a short time. How would that be?"

"That would be wonderful. Kali's going to be my official birthing partner, but only if the baby comes during the day." Jan laughed. "She says she can't stay up all night, not even for me. But I'm happy with that. Thank you, Suman. I'm going to be far more relaxed knowing you're there with me, even some of the time."

"You've got my number. Just keep me updated when it all kicks off and I'll come and find you in Maternity. Otherwise, how are things going for you? Are you still living in your own house?"

"Yes, I'm still there. There's been a lot happening lately with the lawyers. Mr Nath's firm is looking after me, as you know, and they gave me some great news a couple of weeks ago. Turns out I was officially married! The paperwork has all been accepted by the courts, so this means I wasn't 'living in sin' after all. And I fall heir to some of the things Robert left. I'm his next of kin; would you believe it?"

"How on earth did that happen? You always said you weren't married, you were only his living partner. So how come you're married and didn't know it?"

"Well, amongst all the documents the police found in our house, they came across a marriage certificate. I had actually signed it, not knowing what it was. The lawyers have had it confirmed by the courts that the certificate is legal, and this has now been finalised. Robert apparently did it so that he could have money in my name and not pay taxes on it. So I really am Mrs Gupta."

She slipped her feet out from below her sari and removed her sandals, proudly showing Suman a matching pair of silver toe rings, one on each foot.

"See, I've got my bicchiyas on and they won't be coming off again. And not only am I legally a widow, I've been told I can live in Robert's house until the lawyers sort it all out, which could take years. Kali offered to take me in to live with her, but she's not going to enjoy having a baby waken her in the middle of the night for weeks on end. So, as I've nowhere else to go, I've decided to try to be strong and live in my own house for the time being. My cook has come back and is helping me change things inside the house, to take away bad memories. You know, out with the old and in with the new. She'll help me with the baby, too."

"What about money, Jan? Are you going to have enough to live on? It's a big house to keep up."

"Yes, I know. It was a really unhappy house as well, but we'll change all that, me and Cook and the baby." She hesitated for a moment. "Cook's become a friend and I call her Mrs. Basak now. She tells me that makes her sound much more respectable." She laughed. "Just like me!"

"And as far as money goes, they've taken the bulk of Robert's funds and investments away as proceeds of crime, but there were some shares and things in my name only. So I've got a tiny income coming in. We can get by on that. We don't need much. If we fall short, I can sell some of my jewellery and clothes, or take up sewing, and I might even sell some of the furniture." She giggled. "Anything he sat on will be first to go!"

She paused, deep in thought for a moment.

"You know, I signed so many bits of paper without knowing what they were. I certainly hadn't a clue I owned anything. If they can't prove the investment money in my name came from his crime activities, I'll get to keep it, although this is not too likely. Mr Nath says not to count on anything, but I'm not worried. I don't want to benefit from his dirty money anyway. I'll cope."

Suman leaned forward to clasp her hands. "I'm so happy for you. To have a place to stay and money in your purse is a gift that you deserve, for all you've been through. And you'll have a home for your baby when she comes. Have you got a name for her?"

"With your permission, I'd like to call her Su, after you. I've heard Dr Nath call you that several times and I'd love my baby to have your name. You've done so much for me. Would it be okay with you?"

"I'd be very honoured. And is she to have some middle names?"

"She'll be Su Lakshmi Sunny Gupta. Lakshmi after my mother and Sunny after little Sunita. I've kept my promise to you and been staying in touch with Sunny and her mother since she went home, and she's doing well. Her mother is delighted to have her home and she and I have become friends."

Suman was extremely surprised but happy to hear this bit of news, as she had agonised over little Sunny's future once the child had recovered from all her injuries. Persuaded, against her wishes, to approach the authorities about taking Sunny into one of the children's shelters for young victims of trafficking, she and Jan had visited the shelter which had been suggested. Unsurprisingly, after the visit they were in agreement. Neither she nor Jan wanted to put Sunny in there, both worrying about the lack of care and support for the girls who were already living there.

Sunny, when ready to be discharged from hospital, was still in the final stages of recovery, and Suman realised that neither her physical nor her mental needs would be addressed in the shelter. There was a lack of funding, the head of the shelter told her, and Suman could see for herself the effects of this. The place was badly run down, short of staff and, although the resident girls looked happy enough, she could see signs of malnutrition amongst some of them, with one small child displaying symptoms of rickets. In general, the girls looked unkempt, their hair uncombed and matted.

It was Jan herself who solved the problem, offering to take Sunny to live with her again, this time not as a servant in the house, but as a much-loved child needing care and attention. Jan knew she owed this kind-hearted little girl a great debt and was happy to have a chance to try to repay some of her kindness. So, Sunny was instead given into her welcoming hands and taken home to Jan's to be looked after.

However, when Sunny first arrived back, the child's instinct was to work for Jan and try to look after her as she had done previously. As a result, Jan's conscience became riddled with guilt over her treatment of both Sunny and Habi and all the girls who had come before them. She felt ashamed and desperately wanted to find a way to atone for her behaviour. Not sure how she could do this, she decided a little cosy chat with Sunny was needed.

On Mrs Basak's next day off, she and Sunny were in the kitchen preparing some spring rolls for their lunch, which they were going to eat in the park nearby. Amidst the chaos and the fun they were having, she began to question her little charge.

"Do you like helping me in the kitchen, Sunny?"

Sunny stopped what she was doing.

"Am I doing it wrong?"

"No, Sunny. Not at all. But you know that you don't have to do anything at all for me now, right? You're living with me as my friend, so that I can now look after you. So you must tell me what you like to do and what you don't. Is that a deal?"

Sunny grinned. "That's a deal."

"And you know, Diwali is almost here, and I'd like to give you something to celebrate it. If you could have anything in the world, anything at all, what would you choose?"

Sunny's eyes were like saucers. "Anything?"

Jan laughed. "Well, anything I can afford to give you. What would you wish for if a fairy godmother gave you one wish?"

The child's face became serious as she began to consider what she would like. Within moments, her answer came. "If I could have anything I wanted in the world, I would want to see my Amma again. And my sisters."

Jan's heart took a plunge, realising this child knew the same loneliness that she herself had experienced at certain times in her life. That afternoon, she made a number of phone calls and was delighted when she managed to engage the services of a private investigator to try to trace the child's family. It took many weeks, but using the scant information the little girl had been able to recall, the investigator finally gave them the news they had been hoping for. Sunny's family had been found and were longing to have their daughter home. Jan, by this time eight months pregnant, told Sunny at once, throwing open her arms as the child flung herself into them.

Jan, accompanied by Kali, took Sunny home and was taken aback by the warmth of the welcome they received from her family, and the love the child showed for Jan when their parting finally came.

Jan shed tears in the taxi on the way home. She resolved to be the absolute best parent she could ever be to the child she was carrying.

Reminiscences over, Jan took her leave of Suman at last. Now very late for her rounds, Suman scurried about, locking up her files for the day and hurrying out of her office, resigned to the fact that she would be working at the hospital until a late hour that night to catch up on all the duties she had been neglecting.

Unknown to them both, another late night was just around the corner for Suman, as the call from Jan came in just four days later. She had been taken into the maternity department in the morning, having begun her labour pains during the night. Suman visited not long after she got the message, but could see that Jan still had a long labour to go through before the birth, so she left her to the expert care of the midwives at the Sister Irene. She promised Jan she would return in plenty of time for the birth, but it wasn't until nearly eight o'clock in the evening that the labour ward phoned to say Mrs Gupta was in the final stages of labour. Suman made it just in time to see little Su make her appearance, and Jan gave birth to her daughter whilst holding Suman's hand. Kali, acting as the birthing partner, was given the huge privilege of performing the ritual that the baby's father would normally have undertaken at the birth.

Deciding who was to perform the Jatakarma ceremony had worried Jan, since she had no husband to do it. With no other male relatives to ask, Jan had approached Sam to see if he would carry out the ceremony.

Sam had declined as tactfully as he possibly could, feeling he was not close enough to Jan and her baby to do this, but had suggested Kali as an alternative. Once he had convinced her that Shiva would not mind the ritual being carried out by a woman as long as that woman was a good person, Jan issued the invitation to her friend, who was thrilled to accept.

With baby Su in her arms, all cleaned and bathed, Kali sat on a chair and placed Su on her lap. With her little finger, she scooped up some ghee and honey from a bowl held out by Suman and placed a tiny amount in the baby's mouth. Su's hearty cries ceased immediately, and she seemed to relish the taste of the mixture.

As everyone laughed at the tiny baby's contented face, Kali leaned forward and spoke the name of Shiva into the soft little ear, followed by a whispered prayer, asking him for protection for the little infant on her lap.

The people present were silent as they listened to Kali performing this ritual, and there was not a dry eye in the room. The atmosphere of happiness was palpable. To be present at this moving ceremony was a rare occurrence for Suman, and to be experiencing all these emotions was also rare for her, her doctor's stoicism normally coming to the fore. She surprised herself, taken aback at how suddenly she felt a deep, deep longing within her to hold a baby of her own.

She stood up and moved back from the side of Jan's bed, using both hands to brush away the tears from her cheeks. Congratulations, kisses and hugs had to be delivered, and once she had fulfilled this obligation, she quietly slipped away to hurry back to her own room in the paediatric department.

Closing the door of her office, she began to explore these feelings she was having. *No point in thinking about it*, she told herself multiple times, *it's not going to happen*. By the time she had tidied away all the files lying about the room, locked her cupboards and her office door, she was sure she had put the whole thing to the very back of her mind.

It was back to business as usual, and she was almost relieved to hear her pager ring in her pocket. Looking at it, she saw that she was needed at Accident & Emergency, a child in a traffic accident having been brought in. Her steps quickened as she made her way over to A&E, her thoughts now on the job at hand. This was the job that she had always wanted to do, she told herself sternly, the only job she would ever want to do. She was married to her job, and loved it dearly. This was her baby.

Chapter Thirty-Four

KOLKATA, JULY

The monsoon thunderstorms had begun very soon after little Su's birth, giving some relief from the sweltering heat of the season. It was July, and devastating flash floods arrived with the thunderstorms, fast and furious, destroying a number of homes in rural Bengal and washing away many crops in the farming areas.

The monsoon season often brought many landslides, this year being no exception, and Suman heard on the news about recurring landslides happening at Dhapa. She visited Bimla and her family to check that everyone was safe, and was relieved to find them all well and thriving. Bimla's crops were actually benefiting from the rain, with Bimla busy replenishing all her water reservoirs and collection tanks. After a bit of research, she had started growing jasmine to sell at the local markets alongside her other crops. Delighted to see how popular it was, she had taken on the task of uprooting some of her other crops and planting more jasmine in their place.

In early September, with no sign of the rain stopping and no sign of any legal proceedings beginning, Suman took some more time off work and decided to make the promised visit to Maharashtra to visit her mother, her siblings and their families. She phoned her brother Hira.

"I'm coming next week, on Monday," she told him. "Can you pick me up?" Arrangements were made, but thankfully she had not yet reserved her seat on the plane when Vada arrived for a visit.

"You can't go without me!" Vada was adamant. "I've just finished the last round of my exams for now and I can easily get time off. How long are you going for?"

"I thought maybe two weeks. I want to spend a lot of time with Ai. I miss her so much."

"I do too, Suman. Please, please, just go for ten days and take me with you. I can get ten days off."

Suman wasn't immune to her sister's pleas and the flights for the two of them were booked instantly on Suman's computer. Lots of planning and shopping ensued until the time came for the visit. Hira and Kanya were both at the airport to meet them, and the two sisters spent a very hectic but most enjoyable ten days with the rest of their family.

However, by the end of the ten-day break, Suman was experiencing a type of homesickness, and was more than ready to return to Kolkata. She said nothing to Vada, but was surprised to find herself longing for the huge city, aptly named the City of Joy. She was also missing the hustle and bustle of her daily life and her work at the hospital, her colleagues and her friends. However, most of all, she found herself with a deep yearning for a certain Dr Sami Nath, who had slowly but surely become an essential part of her life.

Things weren't the same when he wasn't there, she decided. This time apart seemed to have made her own up to herself that the very strong feeling of friendship she thought she had for him had deepened into something much, much more. She knew without a doubt that it wasn't her apartment she was missing, it was Sam. Not that she knew what to do with this feeling.

It was there in her mind during all the telephone conversations she had with him while she was away, which happened regularly. Having time on her hands, she began to question the nature of this close relationship, knowing that this was not something she ever expected to happen in her life. Indeed, it was not something she had thought she wanted to happen in her life.

Yet it was in her thoughts constantly, popping up at strange times during the day, and always at night. Every night. She went to bed in Hira's home with it filling her head, and tried unsuccessfully to suppress her thoughts, her feelings, and get to sleep. On the nights when sleep totally eluded her, she began to try to rationalise it all.

If we acknowledge we're in a close relationship, where would that lead? Do I want anything more? If we kiss, will this lead to more? Do I want to kiss him, do I want anything more than kissing?

As she asked herself these questions, her memory became her enemy. She was immediately back to her childhood, to Mumbai and Amsterdam, when her days were filled with abuse, pain and horror. Those were the days when she vowed that, if she ever managed to get away, she would never, ever again allow any man to violate her body in any way.

Forcing herself back to the present time, she rationalised that Sam, her beloved friend, was so far removed from those who had badly hurt her that there was no point in comparing him to them.

So she tried to suppress those memories and listen to her current desires. What did she want? She wanted Sam.

She wanted marriage. *Wow*, she thought, *that's the first time I've admitted that!* She only wanted a marriage to Sam, though, not anyone else. What about babies? Did she want that?

That was when it became tricky. At the age of nine, in Scotland, Ellie had taken her to a doctor to assess the damage that had been done to her. Suman remembered Dr Joan's words clearly.

"Whilst I'm hopeful that her ability to carry a child one day has been unimpaired, I can't promise this," the doctor had said.

So maybe no biological babies for me, she thought. *Can I live with that and could Sam?* She'd better explain this to him before going any further with the relationship. What if she lost him over this? Unthinkable. But she had to tell him; she couldn't do anything else.

And so her sleepless nights and endless thoughts continued in amongst the happiness of being with her mother and her family, until the day arrived when they had to pack their bags to return to Kolkata.

She and Vada flew home on a wet Monday afternoon, disembarking the plane to discover Sam standing at the end of the barrier waiting for them, proudly holding a sign which she suspected had her name on it. She waved and smiled, so happy to see him but puzzled by the sign. It wasn't until they drew nearer that Suman could read the words, 'Dr Suman Sudra, a bonnie wee Scots lassie'.

She laughed out loud, as did Vada when Suman translated it for her. She was shaking her head as they rounded the barrier to reach him, allowing him to bestow a warm hug on each of them before querying, "A bonnie wee Scots lassie? Really?"

Taking hold of the trolley, he replied with a grin. "I knew you'd like it. In fact, while you were away, I spent a lot of time teaching myself some braw Scottish words and phrases, just for you. I thought I'd be able to have a good blether with you when you came back."

Stifling her laughter, she leaned in close to his face, their eyes meeting and holding in an intense stare for a good few seconds. Her reply broke the intensity as she said with an enormous grin, "*Did* you, now?"

He continued. "Oh, yes, and I learned some Scottish songs as well. I can sing you a brilliant rendition of 'Will Ye No Come Back Again'. Would you like to hear it?"

They were now walking with the trolley in the midst of the crowds headed for the doors, Suman on his left and Vada on his right. Without missing a step, she replied, "I certainly would. Sing away!"

At this, Vada leaned forward to look at her sister, whose eyes were alight with amusement. She glanced over at Sam, too, all her instincts telling her that, somehow, a major change had occurred in their friendship. She could feel the electricity sparking between the pair of them. She watched closely, surprised and delighted when Sam opened his mouth and began to sing. It was no surprise, however, when Suman leaned over and put her hand over his mouth.

Vada kept watching, knowing that something was going to happen. Her surprise turned immediately to delight as he took hold of Suman's hand, abandoned the trolley and turned round to take her sister in his arms and plant a deep, passionate kiss on her lips. The delight turned to embarrassment when she realised just how long they were going to stand there kissing, however. She described it later as 'almost devouring each other'.

All Vada could do at this point was take hold of the trolley and walk away from this extremely embarrassing couple.

Chapter Thirty-Five

KOLKATA, EIGHT MONTHS LATER

The trial hit the headlines in the national news, on the television and in many local newspapers. It was billed to be a sensation; the biggest trial of its kind, with nineteen traffickers in the dock and over seven hundred rescued victims, a good number of whom were to be called to court to testify.

The evidence was strong, with the witnesses prepped and ready to tell their stories. This was going to change the fate of men and women earning money from modern slavery and debt bondage throughout India and it would surely set a precedent for things to come. India would be a safer place for young girls, women, children, the poor and the elderly.

Devesh warned them not to believe what they read in the papers. He told them it was just sensationalism. Sensational news made phenomenal sales in newspapers, he said, but rarely did this kind of court case live up to the hype created by reporters.

With the main players in this particular trafficking empire all having been annihilated during the shooting, it was left to the lesser underlings in the business to take responsibility for the misdeeds. All of India watched the news eagerly, avidly waiting for the guilty pleas and the sentencing.

They were disappointed, of course. Although not completely. Out of the nineteen accused, fifteen men were sentenced on the lesser charge of possessing firearms or ammunition with no licences. Another two were found guilty of breaching the public peace under the Indian Penal Code, at this moment in time considered to be only a misdemeanour criminal offence. So none of them received a prison sentence. They were forced to pay the grand sum of twenty thousand rupees for their crimes, not a lot to these men who had made so much money from trafficking, but a high price to many people reading the report of the trial.

The last two men, proved to have been working at a higher level within the organisation, received sentences of two years imprisonment each. Their crime was that of 'employment of children under fourteen years of age'. The drugs empire being run by the same organisation never reached the news and was never mentioned at the trial. All other crimes being committed by Robert Gupta's empire, like the trafficking of children and adults, also failed to make it to trial.

Sam, Suman and Vada never received their day in court as witnesses, not being called upon to testify, although they were there in the viewing gallery as Kali and Jan gave evidence in the 'employment of children under fourteen years of age' cases. Ellie and Geoff didn't even get a trip to Kolkata out of it, not being needed in court either, much to Ellie's severe disappointment. She had to make do with faithfully following the reports of the trial in the Indian newspapers published online, plus Suman's daily phone calls.

Eventually, the sensational news prior to and during the trial slowly became yesterday's news, and the furore they had caused died away over time as other headlines took their place. In the Sister Irene Mercy Government Hospital, the gossip about the trial was quickly overshadowed by another piece of news that began to spread like wildfire amongst the staff. The story began one Monday morning, when many of the workers in the hospital arrived to find a very smart, gold-rimmed invitation card in their inboxes, on their desks, or tucked into the side of their lockers in the staff rooms. This invitation brought many squeals of delight, many surprised laughs and many comments of, 'I told you so.'

Around three hundred people replied positively to this invitation, and the hospital began to buzz with excitement as the Saturday of the wedding approached. On the Thursday evening prior to the main event, an intimate dinner took place, with only close family and friends present. The Ganesh Puja was held in Sam's garden, where a marquee adorned with lights, lanterns and flowers was erected. The guests for this important pre-runner to the marriage had been chosen carefully, Suman adamant that everyone she loved should be present. Kanya, as guest of honour, was in charge of the proceedings, surrounded by all of her children and grandchildren, with Vada looking exceptionally pretty in a beautiful, delicate yellow sari trimmed with gold. Sam's family was there in force as well, happy that, at last, they were gaining a daughter-in-law, and a beautiful one at that!

Ellie and Geoff, along with their son Hamish and Suman's Scottish granny, Evelyn, had arrived earlier in the week and spent several days helping with the preparations and shopping. That night, Ellie looked radiant in a new, vibrant blue silk Punjabi suit, her long blonde hair plaited down her back and adorned with flowers, attracting many admiring glances. Suman's young Scottish brother was also attracting glances. Now grown up into a tall teenager with Geoff's dark good looks, Hamish was a handsome young man.

Also part of the Scottish group was Sara, Ellie's best friend, who had been a huge part of Suman's life in Edinburgh. Out in Amsterdam, Sara was by Ellie's side during the rescue of nine-year-old Suman from her traffickers. Suman knew that she was alive today because of these two women and was looking forward to Sara getting to know the man she was going to marry.

Although Sam was well known in hospital circles as being the best-looking doctor on the staff, his ornate kurta was put slightly in the shade by his dazzling fiancée, wearing a stunning, white linen Anarkali dress which reached down almost to her feet. Simple and unadorned at the top, the dress had tulip layers on the skirt, showing off Suman's slim figure beautifully. The first time he caught a glimpse of her that evening, Sam couldn't help but compliment her.

Clasping her hand tightly, he leaned in to whisper, "You look like a flower nymph."

She giggled. "And you look as if you're in your pyjamas, going to bed."

"Oh," he replied with a grin, "this is my wedding kurta. You'll have to wait 'till Saturday to see me in my new pyjamas."

Kanya took charge then, asking everyone to take their seats, ready for the offering of prayers and holy songs to the god, Ganesh. Traditionally performed by the bride's parents, Suman had asked Hira to stand alongside their mother for this ritual, a task he was proud to perform. Geoff, as a non-Hindu, was asked to lay flowers and fruit in front of the god, Ganesh, part of the ritual. The moving ceremony was a beautiful occasion and was followed by a delicious meal for everyone, and then some dancing and socialising well into the night, to allow the two families to become better acquainted.

The next day, there was another event, with many more guests present, the Grah Shanti, when a Manoru ceremony took place, with gifts of fruit, flowers, sugar, coconut and rice offered to the gods, all provided by the groom's father. Wedding gifts were also presented to the couple, who were seated on palatial chairs on the stage, and, as the day before, a delicious meal for everyone was followed by the Sangeet, another party with music and dancing, Bollywood style at Suman's request.

Saturday dawned at last, and preparations for the most important ceremony of all, the marriage, began around nine in the morning, with the Mehndi ceremony. Suman's first job was to welcome in her home the artist who would decorate her with mehndi for her wedding, a tradition stretching back hundreds of years. All the women in the family were present, to be tattooed with the black henna designs of peacocks, flowers, mandala patterns and paisley motifs traditional at Hindu weddings. The marriage ceremony, later in the day, began with the arrival of Sam, resplendent in his gold sherwani, a highly embellished tunic and coat worn over gold churidar pants. To Suman's delight and huge amusement, he arrived on the back of a tall, very skittish white horse, surrounded by his brothers and close friends on foot, all making quite a din, banging drums and tooting horns, the reason for the horse's skittishness.

Suman's amusement dissolved into full-scale laughter as the horse, getting more nervous as they approached the marquee, began to kick up his heels and rear up, almost unseating Sam. As he grabbed the horse tightly around the neck, Devesh took control and pulled on the reins, bringing the horse back gently to a standing position. With massive relief, Sam slid off the horse, having to then endure his brothers' and friends' bawdy comments and thumps on the back. He took it all in his stride, enjoying the fun of it all, and eventually joined Suman with a huge grin on his face.

Dressed in an exquisite red silk sari, Suman's hair was flowing down her back in glossy curls with flowers twisted through them. Dangling down from her parting on to her forehead was a large red jewel encrusted with diamonds. Long gold earrings fell from her ears, matching the gold jewellery around her neck and on her wrists.

She saw Sam looking at her in admiration and touched the necklace around her neck.

"Isn't it beautiful? My jewellery was a gift from your mother. She is so kind."

He nodded, about to tell her it was her beauty he was looking at, when Kanya interrupted to take them inside for the Tilak ceremony, a marriage rite where she applied three dark charcoal lines to her future son-in-law's forehead. On her daughter's forehead she placed a dot of scarlet vermilion powder, the sign that she was about to be a married lady. Ellie took over from there, leading them both by the hand into the circle where the priest sat waiting. She then placed Suman's hand in Sam's, signifying giving her into his keeping, before returning to her seat beside Kanya.

Ellie sat down with a huge lump in her throat, finding it hard to keep back her tears as she watched her beloved Suman being married to the man she loved. At the end of their seven vows and seven circles, the cheers of joy from the crowd brought the tears out in earnest.

All ceremonies over, the couple could relax at last and begin to mingle with the huge crowd of guests. Spotting some special people standing a little way off, Suman sped over to them.

"Daivey, Bimla," she said as she hugged them tight. "I'm so happy to see you. Thank you for coming." She looked around. "Where are Raja and Habi?"

Bimla laughed and pointed. "Over there. They spotted the food being brought out and went to see what they were going to eat. I'm sorry about that. They've got bottomless stomachs."

Suman laughed too. By this time, Habi and Raja had spotted her with Bimla and raced over, Habi shouting her name all the way. The little girl hurtled herself into Suman's arms and received a number of kisses. Raja, much shyer, waited until she had put Habi down and held out his hand to shake Suman's.

"Congratulations," he managed to say before he too, was engulfed in Suman's arms and given a huge hug.

Habi was pulling on Suman's sari. "You look just like a film star," she whispered into Suman's ear. "Do you like my new dress? Bimla took me shopping and bought me this beautiful dress, new, from a big shop."

"I love it. It's you that looks like a film star. And so does Bimla. You're both film stars."

Suman stayed with the little family for another five minutes, managing to get a chat with Daivey, looking very smart in his new trousers and jacket.

"How's business, Daivey? Is it going well?"

"It is, but I have to go to school every day, so I can't get to Dhapa as often as I did. I'm in secondary school now, and the teachers insist I attend. And I do enjoy it. I'm learning an awful lot."

"Daivey, I'm so pleased you're doing that. When you get qualifications at school, you'll be able to run your business even better than before, or you might choose to work in another job. I'm very proud of you."

Several hugs later, she said farewell to the happy little family as they went to get their food. Across the room, guests were beginning to get themselves seated and queues were starting to form at the buffet tables. Halfway along the queue she noticed another little girl she had become extremely fond of, and got the same kind of welcome from Sunny that she had from Habi. Cuddles and kisses were exchanged with Sunny, now fully recovered from all her injuries and looking a perfect picture in her new pink dress and matching headband.

Above Sunny's head, Suman's eyes met Jan's and she smiled. *What a transformation!* she thought. Dressed in a deep turquoise sari with diamonds around her neck, Jan looked every inch a confident, successful woman. The tiny girl perched on her hip was just as beautiful as her mother, with her big, dark eyes intently watching Suman.

"Hello, Su." Suman leaned forward to plant a little kiss on the infant's cheek. The child's smile appeared as she held out her arms, wanting to go to Suman, and Jan happily handed over her daughter. Sunny, by this time, had run off to play with a group of children who were charging around the marquee and making as much noise as they could.

Suman and Jan laughed at their antics while little Su tried very hard to get out of Suman's arms and down onto the floor to play, as well.

"She's nearly walking," Jan said proudly, looking lovingly at her daughter. "I don't think it'll be long before she's racing around after Sunny." She turned her eyes to Suman. "You make a very beautiful bride, Suman. I hope you and Dr Nath will be very happy."

"Thank you, Jan. We appreciate that very much."

"Could I maybe speak to you both? I've got some news."

"Of course, follow me and we'll go and find him."

Unfortunately, Jan's news was not destined to be heard at this time, as Sam and Suman were suddenly commandeered by their bridesmaids, who implored them to come and cut their cake.

"Don't worry." Jan smiled in response to Suman's apologies. "My news can wait."

It wasn't until around two in the morning when a weary husband and wife said their goodbyes to the few guests remaining and made their way up in the lift to their hotel bedroom, arm in arm. In bed, snuggled tightly, their legs entwined, Sam turned the bedside light down very low and looked at his bride.

"Oh, by the way," he commented casually, "I caught up with Jan and she told me her news."

He said no more, waiting with a nonchalant smile on his face.

"So, what was the news?" Suman coaxed when the silence continued.

"Oh, I can't tell you that. It's too awful. It'll kill the lovely romantic mood we've got in here."

"Awful?" she squealed. "What can she have told you that was awful?"

"Nope, I can't tell you. I'll tell you tomorrow," he teased her mercilessly, closing his eyes.

She wriggled around to face away from Sam.

"Well, no sex for you tonight, then!"

"We'll see about that," he replied with a grin, swinging her back over onto her back.

"Sami Nath," she began. "You've got to tell me … " But that was as far as she got, his actions banishing all thoughts of secrets, weddings, and everything else.

He told her the news a good while later, holding her close.

"Jan is giving us a wedding gift, and she wanted to explain what it was."

"Why would she need to explain? What is it?"

"She said she wanted to tell us together, but you were so busy eating and dancing and having such a good time that she told me on my own and said that I could tell you."

She punched him playfully. "I was not eating and dancing. Well, I was, but you could have come for me. What does she want to give us? Come on, tell me."

"She's giving us a house."

She laughed. "Don't be daft. What is she really giving us?"

"A house. Really," he stressed.

"But we've got a house. Why would she give us a house?"

He leaned across and kissed her nose.

"It's not for us."

"Not for us? Who is it for?"

"It's to be a rescue shelter."

"A rescue shelter?" she squeaked.

He nodded. "Yes. She says it's so you can rescue all the children you want and have somewhere nice to take them."

Suman sat bolt upright in the bed, her mouth slightly open.

"For all the trafficked children we can rescue?" He nodded again.

"Where? And how can she do this?"

He lay back with his hands behind his head and grinned.

"It's to be in the hospital grounds so that you can oversee it all. She's been given more of Robert's money and she wants us to have it to build a shelter. It's all been cleared with the hospital. They're going to take it under their wing and help us with the running of it."

Suman was staring hard at him, her mouth again open, for once absolutely speechless. Her new husband took full advantage of the silence, reaching over to her, making speech entirely redundant.

Epilogue

SUMAN AND SAM'S NEW APARTMENT
FOUR MONTHS LATER

Suman was on the phone to Ellie, ensconced on the big, comfortable settee, her feet curled up at her side. The call was a long one, the two of them loving their lengthy chats, catching up with each other's news.

"Budge up," Sam whispered quietly as he joined her. His cup of Scottish tea was in his hand, and he had just filled the dishwasher with the dinner dishes. She moved along the sofa to give him room, and then moved back to snuggle up to him and put the speaker phone on to let him join in the conversation.

Eventually, the call was over and Suman put her phone to one side. Sam hugged her tight.

"You're looking very beautiful tonight, Mrs Nath. New dressing gown?"

She nodded. "New dressing gown and ..." She undid the knot on the belt and held the gown open. "... new nightdress to match. Present from Vada."

"Hmm." Sam laid his mug of tea down on the coffee table and turned to bring Suman in a bit closer. One hand began to sneak inside her dressing gown. "Very sexy. I like it. Thank you, Vada."

"Yes, she thought you'd like it." They laughed and snuggled even closer, his left hand curling around her neck and his right hand working its way further inside the dressing gown.

He was leaning over for a kiss when Suman took a sharp intake of breath. This stopped him in his tracks and he leaned back.

"What? What did I do?"

She leaned over and pulled his head towards her. "Nothing. Don't stop."

However, another wince and intake of breath made him draw back again.

"What's the matter, Su? Am I hurting you?"

She sat up a little. "I'm just a bit tender. My boobs feel a bit sore. Don't worry; probably my time of the month."

Sam waited, watching his wife closely.

After a moment, she propped herself up, adjusting the cushion she was leaning on. He continued to watch as her brows drew together in a frown. He waited some more, a smile playing on his lips.

While Suman's eyes still appeared to be fixated on a wall, her hand very slowly moved from her side and came to rest on the lower part of her stomach. She wasn't aware of what she had done, her mind somewhere else, but Sam continued to smile, and patiently waited.

Seconds later, he was rewarded for his patience as he watched her beautiful, deep brown eyes wake up from her reverie and her lips open in surprise.

She turned to him quickly and whispered, "Sam ..." and then she was silent.

His hand slipped over to lie on top of hers, very gently.

"Another mouth to feed soon, my darling?" he asked, and reached forward to gently wipe two sparkling teardrops that had slipped out from Suman's radiant eyes.

Language & Terms

Aarti - Form of worship used to welcome visitors, brass tray with candle (light) and Puja/prayer materials e.g. flowers, rice, incense, kumkum - is circled three times

Aloo Tikki - Croquette made of potato, peas and curry

Aloo Posto - Potatoes, poppy seeds, nigella seeds and mustard oil

Anarkali dress - Long, colourful, elegant dress shaped like a flower. Anarkali was a court dancer

Auld Reekie - Edinburgh

Bhalobashi - I love you

Bicchiyas - Silver metal toe rings, worn to denote the woman is married

Chai - Tea with lots of different flavours, e.g. ginger, masala, cinnamon, nutmeg etc.

Churidar - Pants/leggings, gathered at ankles, worn with a long kameez or Anarkali dress

Cranachan - Scottish dessert made with whipped cream, oats and honey (& raspberries)

Dalit -   Untouchables, outside traditional caste hierarchy in India

Dupattà -   Long scarf, shawl or stole

Ganesh Puja -   Ceremony of prayers, mantras & rituals performed in front of idol, Ganesh

Grah Shanti/Manoru - Rituals said to remove all negative effects, performed at weddings & events

Kachori -   Deep fried snack made of gram flour and moong dahl

Jatakarma -   Celebration on birth of baby when mantras are whispered into baby's ear

Kurta -   Loose, collarless shirt or tunic

Ma, Amma, Ai -Pet names for Mother/Mum

Macher Jhol -   Bengali fish curry

Majhi Mulagi - Term of endearment for daughter

M G Road -   Mahatma Gandhi Road (most major cities in India have an MG Road)

MC Licence -   Motor cycle licence in India - costs around 200 rupees

Not on your Nellie - From 1930's Cockney rhyming slang, 'Not on your Nellie Duff' rhyming with Puff, e.g. the air in your lungs

Panch Phoron - Indian spice blend of cumin, fenugreek, mustard seeds and fennel

Parle Biscuits - Best selling brand of biscuits in the world

Rangoli - Bright patterns made of powdered chalk drawn in front of the door to welcome visitors, also drawn outside auspicious buildings

Sangeet - Music & Dancing Party to celebrate the union of two families

Seven Vows and Seven Circles - The bride and groom make promises to each other and walk seven circles around a ceremonial fire, each round signifying a specific blessing they request from the gods

Sherwani - Ornate, long sleeved outer coat, buttoned down front and mandarin collar

Suprabhata - Hymns or verses recited in the early morning/a good morning greeting

Tiffin time - Light meal or snack at any time of day

Tilak Ceremony - The groom-to-be is offered tilak, a paste painted on his forehead, to ensure he will be a loving husband and father

Vada Pav Buns - Deep fried masala buns made with potato bhaji stuffed with bread dough

About the Author

Avril grew up in Perth, Scotland, leaving school at sixteen to work in the British Linen Bank, where she met her husband, Bill. Her love of writing began at school, where she was published for the first time, one of her poems appearing in the school magazine. She also won first prize in a poetry competition in Year 4, spurring her on to continue writing both poetry and prose over the years.

Joining Girlguiding UK in the late 1980s, Avril was offered the opportunity to visit a Guide World Centre in Pune, India, and so began a love affair with India, a passion that has remained with her to the present day. Travelling extensively through India, Avril and her Guiding friends encountered the problems of child-trafficking, which inspired them to help in the rescue of young children, offspring of the trafficked women working in the brothels of Pune. This led to years of fundraising to raise money to build two children's homes, allowing the youngsters to live in safety and freedom, away from the violence of the red light area.

Her books, *Diverted Traffic*, and its sequel, *Diverted to Dhapa*, are works of fiction, novels inspired by the stories of the children now living in the children's homes.

Other Works by this Author

Diverted Traffic

To read the story of Suman's childhood and teenage years, *Diverted Traffic* follows her story from the age of nine when she was trafficked from her home in Maharashtra, India and taken to work in the red light area of Amsterdam. Journey with her to learn how she escapes death at the hands of her traffickers.

Avril Duncan

Printed in Great Britain
by Amazon

36514554R00189